LOVE IS IN
THE HAIR

LOVE IS IN THE HAIR

Gemma Cary

DELACORTE PRESS

Text copyright © 2024 by Gemma Cary
Jacket art copyright © 2024 by Agustina Gastaldi

All rights reserved. Published in the United States by Delacorte Press, an imprint of Random House Children's Books, a division of Penguin Random House LLC, New York.

Delacorte Press is a registered trademark and the colophon is a trademark of Penguin Random House LLC.

GetUnderlined.com

Educators and librarians, for a variety of teaching tools, visit us at RHTeachersLibrarians.com

Library of Congress Cataloging-in-Publication Data
Names: Cary, Gemma, author.
Title: Love is in the hair / Gemma Cary.
Description: First edition. | New York : Delacorte Press, 2024. | Audience: Ages 12 and up. | Summary: Follows the endless humiliations, unrequited obsessions, and all-consuming friendships of fifteen-year-old Evia Birtwhistle as she leads a body-hair positive revolution at her school.
Identifiers: LCCN 2023019071 (print) | LCCN 2023019072 (ebook) | ISBN 978-0-593-65126-1 (hardcover) | ISBN 978-0-593-65127-8 (library binding) | ISBN 978-0-593-65128-5 (ebook)
Subjects: CYAC: Body image—Fiction. | Hair—Fiction. | Friendship—Fiction. | Interpersonal relations—Fiction. | High schools—Fiction. | Schools—Fiction. | Humorous stories. | LCGFT: Humorous fiction. | Novels.
Classification: LCC PZ7.C2585 Lo 2024 (print) | LCC PZ7.C2585 (ebook) | DDC [Fic]—dc23

The text of this book is set in 12-point Adobe Garamond Pro.
Interior design by Michelle Crowe

Printed in the United States of America
1st Printing
First Edition

FOR MUM AND DAD,
(THANKS FOR THE HAIRY GENES!)

ONE

WHEN I WAS BORN, I LOOKED LIKE A TINY CHIMP: two-inch bouffant, hairy shoulders and a face furry enough to scare any midwife. Sometimes I feel like not much has changed.

"What if it's hypertrichosis?" I ask over my mom's shoulder while an angry wok spits at her.

"Hyper-what?"

"Trichosis!" I shout over the roaring hood fan. "Werewolf Syndrome!"

Mom flicks off the fan. "Oh, not this again. You're exaggerating, Evia!"

"I'm not." I thrust the side of my face in her direction and stroke my cheek. "My sideburns are definitely getting worse!" As for my eyebrows, they're like tectonic plates. If I didn't pluck them, there'd be a natural disaster. On. My. Face.

"Oh, for goodness' sake, Fluff." Mom whips a bowl of stir-fry onto my place mat, then folds herself neatly into the chair opposite to watch me eat. She'll have hers later, after her class. "I assure you," she says, "you are not turning into a werewolf. You're just . . . at the hairier end of the spectrum."

Great. So there's a Spectrum of Female Body Hair and I'm at the wrong end. Thank you, Mother, and thank you, Destiny!

I stab a squeaky chunk of Halloumi with my fork, then ram it into my mouth. Pah!

It's my dad's fault. He was Greek and he was hairy. And that's all my mom has told me about him. He was Greek and he happened to be working on one of the islands where my mom—in her late thirties—was backpacking. They hooked up for one night, my mom returned to the good old US of A and hey presto, nine months later I was born!

Issues I have with this little episode include:

1. **MINOR ISSUE:** The fact my mom went backpacking in her late thirties. Hands up if that shouts "midlife crisis" to you, too?!

2. **SLIGHTLY BIGGER ISSUE:** The fact that I resulted from a one-night stand. Not exactly the loving scenario you'd hope for, is it? My mother confessed to this when I was eleven.

3. **BIG ISSUE:** The fact she named me after that Greek island, as if I'd grow up to appreciate nothing more than being reminded ON A DAILY BASIS of the exact location of my conception. Every time someone shouts "Evia!" it's like a big, disgusting reminder that my mom had sex.

4. **GIANT ISSUE:** Not knowing my father AT ALL. One day I will track him down. My best friend, Frankie, has promised to help me. We're just not sure how or where to start. . . .

"Anyway," Mom starts up again, "you shouldn't be embarrassed about having body hair. It's completely natural. I've told you before: the only reason women remove it is because they think men want them to."

"*And* because they want to feel beautiful," I add.

"Yes—because society has conditioned us to believe that body hair is ugly! Women naturally grow hair in all the same places as men, but men get to flaunt it while women are led to believe that they must be hair-free. It's totally wrong, Fluff!"

Argh! There it is again! Seriously. Shouldn't my mother have realized by now that reminding her daughter of her furriness several times a day might not be *entirely* sensitive? "Fluff" has been her nickname for me since I was born—for obvious reasons—and lately it's felt more accurate than ever. I tell you: puberty does cruel, cruel things to a girl.

Anyway, every time she calls me Fluff it makes me want to annoy my Mom right back, so I've started calling her Antonia. Or Antonia Birtwhistle in full if I really want to annoy her. You'd think, what with her being a yoga-teaching liberal, that she'd be one of those super-cool parents who likes being called by their first name. She's not.

My mom claims she's a New Age Feminist, whatever that means. Mostly it means that she hasn't lifted a razor in nearly five years. It also means that when her legs are out, I dread a trip to Aldi in case we get stuck in the fruit-and-veggie aisle while a friendly toddler clings to her shin, stroking it. Her knees are just the right height for a two-year-old to mistake her for a golden retriever.

Mom narrows her eyes at me. "Does this sudden preoccupation with hair have something to do with Frankie?"

"What? No!"

"Well. Maybe you should think yourself lucky. You have nothing to worry about compared with that poor girl."

I swallow my mouthful. "Hang on—weren't you literally just saying how natural body hair is? And now you're describing my best friend as 'poor' because she has so much?"

Mom opens her mouth, then closes it again. Ha! I love calling her out on stuff like this.

I eat the rest of my dinner in silence, mostly because she's right. "That poor girl" is my best friend and has been since we first met at eight years old. Frankie used to be this super-confident, hugely talented singer who loved nothing more than persuading me to put on a show with her in her front room, with her family as our audience. But thinking about it, I can't remember the last time we did that. The thought of standing up to sing in front of anyone now—even her own family—would be Frankie's idea of hell.

It's all because of this condition she has called polycystic ovary syndrome, or PCOS. I've since learned that a lot of women have it, and one of the main symptoms is excess body hair. In sixth grade, Frankie had sideburns. In seventh grade, her chin started sprouting hair and, by eighth grade, she was able to grow a beard. Don't get me wrong, the ability to grow a beard is great if you're in a hipster folk band. But when you're a fifteen-year-old girl and you have a five o'clock shadow by the end of the school day, it truly sucks.

I scrape a couple of limp, brown bean sprouts into the compost bin and slide my plate into our tiny dishwasher before retreating to my room.

LATER, AFTER the front door bangs closed behind my mom, I head downstairs and pluck the tub of Halo Top ice cream from the freezer, escorting it triumphantly to the living room. Feet up on the sofa, I flick on the TV and reach for my phone. If this is a preview of what it's like to live alone, I CANNOT WAIT.

I tap open Instagram and start scrolling, scanning for anything newsworthy. There's Adam Johnson showing off his latest tat; Shania Kaminski posting another terrible makeup tutorial; some celeb flashing a blingy engagement ring over her fiancé's shoulder. Getting engaged seems so far off to me that I can't imagine what that feels like. I don't even have a boyfriend yet, just a vague notion that it's something I might have one day—when I have secured some vital intel on HOW to get one.

Swiping through the stories, I suddenly see Madison Cox's face grinning out at me from a fluorescent circle. I should unfollow her; just a glimpse of her glowing orange face is enough to make me shudder. But I began following her one day out of pure boredom and curiosity—apparently her parents are megarich doctors and they live in a mansion—and now I feel like if I unfollow her, she might notice. . . .

I should scroll past, ignore that nagging temptation. But somewhere at the helm of my brain, an overriding voice tells me I need to watch this. My fingertip reacts and before I know it, the video is playing. It's not live but it's recent, having already received 149 views and the reactions still coming. Laughing-face emojis and approving thumbs-up drift across the screen like wayward helium balloons.

The video opens with Madison straddling the doorway of a room, the top button of her school blouse undone, tie discarded, and yellow, strawlike hair tugged forward over her shoulders. My heart implodes to the size of a bullet and fires itself at my rib cage. Because I recognize the black Victorian fireplace in the background. Above it is David Bowie's face with his Ziggy Stardust lightning bolt, and on the mantelpiece is the beaded frame I gave Frankie for her tenth birthday. Inside is a picture of us in our pj's, taken on my first Smith family camping trip. To the right of the fireplace is Frankie's desk, and sitting at that desk, back to the camera, is Frankie.

My bullet-sized heart plummets.

"Why hello, Frankie Smith!" greets Madison, and as she steps into the room, it becomes clear that—despite being the one to post the video—she's not the one holding the camera.

"Come on in, girls!" Madison croons, and the camera moves forward. Aliyah Dobson, Madison's right-hand woman, comes into the shot, parking herself on Frankie's bed, not politely on the edge, but *plonk* in the middle of it.

"Over here, Pix." Madison gestures, and the camera glides toward the desk. So that's who's filming: Pixie Perkins—a robust girl in our year who takes great pride in single-handedly running the black market at school. If you're craving chips or can't get through physics without a Twix, Pixie's your girl.

"Whatcha up to, Fran-kay?" Madison sneers, peering over Frankie's shoulder. Frankie's already snapped the scrapbook shut but it's too late. Madison wrenches the prized possession from Frankie's grasp and starts skimming through the pages. Each spread is about one of Frankie's favorite movies—she wants to be a film critic one day.

"Whoa-ho-ho!" Madison crows. "What do we have here?!" She holds open the scrapbook for the camera to see. It's the Avengers spread, featuring a huge cutout of Thor, surrounded by confetti hearts and cupid-themed doodles. I'm more of a Tom Holland fan, but Chris Hemsworth is Frankie's dream man.

"As if you'd stand a chance with a hottie like Hemsworth!" Madison mocks, pulling out the page and ripping it up.

"No!" Frankie spins her chair to face the camera and dives to the carpet to retrieve the torn fragments. Meanwhile, Cox slams the book shut and tosses it to long-armed Aliyah.

"Hey, Fran-kay! How about we make you look nice for Mr. Thor?" Madison signals to Pixie, who passes her a black tote bag with her nonfilming hand. My stomach churns. What's in there? Makeup?

I shut down the video and immediately call Frankie.

"I'm coming, Franks," I say to her voicemail. "I'll be there really, really soon. . . ."

The thought of Madison Cox and Aliyah Dobson in MY house makes me feel queasy. But seeing them in Frankie's house? In Frankie's BEDROOM?! It's a thousand times worse. Frankie said if they came to watch the prom night prep, she'd stay out of their way; said she'd be fine. They must've slipped out of the kitchen without Frankie's mom noticing. . . .

Head swirling, I lurch for the hallway and shove my feet in some sneakers. Then I start running.

You idiot, Evia. You should have known *something was going to happen.*

TWO

THE EARLY-MAY SUNSHINE FLICKERS THROUGH THE cherry blossoms, throwing speckled light onto the pavement. *It's pretty,* I think, racing through it, but it's not enough to take away my nausea. It's senior prom night. Right now, Frankie's house will be full of older girls. Frankie's mom, Louise, is a hairdresser and it's become school tradition that every year, on the afternoon of the prom, dozens of senior girls head to Frankie's house to get their hair done on the cheap.

This year, Tallulah Dobson will get priority over most because (a) the Dobsons live two doors down from the Smiths, and (b) Tallulah's mom is one of Louise's best friends. So if Tallulah's there for her updo, you can bet your favorite panties that younger sister Aliyah will be there to watch. And if Aliyah's there, Madison is going to be there too. Louise will be so busy, she won't have a clue what's going on upstairs.

When I reach their redbrick town house, the Smiths' front door is slightly ajar. I push it the rest of the way and step into a warm coconut-scented haze. On the other side of the haze, I find Louise, standing behind a kitchen chair, curling iron in hand. It's just past six p.m. and there are only two girls left: one in the chair and one at the Smiths' kitchen table. They take turns glancing surreptitiously at the wall clock.

"Hi," I say nervously.

The girls look up but say nothing.

"Oh, hi, love!" Louise smiles at me before unfurling a perfect chestnut spiral from the iron and gathering up the next tress.

"Have you seen Frankie?" I ask, my throat constricting.

"Up in her room. It's been total chaos down here!"

"Can I go up?"

"Of course, Evia, love. Help yourself if you want a drink." Louise nods to a laminate worktop strewn with half-empty glasses, sparkling cider and a startling rainbow of juice and soda bottles.

I head back through the mist of hair products and up the stripy carpeted staircase. Halfway up, my hand finds the dent in the banister where I once crashed—and broke—a remote control helicopter belonging to Frankie's brother, Jake. He was thirteen and didn't talk to me for weeks. I was ten and heartbroken.

At the top of the stairs, it's eerily quiet. The door to Frankie's room is closed and I pause outside, my feet heavy. I knock so gently I can hardly hear it, so I knock again.

When she doesn't answer, I turn the handle and step in.

I don't see Frankie at first—she's not at her desk. But I

notice something lying in the middle of the taupe carpet: long ribbons of black hair right in front of my feet, hair that was once a lighter brown than mine but is now dyed raven black, hair that she and I have brushed and crimped and straightened more times than I can remember.

Wheeling ninety degrees I see her, face down on the bed, head tucked into her arms. And that's when everything turns to water, blurry and spiraling, as if we're being washed down a giant drain. It's just me and Frankie falling, falling, while the bedroom swirls around us.

I close my eyes and wait for the swirling to stop. Slowly, the water subsides and the bedroom comes back. Carefully— ever so carefully—I step over the hair and sit next to her, taking up as little of the single bed as I can manage. I rest a hand on her shoulder blade.

"Frankie? It's me. . . ."

She turns her head and that's when I see it.

Frankie's had the same hairstyle since middle school: long and thick, parted on the side, with a heavy curtain that hangs over her face when she wants to hide, which is most of the time. Only now she can't hide because her curtain is totally gone. It's been hacked at, leaving uneven clumps sticking out over half of her scalp. The other half of her hair hangs down over her shoulder, untouched.

Slowly and gingerly, Frankie pushes herself up to sitting and hugs her knees to her chest. I climb up next to her.

"I'm so stupid," she mumbles, smearing tears with the sleeve of her hoodie.

I put my arm around her. "No, Frankie. You're not."

She pats slowly at the shaven patches, wincing with every touch. "How bad is it?"

I force myself to look at it. "It'll grow back," I say, squeezing her shoulder.

"Oh God," she whispers, half curse, half prayer. "Oh God, oh God." She squeezes her knees even tighter, as if that might detract from the hurt inside.

"I can't believe they did this."

"You watched it?!" Frankie looks straight at me, her chin trembling.

I shake my head. "I saw up to the part where they brought out the black bag. That's when I called."

"Sorry, I turned my phone off. . . ."

"You don't need to be sorry!"

She slurps up a torrent of snot, then wipes her nose roughly. "I didn't even see them come into the house, Evs! I was watching on and off out my window, but I didn't see them. There was so much noise, everyone coming and going. Then suddenly they were up here—all three of them!"

"And the black bag?"

"Some of my mom's hair things . . ." Frankie looks at me with insistent eyes. "They weren't going to leave until I agreed to something, so I said they could straighten it. That was all."

My stomach clenches and I shake my head. "Was it Madison?"

Frankie nods. "While she was straightening it, she was pointing out all the split ends, said I needed a trim. . . ." She starts weeping again. I rub circles on her back with my palm.

"Madison started cutting, the whole time saying how amazing it was going to look. Then she said my hair was so thick that what I really needed was an undercut to help thin it out. Next thing I knew, she had clippers in her hand. . . ."

Tears spill from my eyes now, too.

"I said no, Evs! I tried to get away, but that just made it worse. As I got down onto the floor, the clippers sort of jerked. . . ." She drapes the remaining half of her hair over her shoulder and combs it with her fingers.

"But she stopped after that?"

Frankie nods.

"And then they left?"

She nods again. "Please don't watch the rest of the video, Evia! Please. I don't want you to see it. Promise me you won't?"

I look into her eyes. It's not that I *want* to watch my best friend being tortured like that, but if everyone else at school sees this video, part of me feels I should at least watch it so I can defend her. Then again, if Frankie's asking me not to . . .

"I promise."

I notice the scrapbook lying at the end of her bed and open it for a quick check. The quartered face of Chris Hemsworth falls into my lap. Frankie must've tucked him inside the first page.

"At least they didn't trash the rest of this. . . ." I mutter, skimming the pages.

Frankie sniffs in agreement and I put the book down.

"What about Aliyah? Did she, you know, *do* anything?"

Frankie shakes her head. "Pixie filmed it and Aliyah just . . . well, watched. At one point Madison asked her to pass the clippers and she wouldn't do it. Madison had to get them herself."

"But she could've stopped her."

Frankie snorts. "And get between Madison and her audience? Ha!"

I pull Frankie into a side squeeze and try to unscramble my brain to find something useful to say. Eventually, two girls' voices move along the downstairs hallway and the front door clicks shut. We hear Louise give a loud, dramatic sigh.

I withdraw my arm from Frankie's back and take a deep breath.

"We need to tell your mom."

THREE

THE FRONT DOOR OPENS, THEN SHUTS AGAIN.
"Daddy's home!" Dom calls cheerfully, his shoes clacking along the hallway. Frankie's eyes fill with fresh tears.

Dom stops in the kitchen doorway and stares at Frankie. "Baby girl . . . ," he says quietly. He slips out of his suit jacket and drapes it over the chair next to Frankie. "What happened?"

I push my back against the worktop, trying to make myself disappear. I usually feel at home here, but with the whole Smith family gathered at their kitchen table, I want to melt into the clutter of cups and chip bags and hair spray.

It feels like a large fluorescent sign has appeared on the wall behind the table, flashing *INTRUDER*. I examine my cuticles intently, waiting for it to melt away.

Jake thumps the table with his fist, pulling me back into the moment. "That whole Cox family has it coming," he says broodily, probably remembering how Madison's older sister, Jess, dumped him. "I'll get them for this."

"You'll do no such thing, Jacob," Louise replies. "It'll only make matters worse."

"You think it can get WORSE?!"

I try not to notice how hot Jake looks when he's angry; he's even hotter when he's playing the protective big brother.

Jake pulls out his phone.

"What are you doing?" Frankie asks, panicking.

"Finding Madison . . ."

"No, don't! Please don't!" Frankie pushes her mom's arm away and reaches across the table toward Jake.

Jake puts down his phone and looks sharply at their mother. "Why did you even let Madison into our house?! You know how hideous she is to Frankie at school."

Louise frowns. "It was so busy. . . ."

She begins stroking what's left of Frankie's hair. "What are we going to do?" she says quietly.

"You could shave it all off," I suggest to Frankie. "Female celebs shave their heads all the time. What was that film we watched? *Life in a Year*? Cara Delevingne rocked a shaved head in that!"

Frankie glares at me. "Evia. She was playing a cancer patient."

Hmm. "What about a headscarf? You can get some really pretty ones."

Frankie sighs.

Louise stands behind her daughter as if she were in the salon, and gently traces a new parting along Frankie's scalp, lifting some of the remaining hair and folding it over to cover the shaven half.

"It's not *that* bad," she says, reaching for a round tabletop mirror. She places it in front of Frankie, who raises it cautiously.

"I'm a balding politician," she says, "with a *really* bad comb-over."

I snort loudly. At least she can still joke.

Louise stands and reaches for the kettle.

"Oh good," sings Jake. "A cup of tea always solves everything!" He rams his chair back so violently it scrapes against the floor. I catch a whiff of his delicious pheromones as he storms out of the room.

"It'll grow back," I say to Frankie. "You're always saying how your hair grows really fast."

"Evia's right," says Louise. "Give it a month or two and—"

"And it'll still look ABSOLUTELY HORRENDOUS! I might as well wear a paper bag over my head for the next year!"

"We could crop it?" suggests Louise. "Most people find—"

"Most people?" Frankie interrupts, her voice unusually scratchy. "Since when have I been 'most people'? I'm taller than average, fatter than average and hairier than average. Why don't I just have it all lasered off, along with the rest of my body?! That would solve the problem nicely, wouldn't it?!"

Dom sighs. "We've discussed this," he says tiredly. "You know we can't afford it."

Most girls wouldn't talk to their dad about wanting laser hair removal, but with Frankie, her whole family knows about it. As well as everyone at her mom's work. And all the neighbors.

"We could go back to the doctor," suggests Louise.

"And what? Have him tell me to lose weight *again*?" Frankie's voice cracks.

"Sweetheart . . ." Dom slides toward his daughter and wraps his arm around her.

The kettle whistles loudly and we are grateful for the noise—for a break from having to find the right words. When it clicks off, Dom leans forward and speaks calmly. "Do you think we should go to the police, love? It is a kind of assault."

"No!" cries Frankie.

"But—"

"No, Dad! It would only make things a hundred times worse. Besides, what are the police gonna say? 'Err, sorry Mr. Smith' "—she makes her voice deeper—"but we understand you let these girls into your house, correct? And your daughter *allowed* them to cut her hair, correct?" She pauses before resuming her normal voice. "I don't want to talk to *anyone* about it. I just want my hair to grow back and to pretend it never happened."

Dom sends a covert message to Louise with his eyes. "Maybe it's time to consider Mayfield," he says, his voice softer.

Mayfield?

Mayfield is the other high school in town—on the opposite side of town, to be precise. And Mayfield doesn't have ME in it.

Frankie looks at him, then at her reflection in the makeup mirror.

I wish she would meet my pleading eyes. *No matter how*

bad things are, I say telepathically, *we can get through this. I'll be there for you next time, I promise. I'll protect you.*

But Frankie doesn't hear me.

She doesn't say a thing.

IT'S DARK by the time Louise drives me home. I close the front door as gently as I can and pad up the stairs, but Mom still comes out of her bedroom.

"Evia!" she begins, her eyes full of questions. I'd texted something vague about going to help Frankie but that was it, and that was three hours ago.

"I'm tired," I reply, turning toward my room. "I don't want to talk about it right now."

Mom launches a spear-shaped pang of guilt, which hits me squarely in the back. Why does she always have to *know* everything all the time? Every time something big happens in my life, I'm not allowed to move on until we've talked about it together—at length. Well, not tonight!

I shut my bedroom door, kick off my sneakers and toss my hoodie toward my desk. Then I climb into bed in my sweatpants and T-shirt.

Are you seriously thinking about going to Mayfield? I message Frankie.

I lie awake, waiting for a reply.

FOUR

THE NEXT MORNING, I'M AWOKEN BY TEEMING RAIN.
My bedroom isn't the biggest, so I have my bed pushed up
against the wall with the window, my curtains just about
within reach. A quick twitch of the curtain reveals raindrop
trails rolling and worming their way down the outside of the
glass. Daylight dims my clock's projection on the wall: 10:15.
Mom must've gone to teach her Saturday class, the one that's
usually followed by a leisurely brunch at the local vegan café.

Suddenly, my phone pings.

Frankie: *Thanks so much for coming over yesterday. xx*

Me: *Duh! What are best friends for? How are you doing?
Wanna come over to hang?*

Frankie: *Nah. Don't wanna be seen. How about you come
here?*

I look again at the window. I will need an umbrella the size of a tent.

Me: *All right . . . Have your mom's biggest hair dryer at the ready! xx*

BACK IN Frankie's room, I am still trying to ignore the Madison ghost. Will she ever be gone, I wonder? Or will she always be here, lurking behind a curtain and ready to spring out at any moment?

"Urgh!" I say, peeling off my wet socks and draping them over Frankie's radiator. "It's gross out there!"

Frankie lobs me fresh socks from her top drawer: an orange pair with bats on them.

"Maybe we should emigrate," she suggests.

"Good idea. Where should we go?"

"Somewhere bearded girls don't get abused?"

"Umm . . ."

"Exactly."

Not sure what to say, I stare for a moment at Frankie's poster of Lettie Lutz, the bearded lady from that Hugh Jackman film *The Greatest Showman*. Sometimes, to make each other laugh, we do Lettie impressions and shake our boobs at one another. I'm not sure now's the time for a Lettie impression.

"I'm sorry about what happened," I say at last.

"Why are *you* sorry?"

"Because I should've been there! I should've come back with you after school."

Frankie hugs me. "It's not your fault. Please, please don't feel guilty about any of this. If I hadn't been panicking so much, I might've called you when they first came in here. But I couldn't think straight, Evs. It was horrible!"

I hesitate, dreading the answer to the question I'm about to ask. "Are you *really* thinking about leaving St. Joe's?"

"I don't know," Frankie says quietly.

"There will be Madison Coxes at Mayfield."

"I know. But not THE Madison Cox. Honestly, Evs, after yesterday, I'm not sure I can ever face seeing her again. Even Aliyah and Pixie looked embarrassed for me. You haven't watched it, have you? The video?"

"No! I promised, didn't I? I reported it as violating Instagram policy, so I'm sure they'll take it down soon. Even if they don't, I think live streams are only available for twenty-four hours."

"Let's hope." Frankie puffs out her cheeks, letting the air out slowly. "You know, you could always come to Mayfield with me. . . ."

I look at her without saying anything. I could, I suppose. But St. Joseph's has a really good reputation for the arts, which is a big deal for me. Mayfield is a science academy, and science is my most hated subject.

Frankie doesn't wait any longer for a reply. "Either way, Dad's right. I need a fresh start."

I reach for my bag and the plastic folder inside it. "Maybe.

But you know who else needs a fresh start?" I pass her the plastic folder and the crisp printout inside.

"Chrissy baby!" Frankie kisses Hemsworth's face.

"I thought we could redo that page in your scrapbook. What d'you think?"

Frankie reaches for her scrapbook and turns to the next available blank spread. "I think that's a perfect idea."

FIVE

ON SUNDAY MORNING, I FIND MYSELF PACING UP AND down, burning holes in my bedroom carpet. While Mom's out grocery shopping, I raid the kitchen for sugary treats. Finally, lurking behind our pungent collection of herbal teas, I find a lone, unopened packet of chocolate wafers. Aha, Antonia! VICTORY IS MINE!

My mom "hides" these things from herself so that:

a) she can pretend she doesn't eat them, and
b) she doesn't have to admit to herself that she failed and bought something in nonrecyclable packaging. In our house, if we can't recycle it, we try not to buy it in the first place. It all started with a school project in fourth grade to try to reduce the amount of plastic at home, which was great at the time. But had I known my little project would evolve into a Lifetime

Cookie Ban and an Everlasting Chip Crisis, I may have reconsidered.

Luckily, my mom is not *wholly* on board. She pretends to be all preachy-preachy, *yogi-yogi* on the outside, but I know her secret! Yes, my mom's life force is in reality fueled by refined sugar, consumed secretly in her boudoir. If I ransacked her room right now, I bet I'd find a package of Oreos stashed in her bedside table or some candy bars under her bed.

Back in my room, I munch through what can only be described as a disgusting amount of chocolatey goodness, until I feel slightly strange. I still can't get the images from Friday night out of my mind. It's like Frankie's head has been freshly tattooed on the inside of my eyelids and every time I blink, it hurts.

I want to do something. I *have* to do something. I just don't know what. . . .

I stare at my phone in the hope that inspiration will appear. Maybe looking at photos of good times with Frankie will make me feel better? Or a little online Jake-stalking?

ARGH! I slam my phone into my pillow. I should be helping my BFF right now, not obsessing over her Beefcake Bro!

Rolling onto my stomach, I reach over the side of my bed and take my mom's old copy of *Jane Eyre* from the shelf beneath my bedside table. I pull the bookmark from page ten and nestle into the heap of mismatched cushions on my bed. But after reading the same paragraph three times, I toss it aside.

Instead, I grab a magazine from the rug next to my bed

and skim through its thin pages. I pause at an ad for swim-wear and Mom's voice immediately erupts from the inner core of my brain, like it always does.

"*Those boobs are NOT HERS!*" the voice screeches. "*Cleavage? In a strapless bikini? IMPOSSIBLE! How did those breasts get there, Evia? I'll tell you how they got there! Someone else's pert little bosoms have been photoshopped onto that poor, unsuspecting model by a badly paid graphic designer.*" I try to turn the page, but the voice won't stop. "*Those legs have been done too!*" it barks. "*See how unnaturally smooth they are?*"

Mom used to be editor-in-chief for a well-known women's magazine. She likes to say she quit over matters of immense moral importance—like whether they should make a model's butt look bigger or not—but in reality, she got offered a massive severance package because she'd been there for about twenty billion years, and she took it. We moved out into the sticks, and a couple years later, the magazine company went bust.

I do hate how smooth that model's legs are, even though I know they're fake. And Mom would tell me that the model's bikini rash has been scrubbed out too. In fact, pretty much everything about her is probably fake. But it still doesn't help me like what I see when I look in the mirror. Speaking of which . . .

My favorite-ever secondhand find is a full-length cheval mirror on wheels. The mirror itself is a bit cloudy in patches, and the mahogany frame doesn't match anything else in my room, but I like it. I imagine its previous life backstage at a theater, being wheeled from one dressing room to another, filled with the dazzling reflection of that night's biggest diva.

This diva looks in the mirror and is dazzlingly mediocre. Okay, I don't dislike my eyes (big and brown) and my skin generally looks like I've just vacationed in Italy. But my hair is big and frizzy, like a dark version of my mom's. Some days, I look at myself and think, *Headbush.* The only way to tame said bushiness is with hair accessories, and having my hair cut into a bob will never be an option. Unless looking like a massive triangle suddenly gains appeal.

Meanwhile, Antonia describes us as petite. I describe us as:

- of average height (short)
- with legs not average enough for regular-length pants (frown)
- and smaller-than-average boobs (double frown; mine are still growing . . . I hope)

Plus, I have two caterpillar eyebrows staring back at me, and an upper lip so furry it could crawl off my face.

BLEURGH.

This is where I am going to regale you with a rundown of my current beauty regime. As Lettie Lutz would say, with or without her bouncing bosoms, THIS IS ME:

1. I pluck my caterpillars (aka eyebrows).
2. I shave my legs (thighs 'n' all).
3. I shave under my arms.
4. I wax my bikini line (generously).

5. I trim (what's left of) my bush. Pretty normal so far?
6. I shave my big toes. Still normal?
7. I bleach my sideburns.
8. I trim my slug (aka mustache) with nail scissors.
9. I occasionally bleach the slug too.
10. I shave my hands, including my fingers.
11. I occasionally bleach my arm hair.
12. I bleach my lower back and the bit between my belly button and my, erm, pants.
13. I shave around my nipples.
14. I bleach the bit of my chest between my boobs.

. . . I think that's it.

And you thought *you* were hairy, right?! Well, I bet you feel much better about yourself now! And yes, I have chest hair. It's not like thick, curly, man-chest-hair; it's what my mom might describe as "fine" or "downy"—invisible to the naked eye, or so she says. But it's not invisible to *my* eyes and I HATE it. When I'm in the bath, I put a washcloth over my rib cage so I don't have to look at it.

I think about Frankie, and how easily Madison & Co. could victimize me if they wanted to. Okay, I can't grow a beard, and my sideburns aren't bushy like Frankie's. But there's no getting away from the fact that I am hairy. I am *a hairy girl,* whether I like it or not, and I can't fundamentally change that.

Suddenly, looking in that mirror, a mixture of indignation and empowerment rushes through me. It's a mixture so dizzying that I have to reach for my creaky old desk chair. I fall into it, wheeling backward until it stops.

Why should girls like me and Frankie—girls everywhere— why should we have to put up with the Madison Coxes of this world? We should be free to live our lives without worrying about them!

I roll up my sleeve, pick up my phone and do the thing that changes EVERYTHING.

SIX

OVERNIGHT MY INAUGURAL POST FOR MY NEW ALIAS,
hairy_girls_club, has accrued 119 likes on Instagram. I'm
totally anonymous—exactly how I intend to stay—but my
initial nerves at sharing the picture are dissolving, bit by bit.
After all, no one knows it's me. I added lots of hashtags, like
#bodypositivity, #femalebodyhair and #bodyhairdontcare, so
people could find it.

I scroll through the comments on Monday, dreading evidence of trolls, but am pleasantly surprised. The first comment on the picture is mine: *Forearm no.1, Hairy Girl, 15.*
Subsequent comments say things like *You go girl!* and *Kudos
for sharing.* One said *I wish more teenage girls would post stuff
like this* and, after a quick flick through some profiles, I realize most of the comments are from older women. They're the
ones following these hashtags.

I look again at my picture. There it is: my unbleached,
furry left forearm in all its glory, resting on my white Ikea

desk, adorned by the friendship bracelet Frankie made me when we were twelve. It seems bizarre that anyone should even care that I've posted this. Why should they? It's a photo OF MY ARM, for goodness' sake! If this were a fair and just society, the comments would be *Why the hell are you sharing this? It's AN ARM.* Instead, people are lapping it up, and I'm already fantasizing about my next post. So I snap a picture of the leg hair I missed in the shower. *Missed a bit!* I type, posting the image with not one, not two, but THREE fire emojis. Because not only am I clearly the epitome of hotness with my patch of stubble, but I am also ON FIRE!

LATER, I head to Frankie's with a bag stuffed full of hats and hair accessories. I mean, it's a long weekend—what else is there to do?! We lie on her bed, flicking through some of Louise's hair magazines and gorging ourselves on bite-sized pancakes. Friday night's live stream has long since vanished from the internet, but we don't talk about it. In fact, we talk about everything *but* Friday night.

"How about a pixie cut?" I suggest, my index finger tapping an elfin celeb with short hair.

Frankie snorts at me. "With these cheeks?"

I flip the page. "Asymmetric bob?"

Frankie sighs. "Maybe." She rolls onto her back and stares up at the ceiling. "I don't know, Evs. It all just feels like everything is . . . too much. D'you know what I mean? Like *life* is too much."

I sit up suddenly, eyebrows drawn together. "You're not thinking about doing anything stupid, are you?"

"What? No! I just wish we were ten again, don't you? Life was so *easy* then."

I nod with a pursed, gentle smile. "You know who we need? Mia & Maya."

Frankie shoots a puff of air from her nostrils, then smiles back.

Mia & Maya are this pair of teenagers—a bit older than us—who have a YouTube channel and post vlogs about boys and stuff. Their followers send them questions and Mia & Maya answer them. Frankie and I do this thing where one of us pretends to be a follower posing a question, and the other pretends to be Mia or Maya answering. Sometimes we record ourselves and watch it back. Once I was laughing so hard I wet myself a tiny bit!

"I'll start," I suggest, clearing my throat. "Ahem. Dear Mia & Maya. I look like I have pubes growing out of my head. It's really getting me down. Is there anything I can do about it?"

Frankie grins. "Well, follower . . . Sorry, I missed your name?"

My face is deadpan. "Headbush."

"Well, Headbush, I'm very sorry to hear that. But no, I'm afraid there is absolutely *nothing* you can do about it. Straightening your head-bush is pointless, so you will have to learn to love it."

"Ouch!"

Frankie shrugs nonchalantly. "Harsh but true. Go again."

I pause for a moment. "Dear Mia & Maya. I am fifteen

years old and I don't have a boyfriend. Please tell me: am I going to be single forever?!" I sniff dramatically and wipe an imaginary tear from my cheek.

Frankie rolls her eyes. "Well, vlog-fan, as I don't actually know you, I feel unable to comment on whether or not you are ready to have a boyfriend. However, after consulting my crystal ball, I'm happy to report that your chances of being single FOREVER are extremely slim. Your chances of being single for the next ten years though . . . who knows?!"

"Hey!" I punch her lightly on the shoulder.

"I've got one," says Frankie. "Dear Mia & Maya. I was recently abused by some girls in my school."

My lips fold in sympathy.

"Should I (a) try to forget about it; (b) post awful things about them on social media; or (c) hire an assassin?"

I ignore the lump gathering in my throat. "Assassin. Definitely. But be careful and *don't* get caught!"

After that, we opt for watching the real Mia & Maya instead. Their most recent vlog is about summer wardrobes and it's a fun, much-needed distraction. And even though we spend most of the day together, munching our way through that entire tub of pancakes, I still don't tell Frankie about my new online venture. It's true—I am partly doing it for her. But after what happened, posting a couple of pictures on the internet seems like, well, nothing.

SEVEN

BY THE END OF THE DAY, I HAVE MORE THAN 300 likes on my pictures. On Tuesday, I ride to school on a wave of female solidarity, hoisted over the weekend's leftover puddles by hundreds of women's arms. My wave crashes at the school gates when I remember I'm Frankie-less. The Smiths talked to our principal, Mrs. Chubb, and explained that Frankie doesn't feel happy—or safe—coming back to school right now. Some admins are going to visit her at home to make a plan of action. Frankie guesses they're worried that if she's off too long, she won't want to come back at all. And that's not something I can bear to think about.

I step into the main entrance and feel like there's a neon sign above my head that reads *LONER*.

I am alone and friendless and everyone knows it.

Gossip-hungry eyes follow me down the hallway. They don't even pretend to look away. I can hear them whispering, speculating. "That's her friend," they say. "She's the one who . . ."

I scan the halls for Karima and Lowri: the only people likely to save me. Karima Bakshi and Lowri Edwards are another pair of wing-women whom Frankie and I often hang out with, when they're not too busy with wind band, orchestra and other musical gatherings. But Kar-Low are nowhere to be seen and my neon sign flashes brighter than ever.

I'm relieved when the bell rings for our Whole Year Assembly and we funnel into the School Hall. I closely follow the person in front, using them as a human shield in case Madison appears out of nowhere. Luckily, I spot Lowri's ginger ponytail swishing above everyone else's heads, and Karima's glossy black bob nearby. I snake through the bodies to emerge next to Karima, and sit on the grimy floorboards with her, tucking my legs to one side.

"How's Frankie?" Karima asks over the bustle of the hall. "I messaged her, but she didn't reply."

My eyebrows flick upward. "You heard?"

"I think everyone heard," Lowri says grimly. "Did you see the live stream?"

I shake my head. "Only the beginning. Did you?"

Karima shifts uncomfortably. Of course they've seen it— they probably watched it together. Kar-Low live in the same neighborhood and seem to spend as much time in each other's houses as their own.

"It was bad," Lowri admits. "It made me feel so angry. . . ."

"How is Frankie?" Karima asks again. But before I have a

chance to answer, a hushing sound breaks like a wave across the hall and Mr. McGovern appears at the front. Before the silence settles, I send my eyes darting around the hall until they find Madison and Aliyah on the other side, like a pair of wolves. I look away, sensing their wolf ears prick up and their noses twitching.

"Guten Morgen, freshmen," McGovern begins, forgetting he's not in one of his German lessons. He's what you might describe as a petite man, with large blue eyes and a mop of curly blond hair. Ever since Frankie found out his first name, we haven't been able to take McGovern seriously. Donald (yes, DONALD!) blasts out Pharrell Williams's "Happy," then delivers yet another talk about mental health. Any moment now, he'll bring up what happened over the weekend, surely? He'll send Madison & Co. slinking out of assembly with their tails between their legs.

Except he doesn't.

Assembly ends with a performance from a good-looking, football-playing freshman named Rupert Clifton, who also happens to be an advanced pianist. Muscle *and* musicality— nice, right? Seeing as I gave up piano last year after failing to master the C minor scale, I am more than a bit impressed. Rupert's crescendos carry me up, up, above the hall and out of the school gates, managing somehow—for a few minutes—to numb my anger about Madison going unpunished . . . until his piece is over, and the indignation comes flooding back.

A robotic round of applause fills the hall and McGovern insists that Rupert bow to his audience before returning to his row. Poor Rupert ducks his head for the briefest of moments.

Two minutes later, Kar-Low and I find ourselves next to Rupert and his best friend, Cameron, in the swarm filtering out of the hall.

"Congrats on the performance," says Lowri.

"Thanks," says Rupert, who is much taller up close.

"You make it look so easy," I add.

Rupert's nose wrinkles. "I hate performing."

"Really?"

He nods. "I don't like people watching me."

Suddenly, someone shouts over the tops of our heads.

"Hold up, maestro!"

Whoever it is, they're addressing Rupert. The fake-deep voice works its way through the crowd and eventually finds us. It's Kenny Fisher: one of the shortest boys in our year and King of Nasty. Everyone knows he wants Madison to be his queen—he's the one who nicknamed her Madison Fox.

"You all good, gay boy?" Kenny sidles up to Rupert. "How's it going?"

Rupert looks down at Kenny and sighs. "Playing the piano doesn't make me gay, Kenny. And even if I were, who cares?"

"It totally does," Kenny says, snorting, while the boys behind him snuffle like pigs.

"Oh, screw you, Kenny," says Cameron, a resigned look in her eyes.

Kenny turns to Cameron, relishing his chance to pick on an easier victim. "I'll tell you what *does* make you gay," he sneers. "Having a girlfriend with a knob."

Rupert's hands ball into fists and Cameron quickly steps between them. "At least I can reach to change a lightbulb," she says bluntly, and Kenny's face turns purple. "Come on, Rupes, let's go."

"Yeah, *Rupes*," spits Kenny. "Don't want to hurt those nice piano hands, now, do we?"

Cameron pulls at Rupert's arm, and eventually Rupert yields. They stride off together and my heart sings at Cameron's tiny victory. Cameron's had a pretty tough time at school in the past couple years. At the end of seventh grade, Cameron Hughes came out as trans and began transitioning. If that's not brave, I don't know what is.

"FREAKS!" Kenny hollers after them before sauntering off in the opposite direction with his pack of snickering reprobates.

"Idiot," snarls Lowri. "Someone needs to take him down a peg or two."

"Totally," I agree, feeling disgruntled. *But who?* Why should the Fishers and Coxes of the world be allowed to do this—to try to make people feel like nothing when actually they're amazing? Did Kenny even *listen* when Rupert was playing? Is he even *capable* of imagining how difficult it must be for Cameron to do what she's doing?!

An idea starts to formulate in my mind. It's the tiniest, weeniest speck of an idea, like the neat dot of a newly sharpened pencil. But it's something.

EIGHT

TOWARD THE END OF SECOND PERIOD, ONE OF THE
school secretaries walks into the classroom and shares hushed
words with Miss Osman, our art teacher.

Miss Osman beckons to me. "Pack away your things,
please, Evia. Mrs. Chubb wants to see you."

The room falls silent.

See me? See ME?!

I put down my lino cutter and start to sweep the tiny,
curled fragments into my palm. Lowri quietly offers to clean
up for me and flicks her hand at the same time, gesturing for
me to go.

"Thanks," I whisper, standing to lift my bag. My legs feel
like they're about to give way. I wish Lowri could come with
me. Where are those hundreds of hairy arms when I need
them?

"You're not in any trouble," says the secretary. But she
doesn't smile.

MRS. CHUBB'S office smells of stale coffee and new carpet. Our principal makes her short, squat frame appear as bolt upright as she can in her black leather chair, while Donald McGovern perches at her side, part teacher, part minion.

"Thank you for coming, Evia," says Mrs. Chubb. "Take a seat."

I lower myself onto one of two chairs in front of her desk, the cushions a dingy imitation of our emerald-green uniforms. I pull my blazer closed across my shirt, suddenly freezing. It's like the Arctic in here!

"You're probably aware," Chubb begins, "that I received a phone call from Frankie Smith's parents over the weekend."

My head won't even nod. It's as if my body is not my own—like I'm watching the whole scene from a corner of the ceiling, through a security camera.

"They told me about a rather horrendous incident that took place at their home on Friday evening. We know who the main culprits are, but Frankie herself is refusing to talk to us about it. We're just trying to drill down to the details so we can punish the right people. Can you confirm it was Madison Cox who cut Frankie's hair?"

I feel like a rabbit trying to cross a road.

"It's okay," tries Donald. "Anything said in this room will stay in this room. You'll be completely anonymous."

Ha! What a joke! My entire art class knows I'm here,

which means most of the freshmen will soon know, including Madison and Aliyah.

Eventually, I nod.

"And Pixie Perkins recorded it, we hear?"

I nod again.

"It's such a shame that these videos disappear after twenty-four hours. We would've had perfect proof. I have to say, it wasn't very intelligent of Ms. Cox to share this footage on social media. . . . So," Mrs. Chubb continues, "what was Aliyah Dobson's role?"

I pause. "I'm not sure, ma'am. I wasn't there."

"We realize that, but we understand Frankie may have told you more than she'll tell us. Did Aliyah do any of the cutting or shaving?"

"I don't think so. Frankie said Aliyah just watched."

"Madison performed all of the, err, hairdressing side of things?"

Hairdressing?! As if Frankie's bedroom were a salon and she emerged with a brand-new 'do?!

"She *attacked* Frankie's hair, ma'am, yes."

The Chubb doesn't drop her gaze. "And were the girls wearing school uniforms at the time, do you know?"

I frown. "Does that make a difference?"

Mr. McGovern chimes in. "The school can't be held responsible for a pupil's behavior at *all* times. The girls weren't on campus and it wasn't during the school day, but if they were wearing the school uniform, it might still be considered under our remit and our Behavior Policy still applies."

I dwell on this for a moment. "So if they *hadn't* been wearing uniforms, what they did would've been okay?"

"No," replies Donald. "It just changes the repercussions slightly."

I think back to the video. "Madison and Aliyah were in uniform; Frankie had changed. Does that matter?"

"No," replies Mrs. Chubb. "Thank you, Evia. Now, we're familiar with how Ms. Cox operates in this school, hence her previous suspensions. But to your knowledge, has Madison done anything like this to Frankie before?" She stares at me tenaciously, her eyes like a giant magnet trying to drag the words out.

I sigh. Our school has a zero-tolerance policy on bullying, but that doesn't mean it doesn't happen, slyly and quietly. Madison's had about five suspensions that I'm aware of—a couple days here, a couple days there, mostly for cyberbullying. But the suspensions don't seem to mean anything to her.

"Ma'am," I begin tiredly, "have you got any idea what it's like to be a fifteen-year-old girl with facial hair?"

Mr. McGovern shifts uncomfortably.

I continue. "Frankie's like a massive target every single day, and for people like Madison, it's too easy. It's not *physical* bullying," I emphasize. "It's lots of little things—like being stared at, being laughed at in the lunch line, people coughing insults over her name during roll call. Being called Frankenstein when no teachers are around."

I hate it when they call her that. Kenny Fisher first said it in seventh grade, and then it sort of stuck. One time, I dared to point out that Frankenstein was actually the name of the

42

scientist, not the monster, but I just got a load of abuse. Another time, Nate Whitehead told Frankie there was someone waiting for her outside the classroom, but when she went out, Frankie found a picture stuck to the back of the door. It was Hagrid from *Harry Potter* with a speech bubble saying, "Give me back my beard." Does Mrs. Chubb want to hear about that, too?

The Chubb leans forward and I notice how white some of her hair is. I don't think I've seen her this close up before.

"But have there been any other *serious* incidents involving Ms. Smith and Ms. Cox in the past?"

Serious incidents? As if the constant emotional suffering and mental anguish aren't enough?!

"Madison once tripped Frankie up with a hockey stick," I mutter. "But that was in middle school."

"I see."

"And I think she takes things. Like, Frankie's always losing her coat and sneakers—that sort of thing. I've never actually seen Madison do it, and the stuff always turns up in the Lost and Found, but . . ."

"Anything else?"

My head mists over. I wait for something to emerge through the fog, but end up shaking my head, disappointed in myself.

"All right, Evia," says Mrs. Chubb, closing proceedings. "If you think of anything else that we might find helpful, please come and see me."

"But what's going to happen, ma'am? You know—to Madison?"

Her mouth moves, eyes unblinking. "I'm sure you'll hear in due course. You may go, Evia. Thank you for your time."

I stand to leave, even though part of me wants to stay and challenge her—make sure something is going to be done. But the bell for next period rings, as if reinforcing the end of our meeting. I step out into the hall and immediately bump into a towering figure waiting outside.

Aliyah Dobson.

Anonymous, eh, Donald?

Aliyah makes a quick calculation behind her deep brown eyes as I walk away, trying not to run.

"SNITCH!" she calls after me, her eyes burning the word into the back of my blazer. Even when I've rounded the corner and am in the sanctuary of the girls' bathroom, I can still feel those six letters emblazoned on my back, smoking around the edges.

"What did I actually say?" I ask myself silently, looking in the mirror. "Something about a hockey stick and some missing sneakers?"

I try to persuade myself that Madison deserves what she gets; that I've done nothing wrong, have nothing to worry about.

But the Evia staring back at me does not look convinced.

NINE

THE NEWS GOES VIRAL AROUND ST. JOE'S PRETTY
quickly. Frankie's asked for daily updates on what happens
at school, so I call her before I'm even through the school
gates.

"Madison's been kicked out!" I announce gleefully. Then I
check to make sure none of Madison's cronies are nearby.

"What? Permanently?!"

"Well, no. It's another suspension—for two weeks."

"Oh."

"Two weeks is the longest they can give. I've only heard of
people being suspended for a few days before."

"What about Pixie?"

"Two days."

"And Aliyah?"

"Off the hook, I think."

"Oh, good."

"Good?!"

"Evs, our moms are best friends. It would be pretty bad if Aliyah got suspended for something that happened to me. . . ."

"Yeah, but she didn't exactly stop Madison, did she? She just sat there!"

"Oh God, I'm worried now."

"About what?!"

"About Madison! About what she might do next!"

"Well, don't worry. It'll all be forgotten before you know it."

"All forgotten? While I sit here looking like this?!"

Silence.

"I was thinking," I begin again. "Maybe you should post a selfie pulling the strong-arm pose or something. You know— show Madison you don't care?"

"Evia, I don't think you understand how *hideous* I feel right now."

We listen to the sound of my feet hitting the pavement. *Pat, pat, pat.*

"Are you almost home?" she asks.

"No, I'm heading into town for a bit."

"Oh, right. Look, I'm sorry for snapping. I just, well, I can't even look at myself in the mirror at the moment, so the thought of anyone else seeing me . . ."

She breaks off and we listen to more of my footsteps.

"Anyway," she says eventually, "if you want to come over, you know where I am. And remember to keep me posted with the goss—EVERY DAY."

"I will. Hang in there."

"Not going anywhere. Literally."

We hang up and I immediately regret not having been

more sympathetic. Then again, I also wish Frankie could see that by hiding at home and protecting Aliyah, she's letting the bad guys win. Sometimes I wish she'd just, I don't know, be TOUGHER.

And love herself more.

BEFORE I know it, my feet have carried me into the nearest shopping center. The speck of an idea that struck me this morning has been steadily snowballing all day, growing from that tiny pencil dot into a graphite boulder. I move on past the chain shops and cafés, past the benches where you can't tell the chewing gum from the pigeon poop, and across the bridge. Finally, I see it: the most colorful display of any shop window in town.

As I open the door, a brass bell jingles and an old man smiles fleetingly from behind the cash register before returning to his yellowed paperback.

The place is tiny and jam-packed with paraphernalia that could comfortably fill a shop three times its size. I fight my way through the maze of display stands and take the rickety stairs down to the basement, where it smells of polyester wigs and slightly damp walls.

My widened pupils scan the hodgepodge of kooky goodies. There are pirates' hooks and wispy voile skirts, in case you want to be a pirate fairy. Shiny capes and too-short nurses' outfits for the sexy flying medics. One wall is a sea of accessories, with everything from wands to walking sticks; another is a mountain range of hats, piled in teetering stacks. Rounding the corner into a musty alcove, I discover a rack of brightly striped ponchos, and voilà!

I lift the packet from its metal hook and hold it for a little while, enjoying the crackle of the flimsy cellophane. Then I choose a second, larger item before carrying my finds upstairs like trophies. I slide them silently across the counter.

"Costume party?" the old man asks.

"Not exactly," I reply, passing him the cash.

"Well," says the man, sliding back the prized items, "I've owned this shop long enough to know not to ask questions. Enjoy!"

I stow my purchases safely in my schoolbag and give the bag a reassuring tap.

"I will," I reply, a smile drifting onto my face.

I certainly will.

TEN

THE PACKET FROM THE COSTUME SHOP STAYS IN MY bag all night Tuesday and all day Wednesday. It had seemed like such a brilliant idea, but going through with it is hard.

By Wednesday evening I have:

- Received 536 likes for my forearm pictures
- Sent Frankie several texts with brilliant arguments for why she most definitely should *not* move schools
- Spent break times with Kar-Low and their clarinet and oboe
- Eaten way too much sugar, mostly in the form of jelly beans
- Decided to stop shaving my big toes. It's an easy one to give up, seeing as they're not that hairy anyway. We're talking, like, three hairs each. If a guy ever comments on my hairy toes, I'll find a picture from *The Hobbit* and tell him that's what I'm aiming for.

My phone vibrates on my desk and I read the message.

Frankie: *Donald came to my house today. He's trying to get me to come back to school* 😣

Me: *Already?!*

Frankie: *Yeah. I told him not yet. I mean, what would I do about the hair situation?! Plus, I'm not ready to see Madison's group.*

Me: *Madison is still off.*

Frankie: *I know. But seeing Aliyah and Pixie would be just as bad—they were there too . . .*

Me: 🙄 *So when do you think you might come back?*

Frankie: *I don't know . . . Donald talked about me returning on something called a reduced timetable.*

Me: *What's that?*

Frankie: *It's where I either go to key lessons or have my own room to study in, away from everyone.*

Me: *What about break times?*

Frankie: *I can have those in isolation too.*

Me: *I'd be there for you . . .*

Frankie: *I know. But you can't be with me ALL day every day. It's the times you're not there that I'm afraid of . . .*

You're an awesome BFF, Evs. But that's not enough to help me deal with the rest of it. Sorry xxx

Not enough.

I put my phone down and stare at the all-important packet I bought yesterday. Heart hammering, I rip open the bag and pull out its contents. Then I strip one of the black mustaches from its cardboard backing and nervously step toward my trusty mirror. Frankie's given me all the incentive I need, and this is my chance to do a test run.

Mustache in place, I smooth the sides down, enjoying how silky it feels beneath my index fingers. I look like a different person! I take a step back and stare for a bit longer. Am I strong enough to do this?

Before peeling the mustache off, I take a picture and share it with about a dozen hashtags, explaining my idea. Then I close the app and distract myself with a bit of hair-removal research.

I had NO IDEA that people had been removing body hair since the Stone Age. Did you?! But back then it wasn't just women doing it; men did it too—for practical reasons. They shaved their hair off so it couldn't get grabbed in battle, and also to keep frostbite at bay. Apparently, by removing the hair it prevented water from getting trapped and frozen against the skin. Who knew?!

I discover that in ancient Egypt, people removed their hair to keep lice away, using pumice stones, tweezers made from seashells, or a sugary mixture used like a wax. Then the Romans came along and decided smooth meant classy. They used razors made from flint and came up with their own hair-removal creams. After that, hair removal seems to go in trends. When Elizabeth I was queen, for example, people started shaving off their eyebrows to make their foreheads look higher, because that's what she did. Much as I dislike how thick my brows are, I decide I'd look pretty weird without them!

Reading the next few paragraphs of this article, something deep within me starts to boil. It seems that one person—a man, of course—came along in 1915 and suddenly decided women should no longer have body hair. King Camp Gillette marketed a razor for women with an ad campaign telling them that underarm hair was gross. All because he wanted to double his razor sales by selling to women.

ARGH! I'm so mad, I have to stop reading!

I click back to my mustache photo and can hardly believe the number of likes staring out at me.

Love it! comments one follower.

Do it! says another.

But can I? It's the kind of thing I'll never live down. The whole school will see me forever as That Weird Girl Who Wore a Fake Mustache. Will people understand why? Is it worth putting myself through all the ridicule?

Yes, I decide. After reading about King What's-His-Face, the approval from my followers is just what I need. It's like the supporters are here in my room, egging me on.

Tomorrow is the Big Day.

Tomorrow, I WILL DO IT!

∿

I AM standing in the school bathroom staring at my naked face in the clean, unblemished mirrors. It's Thursday morning and the cellophane wrapper is sticking to my hand. I recheck that the stalls are all empty, then I take a deep breath.

I am doing this.

For everyone who loved my photo last night. For the girls who have fallen victim to the likes of Nate Butt-Wipe Whitehead or Madison Wolf-Face Cox. For my nine-year-old self. And for all the Frankies: past, present and future. Maybe it's because of Antonia's lectures and attitudes toward grooming, or maybe I'm just fed up with playing a game I never signed up for. But why should the world care that girls have the tiniest bit of body hair? Why should the world expect us to remove it, bleach it, hide it? WHY SHOULD WE PRETEND THAT WE DON'T HAVE IT?!

I squirrel away the rest of my 'stache collection in my schoolbag and swing it over my shoulder. Then, smoothing down my school blazer in the mirror, I let out a long, wobbly breath before reaching for the door.

Here. It. Goes. . . .

The staring starts immediately.

The laughter is brazen, unconcealed.

I spot Nate himself pacing toward me and my heart takes a bungee jump. He stops in his tracks, mouth agape. I carry on walking until I'm past him, my face getting hotter. He shouts back over his shoulder. "Joining your friend in her freaks' club, Birtwhistle?"

I keep walking.

AT LUNCHTIME, I'm relieved when Kar-Low opt for the breakfast bar–style stools lining the walls of the dining hall. I sandwich myself between them so I can get a break from the staring. Somehow, girls staring is not as bad as boys staring. Maybe it's because I don't care so much what other girls think, and because I know, deep down, they'll be able to relate to what I'm saying. But the boys? I feel embarrassed when the boys stare. It's all very well behaving like a feminist, but I still want boys to find me attractive. One day—maybe next decade—it would be nice to find out what it's like to have a boyfriend. But right now, who's going to want to kiss the girl with an upper lip furrier than their own? This must be what it's like for Frankie every day, I realize, and feel a pang of guilt.

"So, math was fun," says Lowri, interrupting my daydream.

"Yeah, thanks for that." I pick a tiny piece from my pita bread and push it into my mouth.

"Why, what happened?" asks Karima, who's top of the class in advanced math. And everything else, to be honest.

I swallow the pita before Lowri can jump in. "Basically, Lowri spent the whole lesson trying to draw attention to my, erm, face-piece, while Cheeseman ignored her."

"He must've noticed it, though?!" says Karima.

Lowri shrugs with one shoulder. "Didn't seem to."

"Mr. Vincent was great, though," I say, recalling my French lesson. " 'C'est une moustache fantastique!' he kept saying, like I was getting into character or something!"

Suddenly, I'm aware of a load of cawing coming from the

corner of the cafeteria, where Madison and her crew usually sit. With Madison suspended, no doubt Aliyah has usurped her throne, but I do not dare look. Lowri swivels around to see what all the squawking is about.

"Hey!" I protest. "Don't draw attention to me!"

Lowri spins back. "I don't think you need *me* to do that, Evs."

There's the patter of sturdy-sounding heels as Mrs. Chubb ploughs her way through the noisy caf, gesticulating at various uniform misdemeanors.

I let out a long sigh through pursed lips, my mustache puckering.

"Miss Birtwhistle!" she announces from behind us.

I turn and smile while my mustache twitches in the manner of a small, hairy traitor.

"My office, please," says Mrs. Chubb. Then she turns and strides off.

My hands suddenly cold, I toss the remaining half of my pita into its plastic container and click down the sides.

"You'll be fine," says Karima.

I take one last swig of water and swish it around my mouth, forcing my throat to swallow.

I bare my teeth. "All clear?"

"Err, no," says Lowri, peering at me. "You've got a little something here. . . ." She pats her upper lip.

"Very funny."

Lowri shrugs, smiling. "See you in class."

Assuming I'm still here, I think.

"GOOD LUCK!" calls Karima.

ELEVEN

I'M BACK IN THE GREEN CHAIR, FROSTY AIR BLAST-
ing from the machine above.

"So, Evia," says The Chubb, propping her elbows on the
desktop so that her ample bosom folds neatly into the gap.
"What's all . . . this?" The palm of her hand sweeps circles in
the air above her mouth.

"It's a fake mustache, Mrs. Ch-Chubb." My teeth are chattering. The Chubb, meanwhile, seems oblivious to the wintry
gale.

"Well, yes, I can see that," she continues. "But what's it in
aid of? And why are you wearing it *at school*?"

I take a deep breath. "It's for Frankie, ma'am. I want to
make a point about . . . what happened to her."

"Ah. Yes. Frankie. You're aware of the . . . cause of her issues? Her condition?"

"Yes."

"But you don't have the—um—syndrome."

"No. But I do have body hair. Like everyone else."

If eyes could sigh, hers would. "Has your mother put you up to this?"

Oof! Even my principal knows about my mom's hairy legs! But the truth is, I haven't told Antonia about my—let's call it—"campaign." I'll be taking the mustache off before I go home—Mom would love it WAY too much. She'd take credit for it right away, congratulate herself for inspiring me, assume that I'm turning into a Gen Z version of her. Don't get me wrong: I love my mom. But no one likes the idea of turning into their mother, do they? I fully intend to conceal this masquerade from my mother for as long as humanly possible.

"No," I reply. "My mom hasn't put me up to it."

"Well, you know I can't condone the mustache. It's not part of the school uniform."

"It's just an accessory, Mrs. Chubb, like a pair of earrings. It's only shocking because it's different and making a point."

Tiredness seeps out of her like a musky perfume. "And what *is* your point, Evia?"

"That society expects us to deal with our 'extra' hair in secret and go around pretending that we don't have it. What sort of lesson is that to teenage girls?"

She looks at me through narrowed eyes.

So I tell her. About the cavemen and the Egyptians and the Romans. About Queen Elizabeth I and the Victorians, all the way up to miniskirts, bikinis and social media. I leave out the part about the Brazilian wax because, well, you can't talk to your principal about *pubes,* can you?!

"Gosh," says Mrs. Chubb when I've finished. "You've certainly done your research."

"Yes. And I think it's important other girls—and guys—know about it."

"Hmm."

"I just think it's totally unfair that if a man gets bored of shaving, he can grow a beard. But if a woman gets bored of shaving, she gets shamed and exposed."

"It is rather a case of double standards."

"Exactly!"

Mrs. Chubb leans back in her chair and stares at my nasal region, as if in a trance. Then she spins one hundred eighty degrees and gazes out of the window so I'm left looking at the back of her chair. The sun streams in around her and, for a brief moment, it's like she's a goddess.

I examine my nails until the goddess spins back.

"Okay," she says. "If we're going to do this, we need to be on the same page. You're an articulate young lady who has clearly researched her arguments, and I'm a woman in her fifties who's spent a lifetime conducting what we shall call *maintenance.* But you need to understand that when you walk around our grounds, you are setting an example to all pupils—younger ones, in particular. I am willing to let you make a point for a set period of time—let's say, until finals."

I make a quick calculation in my head. That's eleven more days of mustache wearing—not bad!

"If at any point this gets out of hand, or starts causing trouble, that will be the end of it. And I don't want it affecting exam season. When finals start, I want this whole crusade over and done with—KAPUT. Do I make myself clear?"

"Yes, ma'am. So, I have your permission to wear the mustache?"

"For now, yes."

A great big grin parks itself on my face.

"You will have to explain yourself to anyone who challenges you about it. But I don't want any propaganda being distributed or any soapbox speeches. Do you understand what I mean by that?"

I nod. I read a book about the suffragettes last summer.

"This is *not* a political campaign."

Well, it sort of is. . . .

"You'd better get to class."

Quickly, before she can change her mind, I pick up my bag and make a dash for the door. Kar-Low are going to be gobsmacked when my mustache and I walk in, intact!

"Miss Birtwhistle?"

I turn around, clutching the door handle.

"I'm not sure many other pupils will be as . . . open-minded. You had better prepare yourself for that."

I swallow. "Yes, ma'am."

Closing the door behind me, I prepare for the onslaught of stares in the end-of-lunch rush. I try to summon my inner tough cookie. But it's a strange thing. Does anyone actually feel tough—or brave—when they're doing brave things? Or do we all feel the same, like we're leaping into the unknown, about to poop ourselves at any moment?

It's a good thing I've got spare period underwear in my bag. Right now, emergency underpants are the only armor I have.

I HEAD straight for Frankie's after school, coat in bag and May sunshine warming my back. Thankfully, my afternoon was easier than my morning. In class, Ms. Wallace even suggested that she set up an interview between me and a writer for the school website, to explain what I'm doing and why. All the way to Frankie's, I predict questions I might be asked, sculpting perfect answers.

Outside Frankie's red front door, I reapply my mustache and smooth it down. Dom and Louise will both still be at work, and I doubt Jake will be home yet.

I push the yellowing doorbell and wait as a pair of feet trundle down the stairs.

I start to panic.

Only a pair of energetic feet could trundle this swiftly. They sound like peppy feet. HUNKY feet . . .

I brace myself as the peppy-footed owner opens the door. *Please don't be Jake, please don't be Jake!*

"Hello, Jake."

He stares at my hairy face-piece. "Evia?"

Yes, my love, my Romeo! 'Tis I!

"Is this some kind of joke?" he blurts.

Frankie emerges from the living room and starts walking toward us, a polka-dot headband carefully positioned over her unchanged hair. She peers around Jake's arm and gasps. Jake blocks the doorway to protect her.

It dawns on me: HE'S PROTECTING FRANKIE! FROM ME!

I'd been ready to jump into her house like an over-wound toy. Instead, I've been pushed over and my robotic feet are shuffling in the air.

"Are you making fun of Frankie?" Jake asks.

"No."

He steps aside, allowing Frankie to join in. "Honestly, Evs, are you? Because it's not funny. . . ."

"No, really, I'm not!"

Jake raises his manly eyebrows at me and lets out a huff from his manly nostrils. Then he simply shakes his head before stalking off back upstairs.

OMG, Jake *hates* me!

I want to cry.

"Have you been wearing that all day?" Frankie asks.

"Yes."

"At school?"

"Yes. The Chubb agreed to it."

"WHY?! Why on earth would she give permission for you to go around looking like Borat? It's like you're taking what happened to me and making a massive joke out of it."

Her words hit me like stones in the face—*pock, pock, pock*—so that my voice comes out all wobbly and pathetic. "I'm trying to make a point about . . . about girls and . . . and body hair. I'm doing this *for you*."

Her head jerks back like a chicken's. "Take it off."

"What?"

"If you want to be my friend right now, I need you to take it off."

"But—"

She stares at me like I'm a monster. I start picking at the mustache.

"You know what?" she says. "No. Just no." Then she folds herself back into the house and slams the door.

I rip off the mustache and let my skin burn. I can't tell whether it's tears or pain, but everything is a blur. I dig into my bag for the other thing I bought in that shop, and wedge it into the mailbox. Then I turn through the watery haze and make my robotic legs run, run, run.

TWELVE

IT'S SATURDAY MORNING AND KAR-LOW ARE IN MY bedroom. We're sprawled over my threadbare rainbow rug, surrounded by the contents of Lowri's backpack: a sketch pad, colored paper and markers.

"So she basically slammed the door in your face," says Lowri, arching an eyebrow.

"Yeah."

Karima cocks her head slightly. "It was probably just shock. She'll come around."

I grimace. "I'm not so sure. She won't answer my calls. I left a message asking if she wanted to join us today because I really want her to be a part of this, but . . ."

"She didn't call you back?"

"Nuh-uh."

Lowri shrugs, scooping a handful of trail mix. "She could've at least heard you out."

"Is that why you skipped school yesterday?" Karima asks.

I nod, feeling slightly ashamed. I'd mustered my most feeble voice and told Mom I felt sick, which wasn't a total lie. Replaying my argument with Frankie and the thought of putting that mustache back on does make me feel genuinely nauseous. Thank goodness Kar-Low announced they were coming over today for backup.

Karima selects a single jumbo raisin from the snack bowl. "Well, listen. Next time you feel like skipping because of Frankie or the mustache or whatever, talk to us first." She pauses for me to respond, not releasing me from her gaze. "I mean it. We may not be Frankie and we might be annoying sometimes because we argue a lot . . ."

"Like, A LOT," Lowri affirms.

"But we're still your friends, okay?"

She's right. Karima and Lowri bicker like a pair of old ladies sometimes. But you could test them on anything about one another, and they'd get it right. In fact, they spend so much time together that the boys at school often refer to them as a couple.

Lowri actually *is* gay—she came out last year, shocking the whole school. She simply said she'd known for three years she was gay, so what was the point in trying to hide it? Meanwhile, Karima has had the same boy crush since sixth grade, but is too shy even to speak to him. It's like just the thought of anything romantic or sexual makes her nervous. One time, we saw an unopened condom on the floor of the girls' bathroom and Karima nearly fainted. It was like getting her to step over a dead body.

There's silence for a bit while we sit there, listening to

Lowri munch peanuts. Then she swallows loudly, clearly itching to ask something. "Did Jake see you wearing that mustache, by any chance?"

My face crumples, betraying my answer.

"AHA!" Lowri blurts violently. "That's the *real* reason you skipped! You couldn't face bumping into Jakey-Wakey in the hallway!"

Argh! I regret ever admitting to Kar-Low that I like-like Jake, but Lowri once found me gazing at a picture of Jake on my phone and wouldn't drop the subject until I'd confessed. I made them promise not to tell Frankie—EVER.

"How did that rhyme go?" Lowri teases, and I cringe all over. Kar-Low once penned a love poem, supposedly written by me for Jake.

"Can we change the subject, please?" I ask hopefully. But Lowri's already whispering into Karima's ear, behind a cupped hand.

"No, no! That wasn't it," Karima says, giggling. "Hang on. . . ." She grabs Lowri's notebook and a red pen. Moments later, Lowri is adding her own finishing touch: the letters *E.B. 4 J.S.* inside a love-heart with a cupid's arrow. She flashes it at me before standing and clearing her throat. "'A Ballad for Jake Smith,' by Evia Birtwhistle," she announces.

I roll my eyes. Undeterred, Lowri begins again, this time in a deliberately feeble, high-pitched voice.

Jakey, oh my hunksome Jakey,
I love you more than cakey-wakey!
You turn my legs all jelly-shaky

and make my heart feel oh-so-achy.
In my future bed you'll wakey. . . .
How many babies will we makey?!

Lowri clutches the notebook to her chest before taking a large, extravagant bow to her audience. Karima applauds emphatically.

I glare at them both with narrowed eyes. "That had better not get airtime EVER again," I threaten.

"Oh, come on," snorts Lowri, sitting down. "It's funny. Not to mention TOTALLY TRUE."

Okay, so I *might* have imagined what my future children with Jake might look like, but would I ever reveal this to Kar-Low? No!

"It is totally *not* true," I insist. "I could never love ANY boy more than I love cake."

And on that declaration, we get down to the serious work of planning a campaign.

THIRTEEN

"JUST TO BE CLEAR," I BEGIN, "THE CHUBB SAID strictly no political campaigns."

"The Chubb just wants to avoid trouble," Lowri replies. "In the meantime, she's repressing us. Muting our voices."

I smile at Karima and cup my hand around my mouth. "Uh-oh. We've stirred Lowri's inner rebel."

Karima rolls her eyes and nods.

"We need a plan," says Lowri. "But first the party needs a name. Any thoughts?"

Mind. Blank.

"How about using a hashtag?" suggests Karima. "Like, #fightforfrankie or #weheartfrankie? Something like that?"

My head swamps with guilt. Frankie will come around when she understands what we're trying to achieve—I'm sure she will—but using her name in the meantime feels wrong.

"They're good hashtags," I reply. "But I'm just not sure they're campaign names. Besides, it's not *just* about Frankie.

It's about all girls and body hair and challenging what's normal."

"Girl power?" suggests Lowri.

Karima frowns.

I take a deep breath and say it fast, all in one go. "So, I've started this new social media account about body hair—sort of anonymous and confessional. It's called the Hairy Girls' Club."

Lowri grins. "Perfect!"

Karima nods. "Says what it is. People always want to be part of a club."

"It's not too . . . gross-sounding?"

"It sounds a *bit* gross," says Lowri. "But isn't that the point? To make body hair NOT gross? Challenge how people think about it?"

"That's exactly the point. But would anyone actually own up to being part of a club for hairy girls? Would they want to be in it in the first place?"

"Only one way to find out," says Lowri, pulling the lid off a marker with her teeth. Then she starts scrawling big, arty letters on one of the sheets. Karima might be the wordsmith, but Lowri is really good at designing stuff.

"Can I see what you've posted?" Karima asks me.

I bring up the images on my phone and hand it over. "I've only posted three so far. I wasn't sure what to do next."

"Hmm," she says. "It's a start. But how about we give the log-in details to our supporters? Then they can post pictures to it too? Join the revolution?"

"Yes!" says Lowri, looking up from her doodling. "Great

idea! That way everyone's involved. Plus, it's anonymous because they're not doing it from their own personal accounts."

"I dunno," I say slowly. "The Chubb said no propaganda. No speeches. How are we going to get supporters without talking to people?"

"Young Enterprise Week starts on Monday," says Karima. "We could bag ourselves a table and work from that. Call it advertising rather than campaigning?"

Young Enterprise is this thing our school does to encourage students to set up their own mini businesses. Most of them sell small homemade items like scrunchies and bookmarks.

"YES!" says Lowri.

"Isn't YE mostly for selling stuff?" I point out.

"We're selling an IDEA," Lowri explains.

"More an ideology," corrects Karima. "A set of ideas or a belief system," she adds, clocking my blank face.

"Could your dad print us some business cards?" suggests Lowri.

I'd forgotten Mr. Bakshi runs a stationery shop and printing business.

"*Join the revolution* on one side, and *#hairygirlsclub* on the other?"

"Yes! And maybe some T-shirts?"

"Oooh," says Lowri, clapping like an enthusiastic sea lion. "AND we could get a ton of mustaches and hand them out like badges."

I promptly tap on eBay.

∿

BY THE end of our session, we've devoured way too many grilled-cheese sandwiches (plain peanut butter for vegan Lowri) and created a huge pile of signs for our YE booth. On a couple of them, we've shortened "Hairy Girls' Club" to the punchier "HGC." We also made posters showcasing statements like:

- *Men told women to shave so they could sell us razors.*
- *Women often shave 10 times the surface area that men do.*
- *Once upon a time, female body hair was a nonissue.*
- *Razor companies made us feel ugly for having body hair.*

If that doesn't make girls stop and think, I don't know what will. Boys too, for that matter.

"Couple of slight issues," I say while my teammates pack up. "First, Frankie isn't actually on board with this. I feel bad going ahead without her approval. . . ."

"Add her to the group chat," says Lowri, collecting up all the bits of paper. "When she sees the bigger picture, she'll totally get it."

"And the other thing"—I'm wondering how to phrase this—"it's, well . . . you two aren't very *hairy,* are you?"

"Err, we might not be as hairy as *you,* Evia," Lowri ducks as I lob a piece of popcorn at her, "but everyone has body hair. You can't exactly vet people before they join the club. I mean, what would you do? Ask people to hoist up a pant leg?"

I picture Lowri stroking people's legs to determine their level of hairiness.

"Besides," she continues, "if you pick and choose your members, it's a bit like saying that a man can't support feminism. Or a straight person can't support gay rights." She raises her eyebrows at me in a way that makes me feel guilty for even considering the thought.

"Besides which, I am PLENTY hairy enough to join a Hairy Girls' Club!" boasts Karima. "Haven't you ever noticed my neck? The hairdresser basically has to shave the hairy bits every time she cuts my hair. She gets out the clippers in the middle of the salon and it's all *buzz, buzz* like she's shearing a sheep! *Sooo* embarrassing."

Karima tilts her head to show us, stroking her neckline. Two lines of dark hair stick out from the bottom of her bob.

"I've never noticed," I say with total honesty.

"As for my legs," she continues, "my mom only let me start shaving them last year. I mean, EIGHTH GRADE?! That's totally ridiculous, right? Everyone else started shaving their legs in, like, sixth grade."

Now that she says it, I do remember noticing her legs last summer in PE. She has dark hair like me, so it showed that she wasn't shaving yet. Luckily, after being called Hairy Maclary in elementary school, Antonia allowed me to start shaving when I was twelve. I was so bad at it to begin with that I kept slicing off long slivers of skin from my shins and ankles, turning our shower into a scene from a horror movie.

I look at Karima pointedly. "How would you feel about sharing a picture of your neck on the HGC feed?"

She presses her lips together for a moment. "Okay."

"Only if you're sure."

"Definitely," Karima insists. So we take a picture of her neck and post it.

"Your turn," I say to Lowri. "Any body hair we can photograph?"

Lowri's nose wrinkles up. "Not really . . . I sort of have the opposite issue. It's handy for swimming because I don't have to shave as often as everyone else." Lowri is a county swimmer and trains several times a week at the local pool. "But sometimes I wish I had *more* hair. I mean, check out my eyebrows—they don't naturally look like this." She wiggles her perfect chestnut brows at us. "How about I clean off my eyebrow pencil and share a picture of my naked brows?"

"Great idea!" I reply, reaching for my makeup remover. "It shows women have different kinds of body hair issues, from having too much to not having enough."

We photograph Lowri's barely-there eyebrows and upload them. Then we wrap things up for the day.

"Did you know," says Karima, on our way out of my bedroom, "in some countries, women have hair transplanted onto them to make themselves *more* hairy?"

"Like balding athletes?" Lowri asks.

"Yeah, sort of." We troop down the stairs together while Karima elaborates. "In Korea, women have pubic hair transplants. I read it online. Apparently, they think it's sexy to have a full, um, bush."

"Wow," I say, pondering this idea. "If that's true, maybe I should move to Korea. It would save an awful lot of wax."

"Nah, don't do that," says Lowri. "We'd miss you too much. And besides, we're leading a revolution, remember?"

FOURTEEN

ON SUNDAY MORNING, FRANKIE'S FACE FLASHES UP on my phone screen. It's her picture from last Halloween, with purple contacts and vampire teeth. I answer after two rings.

"Finally!" I begin. "I must've tried you about five times last night!"

"I know, sorry. . . ." Her voice is quiet.

"I wanted to talk to you about the campaign. Karima and Lowri came over yesterday—we came up with some awesome ideas!"

"Is this the mustache thing?"

"Yes."

"You're still going ahead with it?"

"Uh, yeah. We're called the Hairy Girls' Club and we're going to normalize female body hair to make girls less ashamed of it."

Silence.

"I'd love it if you could be involved. . . ."

Another long pause, then Frankie inhales deeply and breathes out for what feels like an eternity.

"I don't think I can," she says finally. "I'm not in the right headspace for it."

"We won't make it about you, I promise! It's about all girls! Everyone has body hair, right?"

"Right, except I have a lot more than most people."

"I know. But I'm not asking you to be our poster girl or anything, just to be a part of the group. Pleeease . . . I'm not sure I can do this without you!"

Another long sigh. "I'll think about it."

"Awesome. Can I add you to the group chat in the meantime? While you think about it? I hate you being out of the loop like this."

"Ohh-kay . . ."

"Yay!" My heart does a little skip in celebration. Then I tell her about everything Kar-Low and I have planned. Man, it's good to talk! And a massive relief after three days of not talking.

"Is Jake still mad at me?" I ask at the end. It's a risky topic, I know, but I can't bear the thought of Jake ignoring me again, like after the helicopter incident.

"He is pretty mad, yeah."

Oh.

"He doesn't get it. He thinks you should drop the whole thing."

Can't speak. May start sobbing.

"I'm sure he'll come around," Frankie says kindly. "It's just, I'm his baby sister. You know what he's like."

74

Yes. I know what he's like. He's lovely and sweet and protective and big and super, super hot.

I sigh into the phone. "Okay, well, I'd better go. . . ."

"Speak tomorrow after school?"

"It's a date."

"A date," Frankie echoes.

We hang up and I spend the next hour fantasizing about the dates I'll never have with Jake Smith.

ON MONDAY morning I stride into homeroom and take my usual seat next to the longshore drift display. I'm busy picking at the edges of a Greta Thunberg sticker on my tech folder when two figures claim the table in front and push their faces into mine.

Holy Spanx!

Karima grins at me, her mustache crinkling at the edges.

Lowri beams even more broadly, her mustache wrinkling too.

Karima's gone for the classic Poirot—small, neat and curled at the tips. Lowri, meanwhile, has gone all-out with a ginger one. GINGER! Hers is more Wild West–style, fat and bushy, like she's harboring a giant orange slug beneath her nostrils.

"Whose is better? Mine or Karima's?" asks Lowri.

"Umm . . ."

"It's totally mine, isn't it?" Lowri swings her head about, showing off her slug.

"No, definitely mine," says Karima, sticking out her chin. "I think this actually SUITS me!"

I laugh. "I think you BOTH look awesome! You just walked through school with those on?"

"Yep!" says Lowri proudly. "Put them on on the bus. Got a bit of a strange look from the driver when we got off!" Kar-Low catch one of the school buses that rattle in from the outlying neighborhoods.

"Brave," I concede.

"Yeah," mumbles Karima, her eyes wider than usual.

"My parents are loving it!" says Lowri.

"What—you told them about the HGC?"

"Of course! They're beyond excited. Think I've gone all political at last, as if I've declared allegiance to a political party."

Lowri is the product of two *very* left-wing parents. Her dad teaches history at Mayfield and her mom runs a food and baby bank in town. It's cool how open-minded they are, but when I go to her house, I dread all the questions. What do I think about the recent changes to our immigration policy? Is our household zero-waste yet? What's my opinion on such-and-such a party and such-and-such an issue?

We bump knuckles like we're on the football team. Then we take a group selfie in our collective 'staches and post it, giggling like idiots.

'Stache-tastic! I write.

"Ooh!" says Karima next. "Great news about Frankie joining the group chat."

"Defo!" adds Lowri.

"I know," I reply. "I was so relieved. . . ."

Suddenly, the classroom door swings open and Ms. Wallace breezes into the room. She clocks our facial-wear and smiles.

"Good to see you back, Evia," she says, pausing near my row. "I've organized that interview for the school website for after school today—is that going to be all right?"

I nod. "That's great, thank you!"

"Your interviewer is Leo Hobbs and he's going to meet you at the music practice rooms."

"Oh."

"What's the matter?"

"Nothing. I . . . I just hoped my interviewer might be . . . a girl."

Ms. Wallace's eyebrows flicker. "That shouldn't matter, should it? You need to be able to explain your campaign to anyone."

"I guess. Thanks."

Ms. Wallace heads toward her desk and logs into her laptop.

"Either of you heard of Leo Hobbs?" I whisper to Kar-Low.

They shake their heads and I immediately text the same question to Frankie under my desk. "I hope he's not hot. . . ."

"Nah," says Lowri. "He's probably some nerdy type with a comb-over."

Frankie sends an emoji—the girl shrugging. I reply surreptitiously, explaining about the interview and delaying our after-school chat.

"Are we still on for lunchtime?" asks Lowri.

"Yep! Although, don't you guys usually have orchestra on Mondays?"

"Usually," says Karima, looking a bit mournful.

"Oh, ignore her," says Lowri. "She's just sad because she won't get to spend her lunchtime with Ben."

"Shut up." Karima glowers, her cheeks adopting a cerise hue. Ben Ingham is the bassoon-playing boy Karima's had her sights set on since we started at St. Joseph's.

"Anyway, as I was saying," Lowri continues, "we do not have orchestra this week because we have more important things to do." She smiles at me conspiratorially and her orange slug smiles with her.

I RACE out of history at the stroke of lunch hour and sprint the wrong way around the one-way hallway traffic to beat the masses.

The entrance hall is lined with a semicircle of tables and eager-beaver Young Enterprise types. Most tables offer the usual accessories, kitten calendars and lavender bags. The most flamboyant table has pastel-colored bunting cascading toward it from the ceiling and a huge banner that reads *Barty Party*. Bartholomew Hedges from our year stands behind it, selling party "experiences" like plate painting and pizza-making, even though no one's had a themed birthday party since elementary school.

The final enterprise, run by a briefcase-toting sophomore guy, seems to be offering IT advice and gaming tips. Next to Briefcase Boy is an empty table that, I assume, is ours. Brief-case Boy registers me and my mustache, raises his mousy eye-brows, then returns to his tablet.

For a couple of minutes, I watch a pair of girls argue over which scrunchies to put at the front of their display. Then, thankfully, Kar-Low are at my side, armed with bracelets of sticky tape and trusty tote bags. Out come the signs and business cards; on go the T-shirts. We stick up our posters, including some prints of old ads for the first women's razors that say things like *Shave Yourself. It Is a Pleasure.* Now, shaving is a lot of things (the main one being a pain in the ass), but a pleasure it is not.

One ad describes shaving the underarm as "a feature of good dressing and good grooming," while another describes female body hair as "an embarrassing personal problem." *The underarm must be as smooth as the face,* says another ad, written, most likely, by a man who had never known what it's like to get a rash in your armpit, or to have your short-sleeved T-shirt rubbing against itchy, bumpy underarms as the stubble fights to grow back.

We reveal our cardboard mustaches-on-sticks (a temporary, homemade measure until my adhesive eBay ones arrive) and display them in enticing fan shapes at the front of our table.

The other enterprise teams snicker at our signs.

"How is THAT a business?" asks Briefcase Guy, arms folded.

"We're selling *a message,*" I reply, as if it's obvious.

"Yeah, except it's free," says Lowri. "Unlike your"—she scans the contents of his table—"life-changing GAMING TIPS."

He glares at her through narrowed eyes.

OUR FIRST-EVER HGC event is met with:

- giggles from groups of girls who pass us on the way to the scrunchies
- catcalls and taunts from the boys (predictable)
- curiosity from the teachers
- endless questions from younger students, who steal all of our mustaches-on-sticks.

"Same again tomorrow?" says Karima at the end of the hour.

My brain hurts. "Are you sure? That was tough!"

Lowri shrugs, packing up her tote bag. "It wasn't *too* bad." Suddenly, her face drops. She starts hunting through the tote, then her schoolbag. "Oh no," she says, frowning. "I can't find my notebook. I need it for tech—it's got my logo ideas in it."

Karima tuts. "*Someone* shouldn't have been doing their homework on the bus this morning. . . ."

Lowri scowls. "*Someone* should know when to feel sorry for their friend."

"Hang on a minute," I interject. "Which notebook is this? It better not be the same notebook with that—that *ballad*—in it. . . ."

Lowri looks sheepish. Suddenly, my stomach feels like one of those lottery-ball machines, flinging its contents around. I lower my voice and hiss at her. "You're not seriously telling me that Jakey-Wakey Baby-Makey is OUT THERE some-where?!" I jab toward the hallway with an angry finger.

Lowri's lips fold inward and she squints, as if she's trying to make herself disappear, face-first.

"You must've left it on the bus," says Karima, unhelpfully.

The lottery balls in my stomach spring around even more violently. I think one might be about to fire from my bowels. "We have to get it back! We have to!"

Karima rests a hand on my arm. "We'll check on the way home. If it's not there, we'll ask the driver. Don't worry—we'll find it."

Silently, we pick up our bags and head to lunch. Instead of preparing mentally for my after-school interview, I spend the whole afternoon worrying about that notebook. What if someone's already found it? What if it's fallen into THE WRONG HANDS?

FIFTEEN

THERE IS NO COMB-OVER. THERE IS NO NERD. LEO Hobbs is tall, with floppy jet-black hair and blue eyes so piercing I swear he can see straight through my school blouse. He's in the same league of hotness as Jake Smith, but in a less sporty, more slender way.

I push out my lady lumps as far as I can, then panic. What if I look like a pigeon with a stuck-out chest? I retract the lady lumps a bit. I don't want him to think I'm some kind of pigeon-woman hybrid.

"Hi," he says. "Evian?"

"Evi-a," I correct him. "No *n*."

One day, when plastic bottles are a thing of the past, I sincerely hope Evian water disappears from our stores. FOR-EVER.

"I'm Leo." Of course you are. Like Leonardo DiCaprio in *Romeo + Juliet*. All smooth-jawed and beautiful-skinned.

"Hi, Leo." My voice is shaky. Alas! This is not the voice of a fearless feminist campaigner!

Lovely Leo leads me into one of the music rooms, where we perch on two dilapidated old office chairs. Leo's looks like it's been attacked by crows, with bits of sponge sticking out all over the place. Mine's missing a wheel and threatens to unseat me if I lean too far backward. To counter this, I lean forward like a hunchback.

"Your chair's missing a wheel," Leo points out.

I glance down as if I hadn't noticed. "Oh yeah!" Then, deciding that I am going to ooze confidence, I smile at him. "I'll be okay."

Leo pulls an old-school spiral-bound notepad from his scuffed leather satchel. It looks exactly like Lowri's. . . . It can't be, can it? Maybe it is!

Before Leo gets a chance to write anything, I snatch the notebook from him and start thumbing through its pages. It's chock-full of beautiful, slanted boy-scrawl. Not a doodle or ballad in sight.

Someone turns on the radiators in my cheeks. "Sorry," I mumble, sliding the book back. "I thought it was someone else's."

Leo stares at me, mystified. Then he looks down at the page, rolling his eyes. Great. Leo Hobbs already thinks I'm a grade-A weirdo. Good start, Evia!

"Can I just check your last name?" he asks, clicking his rollerball.

"Birtwhistle. Like *bird whistle* but with a *t*."

Bird whistle? My cheeks are now blazing and my heart starts thumping like a Mazda at a drive-through. Oh God, he can hear the Mazda, I know he can!

"Before we start, I just need to, um, take your picture." He whips out his phone like a pistol and takes the shot before I get a chance to arrange myself.

"There!" he says, sliding his phone away.

My mouth falls open. I am sure Lovely Leo wants nothing more than to see the inside of my sticky, dry-tongued mouth.

"I'm sorry," I manage to say with my dry tongue. "Did you just? I, um . . . missed it. Could we, er, review it?"

Leo presents his weapon and flashes the picture at me. I look like a startled pigeon-hunchback.

Leo assesses the photo. "Actually, it is a bit . . ."

. . . unflattering?

. . . awful?

. . . like a mug shot for the Guinness World Records' Ugliest People?

He pauses. "Try again?"

I nod politely. "Please."

I attempt to sit up straight for Take Two and smile nicely.

In picture two, I am less startled and look more like an agreeable, friendly hunchback. Sensing that Lovely Leo wants to get on with the interview, I approve it.

"So," he begins in earnest. "Why did you start wearing the . . . umm . . . mustache?" Leo wags his pen at my face.

I stare back at him, smiling.

My mind is utterly blank. I snatched his notebook. I snatched his notebook!

"The mustache?" Leo prompts again.

I take a swig from my water bottle and swill it around my mouth. Maybe if my tongue feels less like a cactus, I will be able to speak some words?

"Frankie," I begin finally. "My friend."

Leo looks at me with a level of deep concern on his face. Sentences, Evia! Speak in sentences!

"My friend Frankie has a beard."

Good, Evia—a sentence! Leo looks relieved, but I'm still struggling. Maybe if I avoid looking into his crystal baby blues, that will help. I pick a stain on the ceiling and talk to that. The stain bears an uncanny resemblance to the shape of Australia.

"My friend Frankie has polycystic ovary syndrome," I tell the Australia stain. "She can grow a beard and a mustache and basically has a lot of excess hair."

At this point, I swear the stain winks at me. Feeling enthused, I set about thrilling the stain—and Leo—with the same captivating story I told Mrs. Chubb about the history of hair removal, with all my top facts. The speech rolls off my tongue with such ease that I feel quite the orator!

I stop for breath and glance at Leo. "Are you getting all of this?" I ask, eagerly.

"Uh, yes," he replies.

I peer over the top of his notebook.

He's written my name.

Oh.

"Did you want me to repeat anything? Maybe some of the key dates?"

"Uh, no—it's fine. I think, to be honest, our readers will be more interested in you—your hobbies, home life, that sort of thing."

I ignore Leo's hint, avert my gaze to the ceiling, and continue on my diatribe about the patriarchy. THIS is what he needs to get down—not senseless stuff about my hobbies! But Leo will not let it drop. He insists on asking about my family, my interests, my goals for the future. I am beginning to wonder whether Leo Hobbs might be showing more than just a journalistic interest in my life. . . .

"Last question," Leo says while I gaze at the Australia stain. "Who are your role models?"

"Oh." I hadn't prepared for this one. In my haste to identify an answer, I break away from the stain and gawk into the baby blues. My chair wobbles. "I can't remember. . . . Oh yes, I can. But I can't remember her name. It's the bearded lady from the traveling circus—you know . . ."

"No, sorry."

"Oh, what's her name . . ."

Leo smacks his lips together and shakes his head.

"Josephine! Josephine Clofullia!" I clap my hands in celebration of my own genius and throw myself back in my chair.

Big mistake.

Halfway back, I remember the missing wheel.

Three-quarters of the way back, I see my legs swaying in the air and Leo's alarmed face between my shoes.

All the way back and I'm on the floor. That treacherous excuse for a chair has thrown me off like a bucking bronco! I lie there for a bit, pretending it didn't happen and I am still a Lady of Elegance and Poise, seated on my throne. I am most definitely *not* lying on the carpet of a music practice room, surrounded by sticky Kit Kat wrappers and discarded chip bags.

Lovely Leo offers me his hand.

I am a feminist. I should not take his hand.

I take his hand.

"Would you like to swap chairs?" he asks.

I am a feminist. I must not take his chair.

I take his chair.

"Actually," Leo says, scanning his notes, "I think we're pretty much done. Maybe one last question before I go?"

I nod eagerly, eyebrows so high they're practically on my scalp. "Sure!" I reach for my water in the hope that a few gulps might get my breathing under control.

Leo looks straight at me, his perfect eyes gazing into my soul. "Do you have a boyfriend?"

Water gushing. Down throat. Too fast!

Coughing.

Spluttering!

Air filling with particles of saliva from MY mouth!

Lovely Leo recoils as I wipe my chin with my hand. Did I spit on him? Oh please God, tell me I didn't!

I mean, BOYFRIEND?! Wow. Maybe he was romantically interested after all! Maybe, despite my preoccupation with ceilings, I was coming across all confident and sexy and—

Leo slaps me on the back, quite hard. "Are you okay?" he asks, his lovely eyes all worried-looking. "Are you choking?"

Cough, cough. "No!"

Splutter, gasp. "Not . . . ch-ch-choking! Am . . . f-fine!"

"Okay," he says, sliding his pen into the wire of his notebook. "Don't worry about that last question. I think I've got enough. The article should be online about"—he checks his phone—"Wednesday." Lovely Leo packs the book back into his bag and stands to leave.

He looks at me one last time, with genuine concern. "Are you *sure* you're okay?"

I smile confidently between coughs. "Oh, y-yes. I'll be all right in a . . . a minute. You . . . g-go." I raise my hand in goodbye.

Leo stares at my forearm for a moment before leaving. He must be admiring it for its beauty. Perhaps he heard about its fame on social media. Finally, when Leo is able to wrench his gaze from my arm, he reaches for the door and is gone.

Surrounded by sticky keyboards and dated recording equipment, I am alone. I sit back down—in Leo's chair—and replay what just happened.

Stupid water.

Stupid ceiling stain.

Damn those perfect eyes!

Did I answer any questions AT ALL?

Suddenly, my phone pings.

Lowri: *Really sorry Evs but no notebook on the bus. We even asked the driver . . . I'll check the lost and found tmrw in case someone brought it in to school. xx*

Feeling a little weep coming on, I lower my head onto my hairy forearms. That's when I hear it. A strange crackle between my skin and the desk.

I turn my head and there it is: stuck to the back of my arm with its chocolatey goo—an old Kit Kat wrapper.

Ew.

Like the wrapper, my heart crumples. Because *that*, I realize, was the last thing Lovely Leo saw. He wasn't admiring my deep brown eyes or my lady lumps. He wasn't admiring my famous forearm. He was staring at me in pity. Because not only am I a notebook thief and a weird girl who likes to talk about body hair, I am also a Giant Trash Magnet.

SIXTEEN

TWO HOURS LATER . . .

Frankie: *How did the interview go?*

Me: *Don't ask.*

Frankie: *Because you're embarrassed about how superbly well it went?*

Me: *Yes. That.*

Frankie: *How was Leo?*

Me: *Umm . . .*

Frankie: *What did he look like?*

Me: *Leonardo from Romeo + Juliet.*

Frankie: *Oh no . . .*

Me: *Oh yes. I wore a mustache in front of Romeo and I fell off my chair and I spat on him.*

Frankie: *You fell off your chair?*

Me: *Yep.*

Frankie: *And you SPAT on him?*

Me: *Yep. I sprayed him with water from my actual mouth.*

Frankie: *Wow. You really know how to get the boys, Evs!*

Me: *I'm going to die a virgin.*

Frankie: *No, you won't. Unless you die tomorrow, in which case . . .*

Me: *Thanks! Seriously though, everyone at school already thinks I send boys running. Now I'll have a rep for spitting in their faces too! It's Leo's fault. He shouldn't have been so cute. Oh and guess what? He even asked me if I had a boyfriend!*

Frankie: *What did you say?*

Me: *I can't remember. I only remember the spitting.*

Frankie: *Oh Evia . . .*

Me: *In fact, I don't think I answered his last two questions. He basically just gave up in the end. Do you think the boyfriend question was part of the interview? Or d'you think he might've been genuinely interested in me?*

Frankie: *Um . . . Probably the first one. If he was interested, the whole spitting incident may have changed his mind slightly . . .*

Me: *Alright, alright.*

Frankie: *How did the Young Enterprise thing go?*

Me: *Honestly? Not great.*

Frankie: *Oh. Are you doing it again tomorrow?*

Me: *Yes. Because we are masochists.*

Frankie: *Fill me in tomorrow then! And try not to worry about the Leo thing . . . Plenty more fish in the sea and all that.*

Me: *Our school is less of a sea and more of a pond. With pond weed and a layer of scum.*

Frankie: *Exactly! One day we'll be out in the real world with sooooo many more fish . . .*

Me: *We'll catch us some real winners.*

Frankie: *Absolute beauties. Not a blobfish in sight.*

Me: *Blobfish?*

Frankie: *Google it. Goodnight, my lovely BFF. xx*

SEVENTEEN

ON TUESDAY, THE THREE OF US MARCH TO RECEPtion like women on a mission. Karima and I wait hopefully outside the office while Lowri goes to check the lost and found. She emerges a couple of minutes later.

"Not there," she announces. "And no one's handed in a notebook."

My heart does a sort of belly flop but I manage a small smile. "Thanks for trying."

"Don't worry," says Karima. "It's probably in a trash can somewhere. I bet whoever found it didn't even look inside."

Lowri feigns outrage at the idea of her prized notebook ending up in the trash. "Whoever found it should hang on to it. It might be worth something one day—all those quality sketches inside. It's an Edwards Original!"

I laugh awkwardly and concentrate on picturing the notebook in the belly of a dumpster, being poured into a landfill and buried forever. Goodbye, "Ballad for Jake Smith"! Be gone!

We head for our Young Enterprise booth and find our biggest sign has been graffitied. Someone's scrubbed out *Hairy* and scrawled *Scary* above it, each letter scribbled over itself several times.

" 'Scary Girls' Club,' " I read aloud. "That's not bad. Maybe it's a better name for us."

"Yeah." Lowri nods. "It's sort of mysterious. Like, are we scary because of the extra body hair? Or are we scary because we're such brilliant feminists?"

Karima's face crinkles. "I don't think they meant to congratulate us."

"Doesn't matter," I add. "Either way, they're intimidated by us. Which is a good thing."

"I'm not sure anything about *me* is scary," mutters Karima.

"You're a fifteen-year-old girl who knows her own mind," asserts Lowri. "To some people, that alone is scary." She nods at Karima as if that's ample evidence of her statement.

I peel the sign from our table frontage and stick a new one in its place. Next to us, the IT geek snickers loudly.

"What's your problem, Briefcase Boy?" snaps Lowri.

"N-n-nothing!" stammers Briefcase Boy.

"Was it you who graffitied our sign?"

"No!"

Lowri glares at him. "Then keep your opinions to yourself."

Briefcase Boy murmurs something apologetic to Lowri's copper ponytail as she turns her back.

∿

DAY TWO of "advertising" goes *mostly* well. We pass out around thirty mustaches to genuinely interested girls (though they don't put them on), and even consider holding an event of some sort.

"What about a turn-in program?" I suggest. "The police had one where people voluntarily handed in their knives. Maybe we could do something similar. . . ."

Lowri attacks a giant falafel. "With razors?" she mumbles, an ocher chunk escaping from her mouth.

"Razors in school?!" replies Karima, peeling a banana. "Mrs. Chubb would love that!"

"You're right," I add, swallowing a mouthful of peanut butter sandwich. "Too dangerous. But other hair-removal products might be okay: bleaches, creams, waxes . . . Strictly no blades."

"No blades," repeats Lowri, absorbed in chickpea consumption. "Good thinking."

"How about Friday?" I suggest. "Gives us time to make flyers and spread the word. I'll design something tonight and we can photocopy it first thing tomorrow."

"Perfect," says Karima.

We pack away our signage this time, just in case.

"Oh look, girls!" jeers a voice from behind us.

My veins freeze over as we spin to face Aliyah—and the rest of Madison's crew. "This must be the Hairy Muffs' Club we've heard about. Hands up if you want to join!"

No hands go up. Instead, Aliyah pulls out her phone and takes a picture of our stand. She flips the phone to show us our bemused, unsuspecting faces.

"I'm sure Mads will LOVE this," she explains, thumbs tapping.

I immediately go numb and hate myself for it. Karima shuffles toward a curtain.

Lowri, on the other hand, steps forward like a Viking Warrior Princess. She waves a single sticky-backed mustache at the group. "No takers?"

"Are you insane?" says Aliyah, pocketing her phone. "I mean, seriously. No girl actually WANTS to have a mustache. Can you imagine?! Oh, hey, boys! Come and make out with my big hairy face!"

Her cronies elbow one another with a chorus of guffaws. It's amazing how Aliyah's suddenly found her voice with Madison away. Usually it's Madison who does all the talking.

"It's not about boys," says Lowri. "It's about helping each other. Normalizing body hair so girls don't feel embarrassed about their bodies."

"You would know, fire crotch!" scoffs Pixie Perkins.

"Really?" says Lowri pityingly. "Is that all you've got?"

"No," says Pixie. "Fire . . . crotch . . . face."

Lowri snorts hard. "That doesn't even make sense!"

Aliyah sends Pixie a withering look, then turns and stares at me. "I thought your little crusade was all about Frankie Smith?"

My neck prickles.

"You know, she barely fought back when Mads started cutting her hair. It's like she *wanted* her to do it."

My inner angry rhino starts roaring in my ears.

"That's not what I heard," I say quietly.

Aliyah huffs. "Just wait until Mads hears about your little club. You know she's back at school next week? She's gonna *love* this. Oh, and she really appreciated you snitching on her to The Chubb, by the way, Evia."

"I didn't."

"Yeah right!" chimes in Pixie. "I was stuck at home for two days. My mom was pissed. . . ." She makes a face.

"Should've thought about that before going all Quentin Tarantino," says Lowri.

"Quentin what-now?" asks Pixie.

Lowri cocks her head. "Er, famous Hollywood director?"

"Never mind," says Aliyah, turning back to me. "So what were you and Chubb talking about in there? Tips on how to tame your beavers?"

The posse giggles and my rhino starts up again, preparing to charge. "Maybe if Madison hadn't wanted to get found out, she shouldn't have live streamed the whole thing to half the school."

"Good point. I'll be sure to pass that on."

Suddenly, the bell buzzes.

"That's a shame," says Aliyah, turning to the person next to her—a tiny girl named Ellie, whose head barely reaches Aliyah's shoulders. "I was about to suggest starting our own club, ladies." Ellie gawps up at Aliyah with too much adoration, willing her to go on. "Something for *normal* girls who actually *care* about what they look like. So long, Muff Magnets!" And with that, she whisks off, the others speed-walking to keep up.

I feel like I've done ten cycles in a tumble dryer with a studded jacket.

"Well, she likes being honorary leader of the pack a bit too much, doesn't she?" says Lowri. "Mad-Mads won't like it when she comes back and finds Aliyah's taken over."

I nod. "Don't worry. I'm sure Madison will snatch her crown back soon enough. I bet she's asked Aliyah to send her pictures. She'll have a severe case of FOMO."

We swing bags over shoulders and head for class.

"I'm so sorry I didn't say anything, guys," chips in Karima. "I get so tongue-tied when they're around."

"Me too," I admit.

Lowri groans. "Seriously, you two . . . they're just girls! Like us, but mean."

I am so mad at myself. I can stand up to my mom and my friends, even to teachers sometimes. But when it comes to girls like Madison and Aliyah, my head turns into a slushie machine and churns my brains into mush.

"Do you really think they're going to start their own club?" Karima looks worried.

"Who cares?" says Lowri. "If they feel threatened by us, it means we're doing something right!"

Hmm. I'm not sure they feel *that* threatened. And the thought of Madison coming back to school? It makes my peanut butter sandwich want to lurch back up my esophagus, punching with its little peanut fists.

EIGHTEEN

ON WEDNESDAY MORNING, I AM ADMIRING MY FLYER design for our Hair-Removal Product Turn-In when Kar-Low slink into our homeroom. I flash the flyers under their noses.

"They look good," says Karima, smiling weakly.

Lowri nods but says nothing.

"What's the matter?"

"Her notebook turned up," Karima replies. "It was on the floor of the bus this morning."

"That's good, isn't it?" I ask, relief waiting to flood my entire body.

Lowri shakes her head. "There was a page missing."

"*That* page," adds Karima.

The relief turns to dread and hits me like a tsunami.

"Someone on the bus must've found it and ripped it out," Karima continues. "We just need to find out who." She pauses, clocking my worried face. "Don't worry—I'll get my detective hat on."

"She has a really good detective hat," Lowri says, sounding confident.

But the only confidence I have is confidence in the fact that someone has read that ballad. Not only have they read it, but they've decided it's interesting enough to hang on to, suggesting that either they know me or Jake—or the both of us. And although Lowri tries to distract me all through drama class, all I can think about is someone delivering that piece of notepaper to Jake, and him reading it, and him *knowing*. And the thought of him *knowing* makes mini tsunamis strike again and again, sloshing through me in sickening waves.

AT LUNCHTIME, Young Enterprise is a welcome distraction. I am busy displaying my beautiful flyers at the front of the table when a pair of younger girls round the corner into Reception. One of them raises her hand to us and the other smiles. As soon as they've gone, I turn to Kar-Low.

"Did you see that? Those girls?!" I feel like a jumping bean. "They were wearing mustaches! *Our* mustaches!"

Karima nods enthusiastically. "There was another girl on our bus this morning."

"And three in the hallway earlier," adds Lowri.

I can't believe it. "It's working! People are actually DO-ING IT!"

"Let's not get carried away," says Lowri. "That's only"— she does a quick count on her fingers—"nine girls wearing mustaches, including us. Not exactly a revolution."

I shrug. "All revolutions have to start somewhere. By the way, did one of you get us an extra table?" I point to a table on the end, squeezed in between us and the cafeteria doors.

"Nope," says Lowri.

Karima shakes her head.

"Shall we move it? It's kind of cramping our style."

Lowri and I each grab a side of the table and are about to lift it when something jabs me in the shoulder blade.

"Ow!"

"I think you'll find that's ours."

It takes me a moment to recognize her under the platinum wig. It's Aliyah, but she's dressed as . . . What IS she dressed as?

Aliyah takes center stage behind the table while her underlings tack posters to the boards behind. All seven of the girls (seven!) are wearing bouncy blond wigs and red lipstick.

The underlings step forward to reveal posters of Marilyn Monroe, including that famous image of her in the white dress. Suddenly the wigs make sense. Their board is peppered with quotes, scribbled on large sticky notes in capital letters:

I JUST WANT TO BE WONDERFUL.

BEAUTY AND FEMININITY ARE AGELESS.

GIVE A GIRL THE RIGHT SHOES AND SHE CAN CONQUER THE WORLD.

Okay, so the one about the shoes is totally sexist. But who doesn't want to conquer the world? Who doesn't want to be wonderful, or feel beautiful? More to the point, who's going to want to wear a mustache and confess to owning even the tiniest patch of body hair when they've got one of the most famous sex symbols of all time staring down at them? Even a glimpse of Marilyn's leg makes me feel embarrassed about the hair growth on my big toe. GRRRRR!!!

"The Normal Normas?" says Briefcase Boy, daring to read their team name aloud. "Who's Norma and what's she got to do with Marilyn Monroe?"

"It's Norma Jeane, you idiot." Aliyah glowers as girls from the other enterprises flock to the new booth. "Her real name was Norma Jeane. *Everyone* knows that."

"Not everyone, clearly," says Lowri, crossing her arms. "Maybe the link in your *brand* isn't clear enough, Dobson."

But even I have to admit, their brand is pretty strong. *I'm a Normal Norma!* say their badges—i.e., I'm not a hairy freak. *We just want to be wonderful!* says a poster—i.e., We *don't* want to be hairy and hideous. Above all, they're saying that aspiring to be beautiful is a *normal* thing, and Marilyn Monroe represents everything that society holds to be beautiful even today, decades after her death. I mean, she even had curves, for God's sake. She was not one of those skinny supermodels the world has turned its back on. She had boobs and hips and even a fold in her belly in one of the photos, like a real person. She was beautiful and sexy and who wouldn't want to look like her, right?

Boys gather to drool over the Marilyn pictures and girls clamor for the badges. People call to their friends until the crowds are five or six deep. The three of us stand back and watch. One by one, girls pin on their Normal Norma badges while our mustaches go untouched. A couple of our mustachioed recruits even collect badges and wear them WITH their mustaches. My fingernails dig into my palms. Can't they SEE the contradiction?!

With each badge that gets snatched from their table, Aliyah gets more and more smug. She leans back on her heels, plumping up her fake blond tresses.

"Argh," Karima says quietly, scowling. "I hate them."

"Me too," asserts Lowri. "The only consolation is that Aliyah actually looks a bit weird in that wig. I mean, she normally looks hot in anything—even chemistry goggles."

Lowri's right. Frankie told me that Aliyah's mom has been bragging to Louise lately about Aliyah doing sportswear modeling. No wonder Aliyah loves wearing gym clothes so much. It wouldn't surprise me if she had them on right now, under her school uniform.

You look stupid! I want to shout at Aliyah. *You look stupid and your whole idea is old-fashioned and ignorant.* I mean, what does *normal* mean, anyway? What was *normal* about Marilyn Monroe? Sure, she was conventionally beautiful, but she still struggled—her life was far from perfect.

"They could've chosen some decent quotes," Karima mutters. "Wasn't it Marilyn who said something about us all deserving to shine?"

"Twinkle," says Lowri, reading from her phone. " 'We are all of us stars, and we deserve to twinkle.' "

I frown.

"And: 'A wise girl knows her limits. A smart girl knows that she has none.' "

"Why on earth didn't they use that?"

"Because they're not smart?" Lowri goes back to her

phone. "I thought I'd look them up, in case they got something wrong. My personal favorite, though," she scrolls down the screen, "is 'I don't mind living in a man's world as long as I can be a woman in it.' Man's world! Pah!"

"To be fair to Marilyn, it was even more of a man's world in the 1950s," I concede. "Being a woman was totally different back then. Everyday sexism was probably more like hourly sexism."

"Ahh, but 'beauty and femininity are ageless,' " Lowri quotes in a soppy voice.

My top lip curls in a one-sided sneer, squeezing my mustache. I hold up a solitary flyer and flap it wildly.

"Hair Cream Turn-In, anyone?" I call fervently.

But the Normas are so loud, nobody hears me.

NINETEEN

THE ARTICLE GOES LIVE ON THE SCHOOL WEBSITE halfway through math—Lovely Leo sends me a link—and even though I've steeled myself for it, I'm still a bit stunned to see the 'stache-wearing hunchback flash up on my phone. I flash my screen at Lowri, under our desk. "Exciting!" she whispers, trying to give me a boost. But behind us, a few people start snickering. I mean, seriously. Aren't they used to seeing my face-avec-mustache by now?

Before long, a paper plane clips the top of my ear while Mr. Cheeseman's back is turned, and dives onto my desk. As the paper unfurls slightly, I see something written inside. I whip the plane under the table, heart thumping, and unfold it in my lap.

Lowri hears the rustling and looks with me.

E.B. 4 J.S.

The big letters are scrawled inside a massive heart with a cupid's arrow drawn through it—exactly like Lowri's original doodle.

Somebody's got the poem.

Somebody knows. . . .

My heart pounds even harder while Lowri grimaces. Then I screw the paper into a ball and quickly pocket it. We turn around together, glaring. From the middle of the back row, Luke Travers cocks his head at us and makes a heart shape with his fingers. The boys on either side of him crack up. So *that's* what they were laughing at. Not the interview or my big, stupid face, but the thought of me crushing on Jake Smith. There are actual shooting pains in my stomach.

Luke Travers is a pointy-faced boy who creeps under the teachers' radar at school. He's not the loud, punch-you-in-the-face kind of bully, but the sly, cut-you-down-in-seconds kind. He picks on the easy targets—the ones he knows will cry afterward, like Frankie. And he rides the same bus as Kar-Low.

Toward the end of math, I stealthily start packing up my things. As soon as the bell rings, I'm out of there.

"Wait!" Lowri calls, but I'm gone, racing to catch Luke.

"Where is it?" I demand, half running to keep up with him. "Have you got it?"

"Got what?" Luke's thin eyebrows flicker in amusement.

"The poem."

Luke shrugs, smiling, and picks up his pace. I chase after him.

"Please, Luke, don't be a jerk. . . ."

"Please, Luke . . . ," he mimics as Lowri catches up with us.

"*Pleeease don't tell my best friend's brother that I lurrrve him and want to make out with him and have his baaabies!* Guessing I'd better not send it by Bro-Mail, then?"

"What?" I stop walking.

Realizing he's got me where he wants me, Luke stops walking too. "Well, Bradley sees Jake all the time. It'd be pretty easy for him to deliver your little love note."

Bradley is Luke's older brother. And he's in the same year as Jake.

"Please don't," I beg.

"Yeah, don't be mean," says Lowri.

Luke huffs at her. "What's the matter, Lesbos? Not got a secret crush of your own? Slim pickings around here for gay girls, isn't it?" Luke's pointy chin juts out beneath a self-satisfied sneer. "Oh, and don't worry, Birdwhistle—your little ballad will be safe with Bradley." He laughs and starts walking away.

I watch Luke's swagger through a blur of hot tears.

"I'm so sorry," Lowri says gently, turning toward me. She gives me a hug. "Are you going to be okay? I'd walk you home, but . . ." She tilts her head in the direction of Luke and their bus.

I swallow the lump in my throat. "I'm fine. Are you?"

Lowri shrugs. "I'm used to it. I would say I'm stronger than I look, but . . ." She raises her right arm and flexes her swimmer's bicep at me. I smile.

As she starts walking to her bus, Lowri throws me one last tiny, sympathetic wave. I nod at her, then, blinking back the tears, I march—hard and fast and angry. It's only when I get home that I allow the anger to melt into tears.

THERE'S A knock on my bedroom door and it opens.

"Everything okay, Fluff?"

"No," I reply, although my face is so deep in the pillow that it sounds like "dough." I can't tell my mom about Jake, though, can I? It's way too embarrassing.

Mom perches on my bed, stroking my back.

"I think it's wonderful," she says, and I turn slowly to face her.

"What?" What's wonderful?

Mom holds up her iPad and my big, horrid, mustache-donning face stares back.

Oh. That. Somehow, since being sucked up by twin tornadoes Storm Lost Ballad and Storm Bro-Mail, I had forgotten about Leo's article.

"Lowri's mom texted me. What a lovely friend, doing something like this! I have never felt so enormously proud of my baby girl."

I rest my head on that smooth bit between my mom's shoulder and chest, and say nothing.

"Frankie is so lucky to have you. I knew you felt strongly about what happened, but I didn't know you were doing all this." She taps the picture and my hairy face expands to fill the screen. EURGHHH!!

I reach for a tissue.

"My life is over, Mom."

"What?!"

"Jake is about to find out that I like him."

She puts the iPad down. "Evia, it's very common for girls to get crushes on their friends' older brothers."

"I know, but he's about to find out in a really, really bad way."

"Well, it's not like it's a secret. Everyone knows."

I stare at her, speechless.

"I've known you've had a thing for Jake ever since that camping trip. You can barely talk about him without blushing. And I can't say I blame you. . . ."

I snort into the tissue, emptying my nose at the same time. "Jake doesn't know, though, does he? Or Frankie? Please say Frankie doesn't know!"

Mom shrugs. "Even if she does know, she'd probably rather not talk about it. Let's focus on this." She shrinks my face on the iPad and scrolls down. "It's just fantastic!"

I put my head in my hands for a moment. When I dare to uncover my eyes, I say, "Mom, HOW is it fantastic? No boy is EVER going to want to go out with me now. 'Strident feminist,' it says. 'The school's answer to Florence Given!'"

"A huge compliment, if you ask me."

"But he didn't include any of the important stuff! Nothing about the patriarchy or the history of hair removal. It's all about ME! He's put my top interests are raiding charity shops and decorating cushion covers! What a lame-o!"

I'm going to hyperventilate.

"Ujjayi breath, Evia. In through your nose, out via your throat . . . nice and deep . . . *Theeere* we go. It's the warrior breath, remember. You're a warrior."

"I'm not."

"You are! What you're doing takes real strength and courage. I thought I might call Lucy to see if I can arrange an interview. What d'you think? Is the Hairy Girls' Club ready for teen-mag fame?" Lucy used to work at the same mag as Mom until it folded. Now she works for one of the last remaining print magazines for teenagers.

I stare at my mother. "Why? Because my last interview went SO well?"

"Oh, come on. Lu hasn't been up for a couple of years. She'd LOVE to see you and meet your friends!"

I pause. Maybe talking to a woman would be different. Maybe that's where I went wrong with Leo. "I'll think about it."

"Okay, well, food for thought. Speaking of which, I think we should do something to celebrate. My daughter, the feminist! A chip off the old block, eh?" Her elbow prods me in the ribs. "How about pizza tonight?"

"Yes," I whimper. "That *might* help."

"Veggie Supreme? With garlic dippers?"

I attempt a smile. We hardly ever get delivery—Mom can't bear all the packaging that comes with it. This proves it: she must be *seriously* impressed. But even thoughts of melted cheese and crusty goodness can't override the image that keeps forcing its way forward. It's the one where Bradley Travers hands Jake Smith a piece of notepaper. And Bradley laughs and slaps him on the back while Jake squirms, his face burning with embarrassment.

I am going to have to stalk Bradley Travers at school tomorrow and get that piece of paper back.

TWENTY

I ARRIVE AT SCHOOL TEN MINUTES EARLY AND HEAD toward the upperclassman common room—a small gray building set away from the rest of the school. I find a spot outside the science block where I can keep watch over their door and lean back against the red bricks.

Students drift in and out. I watch as they visit lockers, take off coats, wait for vending-machine coffees. They seem so tall and adult that I wonder how, in less than two years, that could be me going in and out through that door, wearing that uniform.

After ten minutes and no Bradley, I am about to give up when someone taps me on the shoulder. I spin around to find Jake Smith—yes, THE JAKE SMITH—staring at me. He smells so good, I wish I could turn this into a scratch 'n' sniff book just so you could get an idea of what eau de Jake smells like.

"Everything all right, Evian Water?"

Oh no, he knows! He's read it!

I nod frantically, like an idiot.

"You waiting for someone?"

"No . . ."

His handsome eyebrows pull together, confused. "Oh, right. Okay. Look, now I've got you here I might as well say . . . Sorry if I overreacted the other day. You know—at the door. I just, erm, wanted to protect Frankie. But she explained what you're doing and it's—well, it's kinda cool."

"Oh!" Maybe he hasn't read the ballad, after all. My mustache dimples above my smile—hopefully in a cute way.

Jake looks at the common room door, then back at me. "Right, well, I'd better get going. Good to see you." He taps his upper lip. "Strong look."

I blush. "Thanks."

Then, as he turns toward the common room, I pick up my bag and start walking to homeroom, like I'd just been lingering by a wall for the fun of it.

Please don't bump into Bradley Travers, I pray silently. *Please, please don't.*

LATER, WE are back behind our little table for day four of campaigning-not-campaigning when suddenly, the Chubb struts toward us with her hurricane face on. Turns out, she's been away for the past three days at an admin conference.

"Girls!" she says, smiling dangerously. Her voice snaps to

ice-cold mode and we all freeze on the spot. "I thought I said no campaigning?"

"We're not really *campaigning*," I begin. "We're . . . educating."

"Are you." It isn't a question. Her frosty gaze flits briefly to the Normal Normas, then back to us. The Normas, I notice, have ushered away a bunch of boys who had been trying on the Marilyn wigs.

"We're selling a message," says Lowri.

"An ideology," tries Karima.

The Chubb's eyebrows flick up. "And what's this?" She picks up a flyer advertising tomorrow's turn-in. "I said no propaganda."

My insides collapse, forcing out a giant sigh. "I'm really sorry, Mrs. Chubb, but we needed to *do* something. Talking to people isn't enough and most people can't even be bothered to listen. If we've only got until finals, I want to use our time to *achieve* something."

Mrs. Chubb returns the flyer to the pile.

"Okay," she agrees gently. "But when did all . . . *this* happen?" She flicks her arm in Aliyah's direction.

"Yesterday, ma'am."

Mrs. Chubb turns toward the Normal Normas. "Miss Dobson? What is it that you think you're doing, exactly? And what *on earth* are you wearing?" The Normas start smoothing and adjusting their wigs.

"We're dressed as Marilyns, ma'am," Aliyah replies coolly. "Or Normal Normas."

"And what has *that* got to do with Young Enterprise?"

"About as much as the table next to us," says Aliyah, her posse silent.

"Is that right? And what message are *you* peddling, exactly?"

"That it's okay to be normal. To *want* to be normal. To follow the rules that society sets for us about what's normal and what's not."

"I see."

SHE HAD BETTER NOT FLIPPING SEE! What rules are those, Aliyah? The same rules that say it's not acceptable for gay people to walk down the street holding hands (in towns like ours, anyway)? The same rules that say if you dye your hair purple or tattoo your face, you're a bit of a weirdo? The rules that aim to keep everything the same forever so that society can't change or grow or get better?

"What exactly IS normal, Miss Dobson? Please enlighten me," The Chubb challenges.

Aliyah looks confused for a moment, as if the answer is totally obvious. "It's all of US, ma'am," she says, drawing an invisible circle around her shiny-haired crew. "MOST people. We're the normal ones. It's them"—she stabs a finger in my direction— "who aren't."

"But Marilyn Monroe didn't live a very normal existence, as I recall."

Exactly, Mrs. Chubb! You are a woman in tune with my own thoughts!

"Besides," she goes on, "I read recently that Marilyn hated being cast as the dumb blond and loathed the stereotype she represented, when in actual fact, she was a well-read woman with an impressive library at home."

Aliyah looks bewildered for a moment, then turns and regurgitates some of the quotes on their display, word for word. If I have to hear these one more time, I swear my ears will explode.

Mrs. Chubb, who seems impervious to Aliyah's arguments, picks up one of their flyers and starts to examine it. Their flyers appeared today in retaliation to ours. I catch a flash of the front: something about a mass hair-removal session at Madison's house. I imagine Mad-Mads sitting tall, like a tangerine-faced empress, surveying her arena while the poor victims are brought in. As they squeal and yelp their way through their treatments, Empress Madison will cackle, holding an entire bunch of peeled grapes above her mouth and plucking one off with her over-whitened teeth.

"Well," says The Chubb at last, "in the interests of democracy, I can't very well let one side continue campaigning and not the other. It's either you both stay or you both go. Which is it?"

Aliyah's chin rises and her neck seems even longer, as if she's some kind of giraffe-girl. My index finger curls. Right now, I'd love to give that absurdly long neck a solid, hefty FLICK.

"But, ma'am!" Karima jumps in. "Isn't our school meant to be about inclusivity? Don't you always say we should challenge what's expected? Challenge the norm?"

Pixie smiles smugly. "I challenge Norm all the time." She's talking about Mrs. Norman—the lunch lady.

Karima ignores her. "The Normal Normas go against everything we've been taught, morally and culturally."

"It's immoral to be normal, is it?" Aliyah retorts.

"It's immoral to *judge* someone for looking different," I join in. "To the extent that you cut off their hair for public ridicule." Beams of loathing shoot from my eyeballs. I am Cyclops from *X-Men* but with boobs. And a mustache.

Aliyah shrugs. "Wasn't me."

Pixie is about to chime in with another gem but The Chubb cuts her off. "We've investigated the incident with Frankie, girls. We must try to move on. Look, I will allow your so-called 'enterprises' to continue for today and tomorrow, but after that, I want no more soapboxes in Reception, no flyers, no turn-ins. Wear your mustaches and your wigs, girls, if you must. But after tomorrow, you simply answer people's questions, okay? Leave the educating to me, please." She pauses but no one speaks. "When finals start, that's it. This whole charade must be done and dusted. Understood?"

We nod.

"Right." She points at the Normas. "Roll those skirts down and lengthen those ties, please, girls. Now!"

"My skirt's not rolled up, ma'am," brags Aliyah, with her super-long legs.

Mrs. Chubb glares at her. "Then take off that ridiculous makeup instead. You look like a cartoon character."

"That's sort of the point," Aliyah mumbles, referring to her anime eyes.

"The receptionist has face wipes, Miss Dobson. Off you go."

Mrs. Chubb watches as Aliyah slinks off to the front desk and the other Normas adjust their uniforms. Then she struts off, melting into the commotion of the cafeteria.

"What's a soapbox?" I hear Ellie ask Pixie.

"Dunno," Pixie replies. "A box of soap, I guess."

TWENTY-ONE

IT'S FRIDAY, WHICH MEANS TURN-IN TIME! YEAH!!

We stand there with our giant cardboard boxes from Mr. Bakshi's shop, and after half an hour have collected:

- a small box of facial bleach (relinquished by me)
- one half-finished tube of hair-removal cream (from Karima)
- a near-empty packet of bikini-waxing strips (Lowri's mom!)
- one home waxing kit (an ancient science teacher)
- one empty shaving foam canister.

"We're not a recycling scheme!" Lowri calls after the canister's owner. But Canister Dumper simply shrugs, then saunters off.

Lowri's shouting attracts the attention of our neighbors, and Aliyah sidles over to take a look in our box.

My whole body sighs.

"Wow," she says, snapping a picture of the meager contents. "I must let Mads know what a success your turn-in has been." She pulls in her smile to maximize its fakeness. "In case you haven't heard, by the way, we're setting up a salon tomorrow at Madison's house to share our hair-removal tips. I'm sure Mads would *love* to see you there. And I bet you all have *plenty* of hair to get rid of. . . ."

I want to swear at her so badly, my face aches. She goes back to her booth, where the other Normas are busy sticking out their bums and swishing their skirts for a gooey-eyed male audience. Argh! Why are boys so predictable? It's *their* fault the Normas are behaving like this. Without boys, would the Normas be standing there in their plastic wigs quoting a woman from the 1950s? But then, without men, would Marilyn have behaved the way *she* did—the way they wanted her to?

I growl inside and try to look busy, lifting the waxing kit from our box for closer inspection. It looks so primeval I am afraid it might explode in my hands. I turn it slowly, looking for clues as to its age while trying *not* to detonate it. But mysteriously, there's no date on it. I run a quick check of the other items in our box. "None of this stuff seems to have a use-by date."

"Really?" says Lowri, scrutinizing the tube of cream. "Surely it must go out of date eventually? I mean, you put it on your skin." She cautiously sniffs the top of the tube.

"DON'T DO THAT!" Karima screeches. "Don't you know what's in this stuff?!" She reads aloud from the side of a box. "Calcium hydroxide, potassium hydroxide, potassium thioglycolate—no idea what that is—titanium dioxide, urea . . ."

"Urea? That sounds familiar. . . ."

Karima smacks her lips together and nods. "Think biology lesson. Think waste product. Think . . ."

"Urine," I realize aloud.

Lowri throws her hand to her mouth and blows out her cheeks.

I do a quick google on my phone. "'Urea . . . Important raw material for the chemical industry. Major organic component of human urine.'"

"Gross!" says Lowri.

"Surely they don't actually extract it from human pee, though?"

Karima shrugs.

We stand there googling other ingredients. That toxic smell you get when you try to remove hair with a cream? It's sulfur, created by the chemicals literally dissolving your leg hair. Yes, it starts off smelling all sweet and lovely with that "new floral fragrance" they promise you on the box. You think, *Ooh, isn't this nice? Much gentler than waxing. And no risk of slashing myself with that treacherous flippin' razor!* But five minutes later, when your leg hair starts to die, your nostrils are assaulted with a smell like nothing you've smelled before: the back end of a garbage truck crossed with rotten eggs and dead mouse.

"Err, just a thought, guys," says Karima suddenly. "But

what are we going to DO with all of this? There's some pretty toxic stuff in here."

"Plus, look at all the plastic," Lowri points out.

I hadn't thought about that. "I guess we can recycle the boxes. I'm not sure what else is recyclable, really. . . ." I pick up the wax bomb. "Sadly, I think a landfill is the only place for this."

"We could donate it to the Normas for their beauty session," suggests Lowri. "Stuff this old might cause all kinds of reactions. . . ." Her eyebrows flick up and down and there's a glint of something wicked in her gray-blue eyes.

For a moment I am tempted. But I shake my head. "I wouldn't wish that on anyone. Not even my worst enemy."

"And certainly not on Madison Cox," Karima says, eyes widening. "Can you imagine the comeback?"

I shiver at the idea, wondering whether Madison has seen Aliyah's photo already.

"Ladies!" calls a voice suddenly. "How's it going?" It's Ms. Wallace.

"So-so," I say, trying not to pout.

She upends a bag and shakes its contents into our box, more than doubling our loot.

Whoa! Either she's just raided our local pharmacy, or she's SERIOUSLY hairy!

"I have roommates," she explains. "I told the other girls about your cause and we had a bit of a clear-out. We've all decided to stop using this stuff."

"Thanks!"

"No problem."

She folds up her bag and floats away like an angel.

"That's more like it," says Lowri, giving our box a satisfying shake.

"Careful!" exclaims Karima. "You might trigger a nuclear war!"

"A hair-removing bomb," I ponder aloud. "Maybe I'll take it home, after all. We might have enough here to make a start on my mom's legs."

Lowri guffaws, but they know I'm joking. I can't even imagine Antonia with smooth legs now. Her hairy legs are as much a part of her as her flappy earlobes and moley back. She'd look totally weird, not to mention the fact that her feminist crown might lose a bit of its sparkle.

"What are we going to do next week when there's no YE?" asks Karima. "We are still going to wear our mustaches, aren't we?"

"Of course!" I reply. "We've still got a full week of mustache-wearing before finals. And it occurred to me that we don't have a mission statement. I think the HGC needs one, don't you?"

"I'm swimming every night next week," says Lowri, distracted by her phone.

"Just you and me, then?" I say to Karima.

"Let's do it," she replies.

"Guys," says Lowri, suddenly back in the room. "Have either of you checked social media lately?"

I shake my head. With all the flyer making and turn-in planning, I'd totally neglected the new group account.

Lowri holds up the screen. "Twenty-six new pictures! Twenty-six!"

I snatch Lowri's phone to check for myself. Sure enough, there are loads of new posts on the club's page, all from girls other than us. They must be the ones we'd shared our log-in details with—the girls who'd seemed genuinely interested when they stopped at our booth. There are hairy arms, hairy fingers, hairy necks. Even a hairy underarm!

I can't stop looking at the posts. "This is amazing!"

Karima leans over to see.

"It's weird," says Lowri. "People are happy contributing on here but not in person." She points to our turn-in box.

"It's not weird at all, when you think about it," I reply. "Online it's anonymous, which makes it way easier. You can be part of the club—own up to body hair being an issue— without actually having to physically walk up to someone and go 'Yeah, I'm hairy' before handing over your hair cream."

"Twenty-six, though! That's awesome!" says Karima.

I grin broadly at them both. "This," I decide aloud, "calls for celebration!"

TWENTY-TWO

FIVE MINUTES LATER, WE'VE PACKED UP OUR YOUNG Enterprise booth for the last time and are hot-footing it to the cafeteria to raid what's left of the dessert section. The dining area is thinning out as people finish their lunches, but I spot Jake near the vending machines, talking to a girl his age with blond hair and perfect makeup. I raise my hand to him and smile as our eyes meet, but he doesn't smile back. Determined not to feel jealous—or worried—I keep that smile plastered on my face until we reach the cake stand.

There's not much left.

"Vegan granola bar for me, then," Lowri says at the only available option.

"Hmm," ponders Karima, who is not known for her decision-making skills. "Maybe I won't have one. . . ."

"Kari, we're celebrating, remember! You've got to." I nudge her gently with my elbow. There are literally two muffins left.

"I'll go lemon curd," I say, to help her out. "You okay with raspberry?"

She nods rapidly. "Perfect."

We're busy paying for our snacks when we hear him—exactly like Luke but louder. "Hey, Smith! Isn't that your YOUNGER WOMAN over there?!"

I catch my breath, looking straight at Lowri. "It's not . . ."

Lowri nods. "Bradley," she mouths, grimacing.

My blood runs cold. I turn, holding my muffin, to see Bradley Travers at the drinks machine next to Jake, with an arm around him. He's pointing to me and laughing. Jake does not look amused. The immaculate blond girl glares at me, frowning, as Bradley says something I can't hear.

"Ignore him," says Lowri, handing Mrs. Norman some coins. But I cannot move. I become aware of my hand clenching the muffin, about to squeeze it to death.

Bradley raises his voice again. "Don't leave her hanging, Smith. Looks like she wants you to buy her a CAKEY-WAKEY!" He laughs uproariously.

Jake shoots me an irritated glance.

The muffin—possibly in a bid to escape being the subject of ridicule—releases itself from my clutches and falls to the floor.

"Oh no! She's dropped it! She's dropped her cakey-wakey!" Bradley holds his fists by his eyes and pretends to baby-cry. By now, half the cafeteria is looking at me.

Jake shakes his head, takes the blond girl's hand and leads her away.

Jealousy and mortification pour through me like wet concrete. They solidify in my veins, and I can't move. I am stuck, frozen like a cold, gray statue.

"CRADLE SNATCHER!" Bradley calls after Jake. Then he looks back at me, sticks out his bottom lip, and swaggers off, just like his brother.

Lowri collects the forlorn-looking muffin from the floor.

"Shall I get her another one?" I hear Mrs. Norman whisper behind me. "There are more in the back."

Mrs. Norman returns with a new muffin and pops it into a brown paper bag. "Here you go, love," she says, handing it to me.

Great. Things must be bad if the lunch lady is giving me sympathy snacks.

"Thanks," I say quietly. But I can't eat it.

I don't feel like celebrating anymore.

Kar-Low take seats at the nearest table and Lowri taps a chair for me to join them.

"I think I need to be on my own for a bit," I say quietly.

"Are you sure?" Karima's voice oozes with sympathy.

"Sure. I'll see you in biology." And I walk shakily away from them, clutching my brown paper bag and racking my brain as to the most private place I can go in school.

Somewhere small.

And quiet.

With no windows.

∿

THE AUSTRALIA stain hovers over me once more, like a small god looking down on its sorrowful subject. Surrounded by inanimate keyboards, I imagine what they'd play for me if they could come to life. A funeral march, perhaps? A piano ballad by Adele? Warbling "Someone Like You" in my head, I start to unwrap my muffin, using the paper bag as a plate.

I am busy staring at my muffin, waiting for my appetite to recover, when he bursts in.

Rupert Clifton—in his football uniform.

With his muscular calves on full display.

"Oh, hi! Sorry!" he says awkwardly. "I didn't expect to find anyone in here. I'm looking for a folder of sheet music. Have you seen it?"

I shake my head.

"It's orange. . . ."

He clocks my muffin.

"Is everything okay?" The door closes behind him and I am alone with Rupert Clifton and his calves. I must be staring because he glances down and apologizes. "I was just at practice." He pushes one of the keyboards back so he can perch on a desktop. "The chairs in here are sketch," he explains.

I would laugh, but I can't.

"What happened?" he probes gently. When I don't reply, his voice adopts a playful tone. "Are you afraid that muffin's poisoned?"

I smile at last. "Well, it is from the school cafeteria. . . ."

"That explains it."

"Do you want some?" I offer. "Assuming it's *not* poisoned."

"How about you tell me what's up and we split the muffin?"

"Deal." I tear it in half, trying not to get lemon curd on my fingers.

"So?"

"So . . . There's been this poem going around."

"About you?" Rupert grabs his half of the cake and takes a hefty bite.

"Sort of. About Frankie's older brother . . . and me."

"Ohhh." Something crosses Rupert's eyes. From where I'm sitting, I can't tell if his eyes are more green or hazel, but I feel compelled to find out.

"And now Frankie's older brother has seen it, and it's just awkward and, well, even if he *weren't* Frankie's brother—if he were any other guy—why would he even want to look twice at me with *this* on my face?" I jab my mustache several times, quite hard.

Rupert laughs and swallows. His half of the muffin is gone already. "Don't be an idiot. Loads of guys would date you, given the chance!"

"It's not just the mustache, though," I continue. "I'm always talking about—you know—body hair."

Rupert shrugs. "So what? Dudes have body hair too. Why would you want to date someone who cares about that, anyway?"

"Don't all guys?"

"I know it's hard to believe, given how many jerks there are at this school, but some of us are good guys!"

I blush.

"We're not all like Kenny Fisher. If I met a girl who I got

along with, and then found out she liked me, I wouldn't care if she had body hair. It would be irrelevant."

Rupert has a smudge of dirt on his cheek. It is suddenly the most endearing smudge of dirt I have ever seen.

"Anyway," he says, standing, "I need to go and get changed before class, and admit to my piano teacher that I've lost my music—*again*—and *you* need to finish *that*." He points at my half of the muffin.

I smile and nod, my stomach suddenly rumbling in agreement. Just to make Rupert feel better, I wrap my mouth around the cake and bite. Lemon curd dribbles down my chin and I giggle. Rupert giggles with me, then turns to go.

"Later, Evia."

"Bye, Rupert."

And he is gone.

In that moment I decide that I want a man who thinks my body hair is irrelevant. And one who still likes me with lemon curd on my chin.

TWENTY-THREE

HOW WILL I EVER SHOW MY FACE AT THE SMITHS' house?! I may never again cross Frankie's threshold or laugh uncontrollably in Frankie's bedroom. I won't sit at their kitchen table or eat popcorn on their sofa. Frankie will wonder why I'm not coming around and she'll stop inviting me and our friendship will be ruined ALL BECAUSE OF MY STUPID CRUSH ON HER STUPID, INSANELY HOT BROTHER!!!

Luckily, it's the weekend. I will not see Jake or Bradley for at least two days and I am trying not to replay our encounter in the cafeteria in my head more than once a minute. To distract myself, I head out to our garbage can and send our turn-in loot crashing into it like a big, fat pile of shame. Then I run myself a lovely, long bath and, in opposition to the Normas' Veet-ing session, I do not shave a single part of my body. Instead, I leave my razor hanging on its little hook in the shower, wondering what it's done to offend me. Ha! Take that, my triple-bladed friend! Today you are the enemy and you shall be snubbed!

After my bath, I do not bleach or trim or pluck ANYTHING. I feel determined to love my body, hair and all, because it is natural. I silently repeat to myself: *I am a mammal and mammals have hair. We are all mammals and MAMMALS HAVE HAIR!*

BY SATURDAY evening, I'm ready for movie night. Mom picks this film about a teenage girl and her relationship with her mother, which as a film choice is about as subtle as a sledgehammer. Mom really doesn't need to worry about our relationship. *Unless* she keeps leaving her menstrual cup right next to my toothbrush or stops me from dating. Or stops buying my favorite ice cream.

Ten minutes into the movie, Mom slides her empty paella bowl onto the coffee table. "Ooh, I forgot to tell you! I spoke to Lucy earlier. She's coming up for that interview next Saturday—she'll meet you in town for coffee somewhere. She said the Hairy Girls' Club might even make next month's issue! Isn't that amazing?"

I stare at her, dumbfounded. "Mo-om!"

"Yes, love?"

I pause the movie for dramatic effect. "Do you even *remember* the conversation we had?"

"Yes."

"I'm pretty sure I did *not* agree to that!"

"Evia, chill. This is your big chance! You can tell the nation—maybe even the world—about your club!"

"You mean it's YOUR big chance to have a famous feminist daughter?"

"What? No! I—"

"What? Thought you'd put me up for national ridicule? Because I love nothing more than everyone at school deciding I'm a feminist freak!"

"You say it like being a feminist is a bad thing."

"It is when most guys at school think feminism means you absolutely positively do not WANT A BOYFRIEND."

"You don't want a boyfriend. Not yet."

"How would *you* know?"

"Take my word for it. Boyfriends only cause grief."

"Oh yeah, and you're such an expert in the relationship department. You don't even know where my dad is! He could be dead, for all you know!"

Antonia holds my glare for a full three seconds, then gets up to retrieve the remote. The lead actress starts moving but I can't hear her. My ears are all *buzz, buzz, buzzzzzzzz.*

Mom's there, seething.

I'm here, seething.

She had no right to talk to Lucy about us! How dare she?! Can I even stomach another interview after my one-on-one with Leo? Then again, if it went well, it would be amazing for the cause . . . for the club.

No, I decide. I do not like this. I do *not* like my mother taking over.

Watch this, Mother: I am going to stand up, pick up my phone and storm off upstairs.

I stand up, pick up my phone and freeze. There's a message from Lucy in my inbox.

Dammit! Mom's interfering even gets in the way of my dramatic walkout. I sit back down to read.

Lucy Green <lucygreen@bigcorpmedia.com>
Saturday, May 18; 8:47 p.m.

Dear Evia,

You are probably aware that I spoke to Antonia earlier today. Wow! Your campaign sounds super exciting! Congrats on having the courage to do it. Not many teenage girls would. In fact, I don't know many grown women who would!

Cutting to the chase, next month's issue is going to have an Eco Girl theme. Think all things sustainable, saving the planet, living au naturel, etc. So an interview with you guys would slot perfectly into that.

I'd need to arrange a photo shoot separately and that would most likely be at our HQ—would that be OK? I'd need you to be able to demonstrate some aspect of your action for the campaign, ideally more than the adhesive mustaches (fab idea, by the way). The shoot would probably take place end of May/beginning of June.

Anyway, I'll see you next Saturday at 11 a.m. at Lady Liberty's. The perfect place to discuss female liberation!

Kind regards,
Lucy

PS: If you want to discuss further, my cell # is below.

I give my mother the mother of all glares. And then I leave the room.

In the Mom-free safety of my boudoir, I close my mail app and go to my top favorite number. Praying Jake hasn't said anything to her about the ballad, I hit Call. She answers on the third ring.

"Frankie?"

"Yeah?" She sounds drowsy.

"Guess what Antonia's done."

"What?"

"She's booked us an interview with her old magazine editor friend. Next weekend. AND a photo shoot."

"Oh."

"I know. I'm annoyed that Antonia organized it without confirming with us first, but at the same time, I'm sort of excited. Hang on, I'll forward you the email. . . ."

I find the message on my iPad and hit Send. I wait a few moments while she reads.

"Mmm," she says eventually.

"What d'you think?"

"About doing an interview? I'm not sure, Evs. I don't mind you guys doing it, but, well, I hate the idea of a photo shoot. Like, *really* hate it."

"But if you were a part of the campaign—if you were the face of it—we'd get so much more attention. And support."

"Are you serious?! I said at the beginning I did *not* want to be a poster girl for this!"

"I know, but you wouldn't have to DO anything. You'd

just have to sit there for the camera. And maybe answer a few questions."

Her voice goes quiet. "I can't believe you're asking me to do this."

Guilt bomb. Heart. *Ker-boom!*

"Okay, I'm sorry," I backpedal. "Maybe you could just do the interview and skip the shoot. Should I talk to Lucy?"

Frankie is quiet for a moment. "No, it's okay. I'll do it."

"Her email address is on there; cell too. But only if you're sure?"

"Yeah, it's fine."

The teeniest shard of disappointment wedges itself in my throat. If Frankie decides not to do the photo shoot, they probably won't want the rest of us to do it either. Let's face it: Frankie's the one with the most obvious body hair.

I pick a new subject to hide my dismay. We talk about the film Mom chose and Frankie tells me how it ends. She's seen it—of course.

"Frankie," I ask quietly, "why do you want to be a film critic?"

"Because I love films, duh!"

"I know but . . . it's not because you want to spend your life in a dark theater, right?"

"Hiding, you mean?" There's a pause. "Maybe a bit. But it's more to do with escaping, I think. Losing myself in someone else's story. Forgetting about what's going on with me. Know what I mean?"

"Yeah." And I do, I get it.

When we hang up, I rerun our conversation in my head. I wish I could make Frankie stronger. And then a second guilt bomb detonates inside my rib cage because I realize that while most of me wants Frankie to be stronger for herself, a tiny part of me wants her to be stronger for our campaign.

TWENTY-FOUR

ANTONIA PARTS THE KITCHEN BLIND, THEN LETS IT fall closed again. She's swanning around in her fuchsia kimono while I sit here prodding my soggy cereal. I decide to try one last time.

"Pleeeeease?!" I beg.

"But why? It's a lovely day. It'll be a nice walk."

I shove my bowl away. "Fine. Don't worry about it."

"Evia!"

"What?"

"If it's because it's Monday, I totally understand. Everyone hates Monday mornings. But that really isn't enough to justify the carbon emissions."

For God's sake. Can't she just forget about the wretched planet for all of fifteen minutes and drive me to school and back? Sorry, Earth: I love you and will make it up to you, but right now I need you to take the hit.

I slam the door on the way out.

Of course it's not about it being Monday morning. It's about speed-walking the entire way to school, feeling too scared to look over my shoulder; it's about walking alone, feeling wide open space all around me; it's about feeling continually sick at the thought of seeing Jake or Bradley, or hearing HER voice.

It's Madison's first day back since her suspension.

She's gonna be out to get me, big time.

THE MORNING drags. At lunchtime, Kar-Low are back at orchestra, practicing for the summer concert. I scarf my lunch on a picnic bench behind the tech block, then spend forty minutes resisting the temptation to bang my idiotic head against a wall. In the Madison-filled smog of this morning, I forgot to bring my water bottle to school. Which means one of two things:

1. Hitting up a school water fountain, exposing myself to God Knows What from that germ-infested mouthpiece (#nothanks).
2. Braving the school cafeteria and almost certainly encountering Miss Cox, Queen of the Lunch Hall.

I hold out for as long as I can and, when there are only five minutes left, I power-walk to Reception. Halfway along the hallway, I pass a huddle of younger girls all wearing platinum-blond wigs and twirling their school skirts like miniature Normas. FOR GOD'S SAKE!

I turn back, unable to ignore them. "Why are you wearing those?"

"Why are you wearing *that*?" comes the reply, its speaker nodding at my mustache with disdain.

"We just want to look beautiful, like Marilyn Monroe," says another of the girls.

"You *are* beautiful," I argue. "You don't need to swish your skirt and wear a wig. There's more than one way to be a girl. Just be yourselves."

They push past me, scoffing.

On the other side of Reception, I hear Madison before I've even crossed through the double doors. Then I spot the back of her long fake-blond mane as she stands at a table, holding out her hand. I swear her butt has grown plumper. Either she's been doing squats solidly for two weeks or she's got balloons up her skirt.

I join the line for the drink machine, keeping my back to Madison. What's she up to? Usually she's on her barstool of a throne in the far corner of the cafeteria, her posse standing around her in an arc of bodyguards.

The laughter builds, then springs to the next table. My back prickles. She's moved on, the laughter getting ever nearer, like the sparks of a wildfire.

My fingers quiver as I push coins into the slot. What vicious rumor has she conjured up this time?

I bend to collect my bottle, then stand and—*SLAP*— middle of my back.

"Hello, my furry friend!" Madison says, beaming, attempting to blind me with her bleached teeth. There's a line where her foundation meets her hair, like a satsuma with a skinny halo, and I can't work out whether her eyebrows have any actual eyebrow hair or whether they're temporary tattoos. "I love the new addition to your . . . uh, face." She stares at my mustache until my top lip feels like it's on fire.

Three of Madison's cronies creep along to join her.

"Did you miss me?" she croons. "I missed you! Although Aliyah's been filling me in on events while I've been away."

I glug a mouthful of liquid, but my stomach suddenly feels full.

"She told me how you went chirping, all Birdy-Birtwhistle to HQ about what happened with Frankie. How you got me suspended."

"I didn't say anything," I begin. "I wasn't there when it happened, for a start."

"So why did you get called in?"

"Because I'm Frankie's best friend, I guess."

She squints like she's using evil superpowers to penetrate my brain. I take a swig from my bottle just to break eye contact. She's still glaring after I've swallowed.

"If you don't believe me, ask Mrs. Chubb."

"I think I'll avoid that topic with HQ, thank you." Madison's face tightens in a grimace. "In other news, have you heard what happened to my main Marilyn over the weekend?"

Main Marilyn? I assume she means Aliyah.

"After your little club bombed at Young Enterprise last week, my main Marilyn set up a pop-up beauty salon at my house on Saturday. Guess how many people turned up."

I move zero facial muscles.

"Thirty-five. Thirty-five girls all lining up at my house to defuzz their arms and legs! I think we can call that a success, don't you?"

Still flatlining.

"D'you know what else happened?"

She whips out her phone and thrusts it in my face.

JEEEEEEEEEEEZ! Poor Aliyah!

Madison slides through the images for me, conducting her smug little slideshow. So *that's* what she was passing around those tables.

Aliyah has a bright-red rash the shape of a handlebar mustache, a similar rash covering her cheeks, and pimples up the sides of her face. And Aliyah NEVER has bad skin. Her face is normally a cross between a smooth brown egg and the inside of a Kinder Bueno. The last picture shows Aliyah in a hospital bed, holding a plastic cup and looking beyond miserable.

"What the . . . ," I begin.

"Well," Madison commences in a high-pitched voice, "my girl did a stupid thing. She took some cream that was meant to be used on her legs and used it on her face." She clicks her tongue against her teeth a couple of times. "Silly Billy. She left it on too long, chatting away, and then—POOF! Her skin goes all burn-baby-burn and she ends up in the ER!"

Whoa.

Madison goes on too willingly. "The doc said it was a chemical burn. And she'd never seen anything like it."

"You went with her?"

"Of course. Someone had to take these, didn't they?!" She wiggles the phone at me.

"Poor Aliyah," I say with genuine sympathy. "Maybe you should complain to the manufacturer."

"Yeah, or maybe next time Aliyah should READ THE LABEL." Madison rolls her eyes. "And anyway, she deserved to be taken down a peg or two. Sounds like she was lording it up a bit in my absence."

The girls behind Madison suddenly look guilty, as if they participated in some sort of betrayal. They're not the only ones relieved to hear the bell for next period.

"Shame," says Madison. "I was enjoying our chat, Birdy. And we haven't even had a chance to discuss your Hairy Muffs' Club!" She starts walking away. "Talk later!" she calls over her shoulder.

TWENTY-FIVE

WHEN MADISON SAID "LATER," SHE MEANT LAST-period later. Specifically in the PE changing rooms.

"So," Madison says, pushing Melissa Mackie out of the way, "tell me: How many guys do you think want a girlfriend who talks about how hairy she is all the time?" She starts unbuttoning her blouse and I turn away, more conscious than ever of my inadequate boobs.

"I wouldn't know. I don't have one."

She chortles. "Of course you don't! Ryan would run a mile if I even started *talking* about body hair, let alone growing it!"

Madison's been dating an upperclassman named Ryan Avery since the start of the school year. That means they've been together eight months now—they're practically married.

Madison stands there in her bra while she fastens her gym skirt. "You think you're EVER going to get a boyfriend while you're growing all your dingly-danglies? Let's see . . ." She grabs hold of my arm and yanks it up for inspection. "Oh-ho-ho!

Little Miss Hypocrite, are we?! Or maybe you can't actually *grow* pit hair yet?"

I wrench my arm away and scowl at the coat hooks, annoyed at having lost the mental battle with my razor this morning. Not only did I shave my underarms, I also shaved my legs from top to bottom in anticipation of having to don a PE uniform this afternoon. That means I only managed a grand total of TWO DAYS without shaving. I am officially pathetic.

"Some of us don't even have to worry about hair removal," Madison brags. "Some of us are naturally smooth-a-licious!" She holds up her forearm and thrusts it in my direction.

"Er—"

"Go on, stroke it!" She runs her hand up and down her arm as if to prove it. "Anyone?" She opens the arm-stroking forum to Melissa and the rest of our bench. Before I know it, girls from all over the locker room are lining up to slide their hands along Madison's arms.

"Not a single hair!" says one.

"How are you so smooth?!" asks another.

Madison shrugs. "Just born this way. Like I said: smooth-a-licious! Girls who have hairy arms or hairy bellies are totally unnatural. They belong in a gorilla enclosure."

I'm burning inside and out. So if I'm a gorilla, what does that make you, Miss Smooth-a-licious? A slippery fish? A slimy salamander? How about a poison dart frog? Yes. I imagine Madison morphing into an orange dart frog, white teeth and all.

Ribbit! says the imaginary Madison-frog.

Right before I squish her with my big, strong gorilla fist.

Frankie: *Hang on, so she literally stood there getting people to stroke her?*

Me: *Yep.*

Frankie: *So weird.*

Me: *I KNOW! And she kept saying smooth-a-licious over and over again. And poor Aliyah. You wouldn't even think they were friends from the way M was talking about her, flashing those pics around. M even said Aliyah deserved it!*

Frankie: *Seriously?*

Me: *Yeah. It occurred to me that M might've used the wrong cream on A's face on purpose . . .*

Frankie: *She wouldn't . . .*

Me: *Oh come on. She totally would! Madison Cox is no one's friend . . .*

Frankie: *You're right there. How's the HGC mission statement coming along?*

Me: *I've drafted it and Karima's taking a look. Would you mind reviewing it too?*

Frankie: *Sure.*

Me: *I'll send it over in a sec. Thanks* ☺

Frankie: *No worries! I think I have a new addiction btw.*

Me: *Spill*

Frankie: *I'm addicted to looking at pictures of hairy women on social media!*

Me: *OMG! Me too!!*

Frankie: *It makes me feel soooo much better—like I'm not the only one out there. There's this one girl, in Germany, who even posts pictures of her hairy belly.*

Me: *I think I know the one you mean. She's so brave . . .*

Frankie: *Not that she should have to be. If the world was a kinder place, it wouldn't matter that she has a hairy belly. Posting a picture of her midriff shouldn't have to be a massive statement, just like it's a massive statement for me to go out with stubble on my face.*

Me: *You're brave too . . .*

Frankie: *But I shouldn't have to be! I wish I could just exist without having to think about this stuff all the time.*

Me: *I know. I get it. I'm gonna stop shaving my hands and fingers. I don't want my future BF to think I have stubbly hands.*

Frankie: *Your future BF? Who is this exactly?!*

Your only sibling, Frankie. You know the one? The one who now thinks I am a total loser and wishes to never set eyes on me again?

Me: *Oh, I dunno. Someone funny who likes Marvel movies.*

Frankie: *I think most guys grow out of the Avengers by the age of 12.*

Me: *Guys NEVER grow out of the Avengers.*

Frankie: *Evs, do you ever find yourself feeling jealous of Madison?*

Me: *Are you serious?!*

Frankie: *I mean jealous of her smoothness . . .*

Me: *Oh, I am TOTALLY jealous of her smoothness. Imagine not having to deal with ALL THE HAIR on a daily basis!*

Frankie: *It's basically hourly with me . . .*

Me: 😬 *But also . . . I think I'd rather have real friends than "smooth-a-licious" arms.*

So there we have it. Proof if you ever needed it that me and Frankie—mostly Frankie—are just too freaking nice. We can't even bad-mouth our archenemy without cutting her some slack. Granted, I could've gone on whining about her for much longer, but Frankie always stops me in my tracks and reminds me of my inner Miss Nice before I go all Little Miss Ragey Pants. (FYI, Miss Nice wears tan oxfords and an excellent fedora; Miss Ragey Pants is crimson all over and wears her undies on her head. I think I know which one I'd rather be.)

TWENTY-SIX

TWO DAYS LATER, I STAND IN FRONT OF OUR FAKE fireplace holding a crisp piece of paper, my fingertips leaving light, damp impressions on the edges. Mom sits opposite me, legs uncrossed, Kindle to one side. Frankie and Kar-Low are with us on video chat. Karima and Frankie have helped me draft the statement, but no one else has seen the finished thing yet and it felt like we needed a sort of inauguration ceremony, hence inviting Mom to listen in. Lowri's mom, Sarah, is in the background too.

I take a deep breath and start to read aloud:

"We, the Hairy Girls' Club, make it our mission to:

   I. Make the world aware that female body hair is natural, whether or not we choose to let it grow.
  II. Challenge negative perceptions of female body hair whenever or wherever we encounter them.

III. Applaud positive perceptions of female body hair and anyone who chooses to flaunt it.

IV. Challenge stereotypes about women and societal expectations of beauty, especially in the media and advertising.

V. Be open-minded and accepting of members and nonmembers alike, however they choose to present themselves.

VI. Promote and celebrate body positivity in all its forms.

VII. Always be kind, no matter what."

There's a slight time delay before the girls start clapping; then Mom joins in, her palms glued together and her fingertips flapping like the tail of a freshly-caught haddock.

"Brilliant, girls! I love it!"

I perch next to Mom on the sofa and turn the split screen toward us.

"Good job, Evs," says Lowri. She has wet hair, post-swim.

"Hear, hear!" adds Sarah.

"It feels kind of real now, doesn't it," I confess out loud.

"Sure does," says Karima.

"We'd better actually achieve something!"

"You will," says Mom. "I have every faith in you, girls. You're the new generation of warriors in this battle."

"Shall I publish our mission statement on the group feed?" asks Karima.

"Yep! Why not?"

"Okay, I'll do it tonight. Bye for now, everyone!" Karima signs off with a wave.

"Bye!" says Frankie. "And good job—all of you."

Lowri signs off with a wave, followed by Frankie. Then it's just me and Mom left in the room with a whole load of quiet.

"We made lots of different versions," I explain to fill the silence. "Some much longer ones. We wanted to get it right."

"It's wonderful."

I realize I'm still frowning at the piece of paper when I look up at Mom. Her eyes are glistening.

"Mom!"

"Sorry. I'm just proud, Evs! Super proud." She pulls me in for a squeeze. "I always thought you were embarrassed by me."

"Oh, I'm still embarrassed. But it's got nothing to do with your body hair."

She shoves me playfully. "I'm always here for you, remember."

I lean in to her and, for a moment, her words comfort me. But then school swims into my head and I think about the random boys who have started sneering insults when they pass me in the hallway. The upperclassmen who shout "Jakey-Wakey!" every time they see me, and the ones who shout "Baby Snatcher!" whenever Jake's in my vicinity. How Madison yells "Hairy Muff!" every time she clocks me, often from behind, out of nowhere. And how, when these things happen, my whole body spasms like it's trying to shoot upward through an escape hatch in the ceiling. I wish I could shrink my mom down and carry her in my pocket, whip her out when I need backup.

It would be really nice if tomorrow no one would call out at me or tap me on the shoulder and laugh, or cough an insult under their breath.

Is that too much to ask?

TWENTY-SEVEN

THURSDAY DELIVERS A SMOOTH WALK INTO SCHOOL.
A jeer-free time at the school gates. The only interruption to
my journey to homeroom is The Chubb, appearing out of nowhere like a doomsayer.

"Last day tomorrow, Miss Birtwhistle," she declares omi-
nously. "Last day." I give her a single nod in return and smile.
My mustache smiles with me, despite having been reminded
of its funeral.

THEN, SOMETHING weird happens. During second period,
my grade gets called into the auditorium, everyone babbling.
There's a frenetic, gossipy buzz around us. Has someone
died? Has there been a massacre? Has McDonald's run out
of pickles?

I file into the next available space and find Rupert Clifton
right next to me.

"Hello again," he says, looking up.

"Hi." I take my seat.

"Any idea what this is about?"

"Nope."

We stare straight ahead at the empty stage, then he leans toward me and whispers, "Got any muffins?"

I smile, then suck my lips against my teeth. "Fresh out of muffins, I'm afraid. . . ."

Just then, Mr. McGovern walks onto the stage and introduces a casual-looking duo called Sexplicit.

Oh. NO. I thought sex ed was gender-specific? Girls in one space, boys in another? But today they're here. And we're here. Everyone is here *together*. Rupert's muscly thigh suddenly seems too close to mine, and I shift ever so slightly toward Chloe Ford on my right. For some insane reason, my brain implores me to look at Rupert's crotch—to imagine those strong, manly thighs inside his pants. . . .

No, Evia! Don't do it!

I feel paralyzed, unable to look anywhere except at the stage. Even looking at my own feet seems dangerous—what if he thinks my downward gaze is directed elsewhere, toward Penis Town? Argh!!! *Eyes, I FORBID you to go to Penis Town!* Why oh why can't I be sitting next to a less good-looking boy for this?

The duo onstage starts talking.

"Hi, everyone! I'm Kate."

"And I'm Jonah!"

A male voice behind me immediately giggles. "Ha! What's his last name? Boner?"

Jonah fake-laughs. "Funnily enough, guys, it's not the first time I've heard that one."

Kate puts an arm around his shoulder and gives it a little squeeze. Has she been to his Penis Town, I wonder?

"In case you haven't already guessed," Jonah continues, "we're here to talk about SEX. *S-E-X,* SEX!" Jonah looks very pleased with himself for correctly spelling a word.

"Everyone finds sex ed a bit cringey," Kate acknowledges. "So we're going to start by getting out all your giggles. We're going to have a competition to find the most cringeworthy nickname for the vagina. Hands up, please!"

All hands stay firmly down.

"Come on, you all know one. . . ."

Rupert, Chloe and I stay statue-still while people around us start whispering loudly. Kate overhears a few of them.

"Foofoo!" she shrieks happily. "Thank you!"

"FANNY!" someone shouts at her.

"FRONT BOTTOM!" yells another, and Rupert's shoulders jiggle.

Suddenly, we are taking a loud and spirited tour through Vajayjay Land. We start with the more polite ones, the *flowers, Minnies* and *honeypots,* before moving on to the sticky-sounding ones like *minge, clunge* and *flange.*

After that, we meet the more animalistic vulvas: the *pussies, growlers* and *bearded clams. Growler,* by the way, terrifies me. I'm reasonably confident I have a friendly vulva, but as no other genitalia have yet approached it, I may be proven wrong. I do hope that when a penis strolls by one day, my vulva does not growl at it.

Before I know it, our *pink canoe* has sailed into a whole new world of *lady gardens, velvety caverns* and *penis flytraps*. As for the most cringeworthy name, we put our votes emphatically behind the creepy, sinister-sounding *whispering eye*. My own vagina responds to this name by squeezing itself shut. My *cave of wonders* may never open again.

"Right," Jonah says. "Penises next!"

Oh good God.

Madison Cox's hand shoots up. "Trouser snake!" she shouts proudly, and my brain quickly conjures up a python in Rupert's pants.

"Knobgoblin!"

"Jackhammer!"

"Indiana Bones!"

The willy talk reintroduces the common names—*stiffy, pecker, woody*—before moving to the edible: *salami, weiner, meat stick*. Some penises sound musical, like *skin flute, pink piccolo,* and *ding-dong,* while *big guy, firehose* and *Hammer of Thor* clearly think a lot of themselves. Eventually, when we have finished guffawing into our laps, we decide on the runners-up. Standing to attention in third place is . . . *throbbing member*. Looking fearsome in second place is . . . *one-eyed monster*. And doing a little wiggly dance in first place? *Disco stick*. I may shun mirrorballs for the rest of my life.

After tackling grooming, contraception and menstruation, Kate and Jonah finally start wrapping up.

"Any questions?" asks Jonah.

Madison immediately pipes up. "What about pubes? Can you tell us what's normal . . . and what's not?"

"Well," Kate begins, "most people start growing pubic hair during puberty. Some grow more than others—"

Madison coughs something inaudible.

"—and while some people choose to trim it, shape it or whip it all off, others choose to leave it au naturel. It's down to personal choice."

Madison coughs the inaudible thing again.

"Sorry? What did you say?" Kate's eyebrows dip. "Evia? Is that a new shape I don't know about? There's the Brazilian, of course, and the landing strip. The Bermuda Triangle. The Hollywood. What's the Evia? I don't know that one."

My cheeks burn so hot I could harvest more energy than a solar panel.

"Oh," Madison begins, all eyes and ears on her. "It's like au naturel but bigger, fuller. Like a really *massive* bird's nest."

The hall turns into a sea of head-bobbing, shoulder-shaking bodies. I wish the sea would grab me and pull me under.

"All right, Ms. Cox," McGovern cuts in. "That's enough." He draws an invisible line in front of his throat as a signal to Sexplicit.

Kate glances at her FitBit and nods. "Right, guys!" she shouts. "I think we've run out of time!"

"Thanks, Kate!" Jonah shouts back. "We hope you've all found our session useful!"

They talk about websites. They make recommendations for sexual-health clinics and people to talk to. But all I can think about is my bird's nest, buried underneath thick gray cotton and burned into the mind of every single person in this hall. I might as well have baby blackbirds flying from my crotch.

Suddenly, the lovely Rupert is leaning toward me. "Ignore Madison," he says breathily. "She's an idiot."

I respond with the feeblest of smiles.

Chloe stands up, ready to join the hordes of nest-haters spilling out of the auditorium. Rupert and I stand too, and as we do, for one tiny split of a millisecond, my eyes flit back to Penis Town.

ARGH! No! Stupid, stupid eyes . . .

What if he caught me looking?

Oh God, oh God!!!

At the hall doors, someone elbows me hard in the bicep.

"Hey, Birdy!" she says, grinning. "How's that nest?!"

Kenny Fisher high-fives Madison as he walks past. I heard he's planning on asking her out, despite the fact she's already with Ryan. Ha! Good luck with that, "King" Kenny.

I take a deep breath through my nose and wish I could whip that mini-Mom from my pocket. "Really well, thanks, Madison. How's yours?"

She snorts in reply. Above her, Aliyah's mouth curls up at one side. Her skin has healed now, but I can't help wondering what that hair-removal "accident" has done to their friendship.

"Admit it," says Madison. "Your campaign is a massive failure. Your turn-in was a flop, and how many people are wearing mustaches? Ten?"

"It's not a disaster," I reply, suddenly finding some confidence. "Why else would a magazine journalist be interviewing us this weekend?"

"Oh yeah? Which magazine?"

"A national one."

Madison opens her mouth, then snaps it shut.

"That's pretty cool," says Aliyah. Madison shoots her a frown.

"What?" I go on. "You mean the Normal Normas *don't* have a top magazine interview lined up?"

"Whatever. Who even *reads* magazines anymore?"

"It'll be online too. Obviously." I roll my eyes at her. "I mean, we'll probably be trending in, like, a week."

She glares, silenced.

Kar-Low appear suddenly to flank me. "Everything all right?" asks Lowri.

"Yep!" I declare loudly. "Should we go to break?"

"Let's!" replies Karima, and they each link an arm in mine.

AT HOME, Mom plants my dinner in front of me. Two veggie sausages roll around on my plate.

"How was your day?" Mom asks.

I stare at the sausages.

"Something wrong?"

"What? No." I slice a sausage and pop a piece in my mouth, chewing carefully while trying *not* to think about skin flutes. I'm too tired to answer Mom properly. Facing up to Madison and her band of foot soldiers all the time is draining, and this militant has had enough of going into battle.

TWENTY-EIGHT

I STAND IN FRONT OF MY LOCKER, BLINKING. DOES IT actually say Evie, not Evia? There are several Evies at school, most of them far more likely to have a note slipped into their lockers than me.

My heart racing, I peer more closely at the blue, hand-written letters. It's definitely an *a*.

I unfold the square of paper and read.

Don't listen to the haters. You're awesome, mustache and all. x

My cheeks immediately flush and my heart does a little bunny hop. Someone thinks I'm awesome! Not nice, or lovely or great. AWESOME. What does Jake Smith's handwriting look like, I wonder? Maybe he's ditched that blond girl! Maybe he's forgiven me for the whole ballad debacle and wants a younger woman after all!

Suddenly, Leo Hobbs appears from a nearby classroom. He sends me a smile, raises his hand—no glimmer of a Kit Kat wrapper—then continues on his way. I smile back, then growl at myself. I should be accosting him for that unhelpful piece of so-called "journalism," not smiling sweetly at his scrumptious face.

Hang on. Leo Hobbs just passed my locker, moments after I found the note! Could it be . . . ? I examine the note, trying to remember Leo's handwriting. He did ask me if I had a boyfriend. . . .

"What's that?" Karima asks, joining me.

I pass her the note, hoping Lowri doesn't appear from the bathroom any time soon. She'd flap this around like a trophy.

"Ooh, an admirer! Who d'you think it's from?!" Karima hands the note back and I stash it in my blazer pocket.

Lowri emerges from the neighboring bathroom.

I try using the power of my mind to reach Karima. *Don't tell her, don't tell her, don't tell her!*

"So," begins Lowri. "I thought we could do a video chat tonight to plan our outfits for the big interview tomorrow. What d'you think?"

Karima pulls a face. "My parents are out tonight, so I'm on babysitting duty." Karima has four younger siblings, so she's got her work cut out for her.

"No worries," says Lowri. "What about you, Evs?"

"I hadn't really thought about it, to be honest. It's not like the photo shoot is tomorrow."

"You never know—she could spring one on us, action-shot-style!"

"Action shots of us sitting in a café?"

Lowri summons a glower.

"Okay," I say finally. "I could probably do with some help deciding what to wear. Let's invite Frankie, too."

"Sure."

"Seven-ish?"

"Eight is better. Got to factor in a swim and dinner."

LOWRI'S FACE appears on my screen soon after eight p.m. "So, no more Little Miss Mustache. How did the rest of your day go?"

"Fine. Uneventful. The Chubb waved at me from her office on my way out, tapping her upper lip."

"She would. I feel kind of sad. . . ."

I glance at the abandoned mustache on my desk. "I don't. I swear that sticky backing has given me a rash for life. Not to mention the evil ripping-out of hair that's been going on every day for the past two weeks." I massage the sensitive patch beneath my nose. "Knowing my luck, the hair will grow back thicker than it was before. After finals you'll be like, 'Evia, why are you still wearing your mustache?' and I'll be like, 'Er . . . This is just my face.'"

Lowri guffaws. "We'll love you anyway. Sooo, who's this note from?!"

ARGHHH!! Can those two keep no secrets?!

"Oh, for God's sake. I don't know! It's the smallest note. All of, like, ten words."

"From what I hear, it says you're awesome. So *that's* pretty awesome! I wonder who it could be. . . ."

"Probably Madison messing around."

"Nah. Definitely a guy, I think. Karima said it had a kiss on the end. Hey, maybe it's a guy with a fetish for hairy women! That's a thing, right?"

Oh great. Can't I receive attention from a member of the opposite sex without it being directly linked to my talent for growing excess hair? "It might have nothing to do with being hairy. It might be because I actually AM awesome."

"Hair fetishes are definitely a thing. Maybe he wants to have a competition to see who can grow the longest leg hair—or pubes!"

"Gro-ossss!"

"Maybe you could braid your underarm hair together so you're joined at the pit."

"Lowri!"

"Or, or, or! Maybe he wants to lather you in shaving foam so he can shave your entire body. . . ."

That would actually be quite useful. And save me a job. But the thought of some guy seeing me naked? Let alone removing my hair for me . . . NO. Just NO.

"Where's Frankie? Have you tried her yet?"

"No reply. She might accept if it's you."

I try, but there's no answer. Oh well. This isn't the kind of thing Frankie would make a big deal about anyway. She'll be wearing her usual black skinny jeans, black band T-shirt and black Nikes. She doesn't like to stand out. Lowri, on the other hand . . .

"How about this?" She holds up a jumpsuit the color of a freshly painted fire truck.

"Wow."

"Too much?"

"No, it's, umm . . ."

"It's my sister's. She didn't take it back to college."

Then I realize it's Gwyneth's bedroom in the background, not Lowri's. The wardrobe spans an entire wall, with mirrored doors parted in the middle. Lowri slides the hangers with a squeal of metal, and flicks from one item to the next.

"It must be awesome to have a sister you can borrow clothes from."

"Yeah, as long as she never finds out. I'm not allowed any-where near Gwyneth's wardrobe when she's home. Ooh! How about this?" She holds up a black blazer with satin lapels and shoulder pads.

"A bit formal?"

Lowri gazes lovingly at it, unperturbed. Then she ransacks the wardrobe again.

"With . . . THIS!" She thrusts a white blouse at the camera and holds it up alongside the blazer. The blouse has ruffles all down the front.

"Are you planning to perform some magic tricks?"

She screws up her nose at me.

"Do you honestly think we need to dress up? Lucy only wants to talk about the club—why we formed it, et cetera. Just wear jeans and a nice top. Be comfortable."

Lowri scowls. "Jeans and nice tops don't tell her WHO WE ARE. She'll want to get an idea of our personalities. By all means, wear jeans if you want to, but I'm going to wear"— the hangers start squeaking again—"THIS!"

This time it's a floral-print midi dress with a Peter Pan collar. But it's mostly burnt orange. And orange with ginger hair . . .

"Maybe not with my hair," Lowri decides. "Did you know Gwyneth was ginger too when she was younger?"

"Was she?" Lowri's sister is now blond with only a hint of strawberry.

"Yeah. Hormones changed her. Lucky thing."

"I thought you loved your hair?"

"I do, but it clashes with stuff, you know?"

"Yours might change."

"Nah, I'm like my dad. If anything, the ginge is only getting stronger."

A pang of envy strikes. I don't even know what my dad looks like. Whenever I try to ask, Antonia shuts me down. I imagine my hair is like his, though, seeing as Antonia's is blond and straight.

"Why don't you try wearing something from your own wardrobe," I suggest gently. "Maybe your denim dress and seventies headscarf? Or that cute burgundy pinafore? Seriously, Lowri, be yourself. If you wear your sister's clothes, you won't feel like you. And if the rest of us freeze, we'll need you to be you!"

Lowri strokes the blazer lapels absently. "You're right," she says finally. "Some of Gwyneth's style choices are pretty out-there." She starts sliding hangers back into the closet. "I guess I'll see you tomorrow."

"At eleven. Don't be late."

"As if!"

"Au revoir, my friend."

"Au revoir!"

I stare at the clothes hanging outside my closet. Lowri forgot to ask what I was planning to wear: a hot-pink cord miniskirt with buttons up the front and a plain white tee. Simple. And anyone who says feminists can't wear pink can think again. A feminist can wear whatever she darn well likes . . . as long as she's brave enough to withstand the public glare. Because if that feminist has even the slightest hint of fuzz on her legs anywhere between her hemline and her heels, society dictates that she shouldn't even *think* about wearing a miniskirt.

The worst thing is, I KNOW I shouldn't care about a bit of leg stubble. I should be setting an example, right? But even though our interview is about female body hair, and even though I'm the one who set up this club in the first place, I still cannot face the prospect of pairing my lovely pink miniskirt with anything less than smooth legs. And so, even though I know I should be shunning my razor in the morning, I know that I won't. I will turn on the shower and reach for my razor like the walking, talking hypocrite that I am.

TWENTY-NINE

WHEN I LOOKED IN THE MIRROR THIS MORNING, I felt good about myself. I even felt good about my body, for once. *Yes, Evia!* I thought. *Hot pink is definitely your color!* And so I trotted into town in my little skirt, delivered myself into Lady Liberty's and parked myself at a table big enough for five.

Moments later, I regret my table choice. The nearby air conditioning unit has turned me into a goose-bumpy mess. Is it just me or does anyone else find that shivering turns your legs from smooth to stubbly in milliseconds? I can go from feeling shiny as an apple one minute to pineapple skin the next, all because I sneezed or shivered or felt a fresh breeze whip around my legs. Oof! I wrap my freezing hands around my mug, then check my phone again. I've been guarding four empty chairs since ten-thirty. Surely the journalist should be the one to arrive first?

I scroll through the Normal Normas' social media feed to

pass the time. In one post, someone is holding a hair dryer under Madison's skirt to re-create Marilyn's famous skirt-blowing-up image while Madison pulls a corny grin. As I scroll through, I realize every one of these photos has a glow to it, or a warming hue, making the girls' skin look flawless, their lips pinker, their eyes brighter. Is it even possible for these girls to post a picture of themselves *without* using a filter?

Turning my phone face down, I finally see Kar-Low sweep past the front window. Karima opens the door so Lowri can make her grand entrance. I can't stop my eyes from rolling.

"What?" she says, the biggest grin on her face. She's worn the red jumpsuit—of course.

"It does look good on you, to be fair," I admit.

Lowri shrugs with a smirk and picks up the menu. "I know."

Karima slides into the chair next to Lowri. "Say the words *photo shoot* and *somebody* can't resist the chance to show off."

Lowri shoots a glare at her. "You're just jealous of my model legs."

Karima sighs. "I am, actually." She's wearing her favorite emerald-green top with dark-blue jeggings. "Wow," she says, looking around at all the Statue of Liberty posters. "I've never actually been in here. I feel like I'm being watched!"

"I know," I add. "I particularly like that giant mural behind you."

Kari glances up and shudders.

"Lucy's not here yet?" asks Lowri.

I shake my head.

"Cutting it a bit close, isn't she?"

I check my phone again: 10:54. "She is coming out from the city, I guess."

"It's not *that* far," says Lowri. "Do we have time to get drinks?"

I eye up the line. "Maybe. But be quick."

BY ELEVEN-THIRTY we have all finished our drinks and I'm squirming on the rock-hard seat.

"Just go!" says Lowri. "How's it gonna look if Lucy walks up and our team leader has a wet patch?"

"Do you think one of us should call her?" Karima says, and I check my phone for the millionth time.

"Nah, she'll call us. Maybe she lost a signal—you know what trains are like. Plus, I don't want to hassle her. She's this big-shot magazine editor—she's probably busy doing other work on the train."

Karima starts picking at her nails while Lowri taps hers on the table. They're mushroom—her current favorite polish color.

"I'll call Frankie," I announce. "It's not like *her* to be this late."

Frankie doesn't pick up. That's two days in a row.

"I'll go to the bathroom," I blurt out. "You guys stay here. And message Frankie in the group chat."

Lowri sighs through her nose and Karima nods with a pursed-lip smile. I wish Lucy would hurry up and get here.

I go to the bathroom.

We order brownies.

We eat the brownies.

At noon, I finally agree to phone Lucy and she picks up after two rings.

"Oh! Hi, Lucy, it's Evia. Antonia's daughter."

"Hi, Evia! How are you?"

"Good thanks. Umm. I was just wondering . . . We were just wondering . . . If we had the wrong time?"

"Sorry?"

"Are you, um, on your way?"

"On my way?"

"To meet us."

"Oh right! The interview! Yes, that was going to be today, wasn't it? Did Frankie not tell you?"

"Tell me what?"

Lowri lifts her hands, palms up, and mouths "What?" at me. I put my phone on the table and switch Lucy to speaker-phone. I'm doing this weird shaky-shivery thing.

"Oh dear. I'm so sorry, Evia. I should've emailed. I just assumed that because you were all such good friends, Frankie would tell you herself. Oh goodness."

"Tell us what?"

"That I canceled the interview. Frankie told me she didn't want to do it. She said she'd pass along the message."

My eyes fill. I can't look at Kar-Low.

Lucy continues. "Frankie said she couldn't go through with it, that it was too much after—you know—what happened with that girl from school. She's not ready to talk about it. I am SO sorry, Evia. It's just, well, if I'm honest, the magazine was mostly interested in Frankie—her abuse and the symptoms of her condition, what she has to live with. Your campaign is great. It really is. But the club alone isn't really big enough to justify a feature for the mag—not at this stage, at least. Frankie's story would've given readers so much more to think about."

To ogle, she means. To point and laugh at, like Josephine Clofullia all over again.

Even Lowri is quiet. When I dare to look up, both Karima and Lowri are staring at my phone screen, unblinking. Disappointment crashes back and forth between us.

"I really am sorry to have wasted your Saturday morning, girls. Evia, I'd love to meet you another time anyway—and your mom. It'd be lovely to catch up." An oven starts pinging in the background. "I have to go, I'm afraid. Enjoy the rest of your Saturday!"

"Okay, bye, Lucy."

"By-ye," Lucy sings emptily. Then she's gone.

I stab at brownie crumbs with my fingertip. "I should've guessed something was up with Frankie."

"You couldn't have known," Karima says gently.

Lowri crosses her arms against her wasted jumpsuit. "I say we go to Frankie's and find out what the hell she's playing at. Why didn't she just tell us she didn't want to do it? I'm gonna message her right now!"

"No, don't!" I say, nearly shouting. "She'd already told me she didn't want to do a photo shoot. But I thought she was okay with the interview. Maybe she was never really okay with any of it."

We sit there, silent, for a bit. Part of me can't wait to get out of here, get home, pretend this never happened. The other part feels like once I leave, I'll have to admit I failed: failed in missing the biggest opportunity our club might ever get, and in missing the big flashing signs that my BFF wasn't happy.

Antonia will be so excited, waiting to hear all about the big interview. And what can I tell her? It didn't happen and it's all because I'm a gigantic fraud. Not only am I a terrible friend, but I am also spearheading a too-small campaign that (a) is going nowhere, and (b) probably wasn't mine to conceive in the first place.

Lowri can only hold a silence for so long. But she manages to maintain her pout, even when talking. "She could've at least told us she canceled, instead of letting us sit here like numbskulls for two hours. And now Madison's going to find out our interview didn't happen. Can you *imagine* how that's going to go down?"

My insides tie themselves in knots. Why-oh-why did I have to blab to Madison about this? Why couldn't I have kept it quiet until it was a done deal?

"Are you even going to ask Frankie to explain?"

I speak to my mug. "I'll talk to her."

"Good. Then you can find out—"

"I SAID I'd talk to her." I pick up my bag and throw the fake-gold chains onto my shoulder.

Karima looks up at me, all sympathetic. "Don't go," she says soothingly. "We need to discuss the club—I mean, what do we do next?"

I turn away, my eyes brimming. A leading journalist for one of the country's most famous teen mags just told me my campaign is basically pointless. We had one chance to make it bigger—far, far bigger—and we lost it. Just like that.

Maybe I'm just wasting everyone's time.

THIRTY

ON SATURDAY EVENING, MOM PULLS ME IN FOR A snuggle like she used to when I was little. When I got home and told her what had happened, she immediately called Lucy demanding an explanation. I can tell she feels bad for helping organize The Interview That Never Was.

Suddenly, my phone rings and Frankie's Halloween face appears on the screen. I take a deep breath and signal to Mom that I'm taking the call upstairs.

"You've been ignoring me," I say on my way up.

"I know," Frankie replies. "I'm sorry. I didn't know how to tell you about the interview."

I climb onto my bed and lean back against the cold wall, saying nothing.

"I wanted to be able to do it, Evs. I really did. But the more I thought about it, the more tense I got, until it felt like I couldn't breathe."

"That doesn't explain why you pulled out without telling us."

"I didn't ever agree to doing the interview, actually. . . ."

"You did!"

"No, I didn't."

The tension between us is palpable. I switch Frankie to speakerphone and set my phone on the duvet in front of me.

"I'm going to leave the group chat," she announces, just like that.

Silence.

"It's not the right time for me."

I grunt loudly. "There'll never be a right time."

"What did you say?"

"I said there'll never be a right time! This is the perfect opportunity to do something, Frankie! To make a difference! Raise awareness of PCOS and body hair! But will you do it? No. Because it's too hard. You're not brave enough."

"Wow," she replies calmly. "You really have no idea, do you? I don't want to have to be 'brave' just to leave my house. To show my face. Why can't I just exist like everyone else? Why does walking around with my face have to be such a . . . such a *statement*? It's not fair."

"*I know!* That's why I came up with the HGC in the first place!"

She sighs. "You honestly think you know what it's like for me, don't you?"

"Well . . . sort of."

"Do you have to shave your face twice a day? Do you have

to put up with people constantly staring and making jokes about you?"

"YES! All the time—when I'm wearing that mustache—"

She snorts into the phone. "And there it is. The key difference between us. You *choose* to put that mustache on, Evia. You can take it off whenever you like. And do you know what that makes you? A hypocrite. A massive, fake-mustache-wearing hypocrite."

My brain scrabbles for the right words, but she hasn't finished.

"You wanting me to be stronger all the time—braver—it's . . . it's . . . *patronizing,* Evia. Like I'm some two-dimensional cartoon character who can suddenly flip from being the butt of the joke to the hero. Well, I can't. And I've had enough of trying."

There are three short beeps and I stare down at my phone. She's gone.

She hung up on me.

Slumping down onto my duvet, Frankie's words bounce around my head like balls in a malfunctioning pinball machine. I try to nail down my thoughts, but I can't.

Hypocrite.

Patronizing.

Demeaning.

New balls keep firing into the machine with loud pinging noises, striking the sides violently with each bounce. *Ping, ping, ping!*

I feel sick.

I lie back and close my eyes, waiting for the nausea to pass.

Thank God we're on break from school. All I need to do is go to my neighbors' house every day, put up with their ten-year-old daughter from nine till five, and collect my money. The way I feel right now, Lola's going to be looking after *me*.

LATER, I scroll through my news feed, hoping to find something to cheer me up. A new makeup tutorial from Shania Kaminski would do nicely. In one classic clip, she spilled liquid foundation all over her carpet. Another time, she turned her five-year-old sister into a grunge girl and filmed their mom going totally ape.

Notifications flag that I've been tagged in something by Kenny Fisher: a picture of someone else's legs. The legs are poking out from the hem of a knee-length denim skirt. And they're hairy. Super hairy.

Evia Birtwhistle IS THIS YOU?!?!

I skim the comments, my heart already racing.

This is disgusting.

Fugly. No man will ever want a woman with hairy legs.

Totally agree! Gross.

WTF? The last three comments are from people I don't even know!

My thumbs start typing, my heart sending reverberations up and down my spine.

No, it is not me, Kenny Fisher. But if this woman chooses not to remove her leg hair, THAT'S HER CHOICE. No man should ever judge her for that. How many men have leg hair? All of you. How many women have leg hair? All of us. Just stating facts.

I hit Post. Ha. In your face, Kenny Fisher!

No. In YOUR face, Evia Birtwhistle.

Because now I'm discovering that every picture on the HGC's account—and I mean EVERY picture—has been trolled. Not just by Kenny, and not just by guys, but by a truckload of female haters too. It turns out a whole host of random people have been colossally offended by the idea that girls have body hair.

The first comment on several threads belongs to Madison Cox or one of her Normas.

Body hair on women is unnatural. It looks wrong wrong wrong!

Vile.

What's the sudden trend for letting everything grow? It's beyond gross.

Januhairy was months ago! Shave it off or put it away. Like NOW!!!

Some things should just not be allowed to grow. Tumors are one. A girl's leg hair is another.

Whoa!

It takes me two hours, but I respond to every single comment. To start with, I am nice. Well, as nice as I can be. Mostly I write things like *Show some respect* and *It's just a leg!*

Some of my responses get replies right away, and before I know it, my heart is racing and my thumbs are pitter-pattering so fast it's as if each thumb has been personally offended.

Suddenly, there's a light tap on the door. Mom pokes her

head in. She looks at me with kindness in her eyes and that's all it takes: I burst into tears.

"Oh, Evia! What on earth is the matter?!" She plants herself on the bed and squeezes me into a side-hug.

"People hate me, Mom," I sob. "Look!" I thrust my phone at her. "This guy says he would break up with me if I were his girlfriend. And this one"—I scroll back to my original hairy-armed picture—"says my arms are hairier than his and that I should kill myself!"

"Dear God." Antonia pushes her reading glasses back up her nose and looks over all of the vitriol.

Don't get me wrong, there are some positive comments in there too—mostly from other girls saying things like *Keep going* and *Thank you for sharing.* But probably half of the comments are spilling over with misogyny and disgust and, perhaps worst of all, pity. Because they assume girls like me can't have a life if we parade our body hair. Because we must hate ourselves or be mentally ill or hate all men and therefore have zero chance of ever leading a happy life.

"This is ridiculous," Mom mutters. "Diabolical . . . Ignorant, sexist pig. Oof! And all of this is directed at you?"

I nod, sniffing. "Well, me and my friends. But mostly me for starting the campaign in the first place."

She puts the phone down and gives me another squeeze. "I'll reply to them for you, if you want. I can't believe the stuff these people are coming out with. Anyone would think you're the first girl in the world to bare some body hair!"

"Mmm."

"This has been going on for years now. Years! These kids seriously need to get with the times. Do you know when I first started growing my leg hair?"

"Er . . . I was about ten."

"Yes. And do you know why I started growing it?"

"No," I sniff, dabbing my eyes with a tissue.

"To begin with, I just wanted a break from shaving: to see how it would feel if I just left it. Then, after a while, I started to like it. I liked how it wasn't stubbly—how natural it felt. And then, I don't know, it became a statement. Like: this is me, and if you don't like it, I don't care. It was liberating to realize I didn't need to rid myself of body hair ever again if I didn't want to."

"Was it scary, walking out for the first time with hairy legs?"

"Yes! I think that summer I wore the same maxi dress for about two months. But eventually, I worked up the courage to step out of the house bare-legged. Do you know what my biggest motivation was?"

I shake my head.

"You, Fluff."

"Me?"

"Yes, you: my daughter. My only daughter. Because the only way to normalize this thing is for people to see it—every day. When they first notice, people are a bit shocked; they stare. But the next time, they're not so shocked. By the hundredth time, it's not shocking at all. It's just . . . different. And I wanted you to see it every day, three hundred sixty-five days a year, so that you would feel you had a choice." She smiles the simplest of smiles. This massive thing she has done begins to sink in.

"I'm not sure I'll ever be brave enough."

"That's okay. I was forty-seven when I did it. What you're doing now is brave enough, believe me. And next time you need some help responding to these heartless excuses for human beings, just ask. I mean it, Fluff."

"Okay. On one condition."

"Anything."

"Stop calling me Fluff."

"But—"

"You said anything!"

"Okay, okay. I'll try. Now, it's supposed to be movie night. How about you come down and we find something really terrible and cheesy on Netflix to make you feel better?"

THIRTY-ONE

FRANKIE LEFT.

That's it. No goodbye. Just an automated notification that my BFF is no longer part of the group chat.

Lowri: *Err—what just happened?*

Evia: *Frankie left the group.*

Karima: *What? WHY?!*

Evia: *She doesn't want to be part of the campaign anymore. She made me feel really terrible, guys . . .*

Karima: *What? Why?*

Evia: *She pointed out that I can wear my mustache any time I like, but for her, it's not a choice. And she's fed up with having to be brave all the time.*

Lowri: *What about the interview? Any explanation?*

Evia: *She said she never actually agreed to it in the first place. I think she's probably right. I think I got sort of swept along in the excitement and thought she was okay with it.*

Lowri: *Oh.*

Karima: *Are you alright to keep going without her? With the campaign, I mean?*

Evia: *I guess so. I mean, I'd be happier if she was on board. But she's got to do what's right for her.*

Karima: *Totally.*

Lowri: *So I guess it's Lucy's fault that the interview fell through, not Frankie's.*

Evia: *Yeah. Stupid Lucy.*

Lowri: *Stupid Lucy.*

Karima: *BTW, did you guys see all that awful trolling on our account?!*

Evia: *Yep.*

Karima: *I think we should report it.*

Lowri: *That bit about tumors . . .*

Evia: *I know. My mom offered to help reply to some of these cretins.*

Karima: *Are you OK? Tagging you in that picture wasn't nice . . .*

Evia: *Yeah, I'm OK.*

Lowri: *They'll get bored and go away soon.*

Karima: *Let's hope!*

Evia: *Hang on a moment . . . *Sniffs air* I think my mom is making pancakes!*

Karima: *Amazing! Go go go!!*

Evia: *Talk later. X*

I slide my arms into my baby-blue bathrobe and my feet into slippers, then pad down the stairs, led by my nose. By the time I reach the kitchen, it feels like the nerve endings of my brain are dripping with maple syrup. It's like the Batter Fairy has been hard at work, then fluttered off without a trace!

I grab a fork and help myself to the large stack in the middle of the table. I'm just squeezing the syrup bottle when music suddenly blasts from the speakers, diverting my aim. The bottle does a gigantic fart in my lap.

Great.

Syrup on pj's.

A woman's voice starts whispering loudly, then a piano and violin blast into the pancake air, filling the whole of our house with their opening bars. The voice returns, humming in a melodic, warbly sort of way, and the utility room door BURSTS open. Mom surges into the kitchen like a whirling pink tornado. She grabs a balloon whisk from the utensil jar and holds it up, balloon to mouth. Before I know it, she's waltzing around the kitchen in her kimono, crooning.

God.

I know what the song is. It's Christina Aguilera. You know—the old one about being beautiful?

Well, Christina is in my kitchen with hairy legs and a kimono. I don't know whether to stay and watch or run and hide. But I want the pancakes. I stay, shaking my head but breaking into a slow grin at the same time.

As the chorus hits, my mom swings a hairy leg out of her kimono and sweeps her foot up onto the table so it's right there in front of me, like a giant, slightly bony teddy bear. Then she sings into the whisk all deadpan, stroking her shin lovingly, going on about how beautiful she is.

She straightens the leg for me to stroke and I give it a reluctant ruffle. Oh, Christina, I am sorry! I know this song is all about inner beauty and stuff, but I fear my mother may have taken it too far. Never again will I hear this song without an image of Antonia's fuzzy calf on the kitchen table.

Fuzzy calf.

"... *beautiful* ..."

Fuzzy calf.

"... *bring me down* ..."

Mom butchers the second verse. Then, as the chorus is about to strike again, she pulls a chair right up close and stares into my eyes. She drops the whisk and cups my face in her hands. She is trying to sing about how beautiful I am, except she has quite outdone herself with her dance moves and is running out of breath. Finally, she kisses me on the forehead, which I interpret as a signal that she has reached the end of her routine. But I am wrong, because the kiss seems to signal the beginning of a whole new segment of choreography. I think I will call this segment "slow moshing." Slow moshing is where my mother zigzags over the kitchen as if something is pulling her by her shoulders, lurching her from one side to the other in a haphazard way. She is also pecking her head in a semi-rhythmic fashion, like an ostrich in distress.

As the outro dwindles, Mom sweeps toward me and lands dramatically in a chair, panting. She snatches the other fork from the middle of the table and spears a pancake. "Carbs!" she hollers. "Give the woman carbs!"

She wolfs down a couple of mouthfuls while I shake my head at her.

"What a song," she says eventually, still breathing heavily. "I used to sing that for karaoke, moons ago."

"Isn't that a bit of a depressing choice?"

"No! Not at all! It's empowering. And I thought it would be a nice way to start your Sunday morning."

"Let's hope the neighbors agree."

"Oh, they won't have heard a thing."

I arch my eyebrows.

"I'm fifty-two years old, Evia. I'm probably over halfway through my life. If I want to sing Christina Aguilera at the top of my lungs in my own home on a Sunday morning, I'm going to do it."

"Don't say that."

"What?"

"About being halfway through your life."

"Well, it's true! If I live past a hundred four, I'll be a wibbling, dribbling wreck!"

"Nah. You'll be showing the nursing home staff how to hold their planks and do a tree pose."

She smiles. "Maybe." She nods. "Although if my only daughter banishes me to a nursing home, I'll be a bit annoyed. You're my insurance policy, girly!"

For a moment, the realization she just called me "girly" rather than Fluff adds a warm feeling to the fullness in my tummy.

Suddenly, my phone vibrates in my robe pocket. I lick my fingers and glance at the message on the home screen.

Did you find my note? x

My stomach does a backward somersault. It's from an unknown number. Between everything that happened—or didn't happen—at the café, my fight with Frankie, and feeling like I'm under attack by an army of razor-wielding trolls, I had forgotten all about the note on Friday.

What do I say? Should I reply? I make a mental list of all the plausible identities of its sender:

1. A hot guy who is genuinely interested in me (chance: VERY LOW)
2. A man with a fetish for hairy women, as per Lowri's suggestion (LOW)

3. An overly friendly girl who is worshipping me a bit too much and wants a photo of me for her shrine (chance: MEDIUM)
4. A troll in disguise (HIGH).

I slide the phone back into my pocket without replying. I can't face any more trolling. I stab another pancake.

THIRTY-TWO

I'VE BEEN BABYSITTING FOR LOLA SINCE I WAS NOT-
quite-fourteen. She lives across the street and when I'm there,
her favorite things to do include (a) playing with the filters on
my chat app, and (b) leafing through trashy magazines. She
thinks we're the same age and that she's my BFF. To be honest, this week she might be.

By Wednesday, it's a miracle I've managed to keep her off
my phone for so long. Midmorning, I come back from the
bathroom to find she's clocked my passcode and she's in.

"What's a fem-i-na-zi?" she sounds out.

Oh crap.

"Lola! I said *don't* go on my phone!" I snatch back my cell
and stare at my feed. It has fifty-seven new notifications since
I last checked.

The word *FEMINAZI!* flashes at me, bold and big, alter-
nating in black and red like a swastika. The image belongs

to Luke Travers, who's tagged me. Kenny Fisher replies, *Ha! Good one!*

"So?" says Lola, reminding me she's there. "What does it mean?"

"To be honest, Lola, I don't know. I guess it's a cross between a feminist and a Nazi. D'you know what a feminist is?"

"Someone who loves women?"

"Well, sort of. It's someone who believes in women's rights—that women should have the same rights and opportunities as men."

"Oh."

"And do you know who the Nazis were?"

She nods.

"Well then, you know it's a horrible thing to call someone."

"But why is that boy saying you're a femi . . . fem-in-azi?"

I sigh, my shoulders dropping. "I've started this campaign at school. It's about female body hair."

Lola frowns.

"We point out that all girls have body hair and say they shouldn't feel bad about it. We shouldn't get rid of it just because society says we should."

"What, so you don't shave your legs? Or under your arms? That's gross, Evia!"

"Lola!"

"I'm going to shave under my arms as soon as I start getting hair under there. And Mom says I can go to the salon with her the week before I start middle school."

"What for?"

"My first leg wax."

"Oh, Lola. You're only ten! Besides which, waxing hurts! Why are you even thinking about it?"

"Because everyone else is! Two girls in my class have started their periods already! I can't wait to get mine."

I sigh again. I try to explain my arguments a bit more, but Lola won't budge. It's bad. I mean, if I can't persuade a ten-year-old to come around to my way of thinking, what chance have I got of persuading anyone else?

Later, I get busy replying to the trolls. Some of the things they say . . . I can't let them get away with it. When my chest starts getting tight, I put my phone down or pass it to Mom. She's being a total legend. She even used her Yogi Bear handle to post a picture of her legs to our group feed. She captioned it: *Women have body hair. Get used to it.*

The strong-arm emoji was basically invented for my mom.

ON WEDNESDAY night I hit the bowling alley with Karima and Lowri. Kar-Low head straight to the desk to change their shoes while I head to the bathroom. After drying my hands, I nearly walk straight into him.

Jake.

Alone, outside the bathrooms, waiting for me.

"Oh!" I manage, hoping that the bowling alley's strange purple lighting will hide my flushed cheeks.

"Hi," he says. "How are you?"

"Um, good. You?"

He nods. "Yeah, fine. Look"—and I wonder if he's tracked me down on purpose to make this speech—"don't worry about the whole poem thing. Bradley should never have given it to me. It was a harsh move."

I smile like a fool.

"Let's just forget about it, okay?"

I nod again. "You haven't told Frankie, have you?"

Jake snorts. "Course not. She'd never speak to you again!"

My heart crushes a little. I deliberately haven't contacted Frankie since Saturday and it feels like there's an open wound in my chest growing deeper every day.

I adopt a deliberately cheerful tone. "Have you been bowling?"

"Yeah."

"On your own?"

"Er, no . . ."

At that moment, the blond girl from school emerges from the bathroom, looking more immaculate than ever in a white minidress and denim jacket. Jake nods at her. "Evia, meet MJ. MJ, this is Evia."

Of course. They're on a date. Jake was never waiting for me—why would he be waiting for me?

MJ smiles, but says nothing.

"MJ . . . ," I say, wishing Kar-Low would come save me. "Like Peter Parker's girlfriend."

MJ rolls her eyes. "I haven't heard that one before. . . ."

My cheeks must be burgundy by now.

"Well, let's hit the road," Jake says to MJ. "Good talk, Evian Water. Catch ya later."

"Later," I echo as MJ reaches for Jake's hand. Then, while they head to Jake's car to drive away like actual adults, I book it toward Kar-Low faster than you can say "Spider-Verse."

"Who wears a dress bowling, anyway?" Karima asks during our third frame.

"MJ, apparently," I reply sulkily.

Meanwhile, Lowri has just scored her fourth strike and celebrates with even more flamboyance than usual, having noticed a group of older girls taking occupancy in the next lane. Karima and I groan—neither of us has scored a strike EVER.

"Are you good at *all* sports?" I ask Lowri when she returns to the booth.

She shrugs. "I guess I'm just multitalented."

Suddenly, my phone buzzes.

I think we should meet up. x

"What's up?" asks Lowri, sliding across the booth.

I show them the messages from the unknown number.

"You mean you didn't reply to the first one?" asks Lowri. "Evia! Don't leave the poor guy hanging!"

"But what if it's not a guy? What if it's Madison or Kenny? Or a weirdo with a fetish—like you said!"

Lowri's mouth twitches. "I was only joking."

"It's not Jake, is it?" asks Karima. "Because he's just seen you, so that would be a bit weird."

I shake my head. "I've got Jake's number. It's not him."

"Well, you should *definitely* reply," says Karima. "Whoever it is, he sounds genuine."

"Do it, do it, do it!" says Lowri so loudly that we get looks from our neighbors.

"All right, all right!"

"Start by asking who he is," says Karima. "No harm in that."

My thumbs hover expectantly, awaiting instructions from my tangled mess of a brain. Finally, my gray matter talks to my thumbs.

I don't talk to strangers, I type, feeling proud at my bold, semiflirty tone. I've barely hit Send when the damned thing vibrates in my hand.

I drop it like a hot potato.

We all sit there for a bit, staring at the potato on the floor.

"Honestly!" says Lowri, climbing down on all fours and reading from the sticky carpet. *"I'm not a stranger,"* she recites. *"We've been at school together for four years.* Ooooh! I wonder who it could be!"

Before I can grab the phone back, Lowri's thumbs start moving. *"So—who—are—you?"* she reads, typing ON MY PHONE.

"Lowri Edwards, give me that back RIGHT NOW!"

Lowri rolls her eyes and hands me the phone. She pulls herself up from the damp, Coke-soaked carpet and looks down at the knees of her jeans. "Great," she says, glancing over at the girls next door. "Now I have wet patches."

"Serves you right," I gloat.

There are new vibrations in my hand, but this time I keep a firm grip on my phone.

Meet me at Shake It Up tomorrow, 7pm and you'll find out. X

"Oh God," I say, frowning. "He wants a date."

Karima's smile widens and Lowri rubs her hands together with glee. "Excellent," she says. "Now, please accept so I can finish thrashing you both at bowling and get out of here with my wet knees."

THIRTY-THREE

TRIPPING ALONG THE PAVEMENT TO THE MILKSHAKE
bar, I regret my choice of outfit. I'm wearing a long-sleeved
ditsy dress and Doc Martens, which, on the way here, seem to
have set my feet on fire. I pat my upper lip and clammy forehead. Why on earth didn't I accept my mom's offer of a ride?
Actually, I know why. Because I didn't want her grilling me
and realizing that I know nothing about my date except that
we're at school together. Eeeeek!

I put my hand on the door, then freeze. *Come on in!* invites
the sign in retro lettering. Behind me is my comfort zone and
on the other side lies a vast, crumbling precipice. As soon as I
step over that threshold, the floor will give way and swallow
me up. I'll be entering a new and uncertain world—one where
Evia Birtwhistle goes on actual dates with actual boys and
explores the possibility of Having a Love Life.

Finally, I push open the door and step onto that precipice. Beneath my feet, the floor is checkered with squares

of custard cream and duck-egg blue. The walls are painted bubblegum pink, the bar area a saccharine pink-cream-blue. I have stepped into the lair of a cotton-candy monster! The monster seems to have scared all the customers away from the backless leather stools at the counter to the small round tables below, where they're busy slurping and laughing. Are they laughing at me? Is my makeup running off my face?

Suddenly, I wonder whether my date is still even here. I am more than fashionably late. I could leave. Maybe he hasn't seen me.

"Evia!"

Oh.

A hand goes up from a booth in the far corner. "Over here!"

My heart quivers with nerves while my mouth smiles with relief.

"Hi," I say, arriving at his booth. It's Rupert Clifton—piano-playing python owner Rupert Clifton. It's not some alien boy with three eyes, it's not Luke or Kenny or a troll in disguise. It's Rupert Clifton, a real-life, hunksome boy my own age who knows me and still wants to go out with me!

Still pondering this whopping miracle, I maneuver myself into the booth and slide my arms out of my denim jacket.

Rupert's tall, Oreo-stacked freakshake sits untouched.

"Sorry—the waitress kept pestering me for an order."

"That's okay. I'm so sorry I'm late."

God, it's hot in here. As hot as that music practice room. Maybe I should wear more layers when I'm around boys, so I can strip off. (Not *completely,* but you know what I mean.)

"So . . . You didn't guess it was me?"

"No! I really didn't."

I pick up the menu and start browsing. There are fruity freakshakes, dessert-themed freakshakes, movie-themed freakshakes, as well as the more standard smoothies and milkshakes. Nearby, some kids' eyes light up as a waitress delivers two enormous dessert drinks to their table, their mother gasping. One is topped with whipped cream, cookies and large chunks of honeycomb, while the other is decorated with a rainbow of sweets, mini doughnuts and a cone masquerading as a unicorn horn.

Rupert looks at me, his green eyes twinkling. Yes, I observe in a gratified way, Rupert's eyes are light green around the outside and hazel around the middle, and I am going to look into them A LOT.

"I hope you're ready for a sugar high," he says, and I grimace. I've been to the bathroom three times in the past two hours. My nervous system seems to have relocated to my gut. "Er—I'm not sure. I can't decide. Do you think the Vanilla Beet Shake sounds nice or gross?"

"Honestly? A bit gross . . ."

"Hmm. I think I'll get it."

"Are you sure?!"

"Yep."

Rupert slides toward the edge of the booth to get out to order my drink at the bar. I can't help but notice his biceps in his tight gray T-shirt. Do I dare to imagine those arms around me? I can't believe he actually likes me. Me!

"Hang on!" I rummage in my bag for my coin purse. It's a black velveteen number with an old-fashioned clasp, from my granny. My mom's parents live in Canada, so we hardly ever see them.

"It's fine," Rupert protests. "Let me . . ."

I thrust some cash into his hand. "Please."

I watch as he walks to the counter. Rupert is tall for our age—about six foot one—with dark blond hair and the kind of neck that makes me go a bit wobbly. I have this sudden overwhelming desire to stand behind him and touch his neck—to stroke the hair along his hairline. He turns to smile at me and I look away, blushing hard.

While I wait, I find myself staring at the back of a head on the other side of the room. This girl's bob is so sleek, her hair so amazingly shiny! Suddenly, the girl's dining partner pops her ginger head over the top of a menu and gives me a sneaky wave.

Goddammit!

When did *they* sneak in?!

I've barely had a chance to glare at them when my phone buzzes.

Karima: *Don't be mad at us! We just wanted to check you were all right and make sure your date wasn't a complete weirdo!*

Lowri: *You've lucked out majorly! Rupert's a hottie.*

Karima: *Says the gay girl*

Lowri: *I can appreciate a good-looking guy.*

Karima: *Can you though?!*

Lowri: *Well, he's got nothing on Allegra Mackenzie but . . .*

Evia: *WILL YOU TWO PLEASE STOP BICKERING AND LEAVE ME ALONE?! IN CASE YOU HADN'T NOTICED I AM ON A DATE!!!*

Rupert returns to his seat, sliding me my change. Lowri ducks behind her menu once more and I turn my phone face down on the table.

"Everything okay?" Rupert asks.

"Yep!"

"They're going to bring your drink over."

"Thanks." Luckily he doesn't seem to have noticed Kar-Low in the background. "So . . . How's your break been?"

"I haven't been up to much, really. Mostly hanging out with Cam."

So that's how he got my number. Cameron and I did a drama production together last year.

"We've been trying to do a bit of studying, but mostly we end up playing computer games. How about you?"

I realize I'm playing with the clasp on my coin purse and put it down. "I'm babysitting my neighbor's kid."

"Oh, right. How old?"

"Ten."

"Same as my sister."

"I didn't know you had a sister."

"Yeah, Ella. She'll be coming up to St. Joe's next year." He also has a brother named Toby, who I think is in seventh grade.

In my peripheral vision, Lowri springs from her seat and stalks toward the bar like a lumbering moose. Halfway there, she trips over a chair leg and disappears with a clatter of furniture, making Rupert turn toward the commotion. By some small miracle Lowri remains floored until Rupert turns back, shrugging. When Lowri recovers to full height, she gives me an exuberant double thumbs-up and starts limping toward the bar.

"You're an only child, aren't you?" Rupert asks.

I try not to look at the bar. "Yes."

"I just remember from French. You know, in middle school all you do is say the same things over and over again. *Je m'appelle Rupert. J'ai onze ans. J'ai un frère et une soeur.* Sorry about the accent—my French is bad."

"Sounded great to me," I lie.

Our legs collide under the tabletop. I panic and cross mine out to the side.

A waitress appears with my drink—a tall glass filled with a thick, incandescent purple liquid and topped with vanilla ice cream and a sprinkling of nuts. I take a long, cold slurp before coughing.

Rupert raises his eyebrows at his own cookie-topped nemesis. "I have no idea how I'm actually going to eat or drink this." He opens his thumb and forefinger like pincers and liberates an Oreo from the calorific mountain. "Probably not the best choice for a first date." He instantly blushes, then wipes his mouth with a napkin.

I look down, at the same time realizing that my body temperature seems to have returned to normal. Maybe I am not going to mess this up Leo-style after all. I haven't stared at the ceiling once!

"So," Rupert asks, changing the subject. "How's the club going?"

"Er . . ."

"Bad question?"

"I just . . . I'm sort of regretting starting the whole thing. Frankie's left the group and there have been some pretty harsh comments on social media."

"Really?"

"Mmm. Wanna see?"

We spend the next hour poring over the insults, Rupert reading and listening. He is sympathetic, says the right thing at the right time, he is pretty, well, perfect. My eyes keep finding his neck, his chest, the smooth line of his jaw.

As he hands back my phone, our fingers touch and there's a silent fizz of something that makes my heart race. There might as well be a giant arrow above our table, blinking with the words *She likes him! She likes him!* I blush, even though I know it's not there.

"So," he says when we've both somewhat miraculously slurped to the bottom of our glasses. "Do you think you might be up for a second date?"

His words park themselves on top of my brain and sit there like a double-decker bus. Suddenly, all the fizzing and excitement turns to dread. What if I'm not ready for a boyfriend? What if I don't know what to do?

"Yes. Maybe. I . . ."

"Don't worry—you don't have to answer now. Sorry, I didn't mean to put you on the spot."

"No, it's okay. Look, I'd better be going soon, to be honest. I'm on Lola Duty again in the morning."

"Okay," he says. "Can I walk you home?"

I know I shouldn't like his chivalry, but I sort of do. "No, it's fine. I'll text my mom. She's expecting to pick me up."

We sit in silence while I type. "I might wait outside," I say, suddenly craving fresh air.

"I'll come with you."

Oh no. I am not ready for Mom to meet Rupert yet. She'll be like a barnacle latching onto a whale.

Outside it is light but cool. I cross my legs and sway, trying to ignore my bursting bladder. We talk about the weather and teachers and vague plans for the summer. Finally, I spot a battered red Kia approaching the bus station. I wave like I'm hailing a cab and start moving quickly to create distance between Rupert and Mom's ancient car.

"Bye, then!" I call, running backward.

"Watch out!" Rupert yells.

"What?" I yell back and run smack into a concrete pillar.

"Oh," I mutter, falling butt-first onto the pavement.

Rupert runs toward me, his face all concerned.

I raise my hand in a gesture that is meant to say "Don't worry—I'm a super-tough woman" but probably just says "Oww!"

Before he can reach me, I push myself up to standing and

limp across the street. My mom pulls up to the curb in the nick of time.

"Are you okay, love?" she asks as I open the passenger door. "That was quite a tumble."

"Drive," I growl, caressing a buttock.

In his concern, Rupert has caught up with us on the other side of the road. Mom lowers her window and leans out. "Hiiiiii!" she screeches, waving her entire forearm.

Rupert waves politely from the opposite pavement.

"WHO ARE YOU?!" Mom bellows.

"Rupert!" Rupert calls from across the road. "Rupert Clifton!"

"HELLO, RUPERT! I'M ANTONIA!"

Is it possible to die from embarrassment?

"GOOD TO MEET YOU, RUPERT!" Mom yells out the window. "COME FOR SUPPER SOMETIME!"

Supper?

SUPPER?!

Who even says *supper* anymore?! We *never* say *supper*!

I reach over to shut Mom's window but she bats my arm away. Finally, with one last wave to Rupert, she takes the hint and drives.

Argh! I am so mad at her! And at Kar-Low for trespassing on my date, good intentions or not. When we get home there is only one person I want to talk to. I scroll to her name and record a voice memo.

"Frankie, I miss you. I'm sorry about everything, I really am. I just want my best friend back. Something happened today—I had a date. It started off okay, but then it all went wrong. Please, when you get this, can you call me back? I miss you." I tap the Send button, then fall back into my pillows.

A message comes through almost immediately: *It felt like you were running away from me earlier. . . . Sorry if I talked too much. x*

Argh, not Frankie. And now I feel bad. What do I say? *Yes, I was running away from you, Rupert. No, you didn't talk too much. I had a wonderful time.* How much is too much to say after a date? I don't know! This is precisely why I need my BFF!

I keep my reply simple: *I had a lovely time. You didn't talk too much. x*

My phone pings again as I'm delivering my limbs into pj's.

Dear Mia & Maya, my best friend recently went on a first date. I want to be excited for her but I'm going through a bit of a tough time at the moment and have just started therapy. Is it OK if I hear about her love life another time? I'm really sorry . . . x

Therapy? Therapy?! Why didn't she tell me before? Now I feel terrible about trying to share the excitement of my date with her!

I text back: *Frankie, I'm so sorry—I didn't know. I hope you're OK? I'm here when you want to talk. xxx*

I read and reread her message until there are a dozen ghost-like Frankies in my room, all eerily quiet. One by one, they sink to the floor, crying, then melt into the carpet.

204

THIRTY-FOUR

FIRST THING ON FRIDAY, I GET MESSAGES FROM Karima and Lowri badgering me about the date, so I debrief them instead. Afterward we start making plans for the future of the HGC. The whole time, there's a tiny rodent gnawing away at the Loyalty to Frankie section of my brain, trying to distract me.

I put the tiny rodent in a box.

I finish looking after Lola.

I collect my money.

ON MONDAY morning, there is only a small pool of dread in my stomach as opposed to the reservoir I had before break. No more mustache-wearing equals no more stares, no more having to defend myself wherever I go. Frankie's comment about my hypocrisy rings in my ears and I am reminded, once again, that she was right.

On the way to school, I notice a new ad at the bus stop. A woman's face looks out at me, her lips parted and one shoulder slightly raised as she peers over it toward the camera. Perfect "nude" foundation, it advertises; "magic" flawless coverage is the promise.

PAH! Mom's voice starts up in my head. *Those cheekbones are impossibly high, Evia! And her eyes are practically lilac! Magic indeed. The only magic involved is via a digital paintbrush in Photoshop!*

I know my inner Mom voice is right. I *know* the ad is drawing on my insecurities and trying to make me feel inferior. Yet I still find myself wanting to reach for the concealer. It doesn't help that a new pimple appeared on my chin overnight. I'm basically transporting a volcano on my face.

Thankfully, I see something that cheers me up—or at least I think I do. The girl runs ahead and I do a double take.

Inside the school gates, there's another one. Am I dreaming?

Crossing over Reception, another two. One of the girls raises a hand at me, then bows her head toward her friend and giggles.

No, I am not dreaming. These are GIRLS. WEARING. MUSTACHES.

On the way to homeroom, there are four more, appearing in pairs, like soul mates.

Karima and Lowri are already in the room, their faces looking strangely bare without their upper-lip embellishments.

"Your bus got in early," I declare.

"Never mind that!" says Karima, her eyes gleaming. "Have you seen any? Mustaches, I mean?"

"Oh yes, a few. What's going on?"

Just then, Chloe Ford walks in, arm in arm with Hannah Bayliss. They are both donning fake 'staches and grinning like madmen.

"Hey, Chloe!" I call. She comes straight to my desk. "What's going on with the . . ." I tap my philtrum.

"Haven't you heard?" she says. "People have seen all the trolling on social media and are really shocked by it. Some of the things they've said about you are just, well, vile. We wanted to do something to show we're on your side."

Hannah chips in, "Us girls have got to be in it together!"

Then they giggle and go to their usual seats on the other side of the room.

More probing of Chloe during English reveals that the chief organizer of the demonstration is a new girl named Jemima Drake. I make it my mission to track her down by the end of the day, despite having no clue what she looks like. Every time I see a mustache, my heart does a little wiggle. If only my own furry face-piece weren't banished to the bottom drawer of my desk at home . . .

AT MORNING break, I spot dozens of mustachioed girls from various grades, and not a platinum wig in sight. Some of the younger girls even give me a wave from across the cafeteria, like I'm some kind of school celebrity. I find myself hoping that, from her throne in the corner, Madison has seen them waving.

"Miss Birtwhistle!" The voice pierces me like a stalactite to the ribs.

I turn from the vending machine to face The Chubb, who struts up to me as fast as her long plaid skirt will allow.

"I thought we agreed that after the break there would be no more funny business?"

"I didn't have anything to do with this, Mrs. Chubb."

"You didn't?"

"No, honestly. See?" I point to my mouth. "I'm not wearing one."

Her eyebrows bounce while she thinks. Maybe she's going to let me off the hook.

"Detention after school, Evia. All week. Mr. McGovern's classroom till five p.m."

"But, ma'am! It wasn't—"

"It's not open for debate. We agreed to the plan. Your time is up."

The hubbub of the cafeteria prevails, but dozens of pairs of eyes burn into me.

"If I see a single mustache in school tomorrow, your friends will be joining you." Mrs. Chubb pivots on her clunky heels and marches out of the cafeteria. I watch her go, dumbfounded.

"Oh dear, oh dear," comes a voice from behind me. "Sounds like that's it for your little 'campaign.'" Madison has moved from her stronghold with a throng of Normal Normas. Only Aliyah hangs back, flirting with a tall sophomore named Cole.

"How did your magazine interview go?"

I swallow hard.

"Busy trending, are we? Oh, and I heard your BFF quit

too! Frankie's mom has been busy telling Aliyah's mom everything: how poor Fran-kay had been stressing about this big interview . . . how the interview got canceled . . . how you two have had this big falling-out. Happy times!"

I can't help it: my whole body sighs. A few younger kids with mustaches hover nearby in a halfhearted display of loyalty, but hang back when Madison laughs at them.

"Oh, come on!" she gloats. "Am I meant to feel *threatened*?!"

The kids don't disperse but they don't edge closer either. Madison doesn't stop.

"Let me get this right: first, you get ditched by the big national magazine, then you get ditched by your best friend. Which MUST mean that she doesn't want to be a Hairy Mary after all. Hey, if your BFF wants to be smooth-a-licious, maybe *we* could recruit her!"

"Frankie would never join the Normas."

"Oh, who cares! It's not like we need her anyway." She gestures to the girls around her, festooned in badges. Meanwhile, Aliyah has started making out with Cole in full view of the whole cafeteria. Madison turns to see what I'm staring at.

"Urgh," she groans.

"Looks like you might be in need of a new BFF too," I observe bravely.

"Oh, shut up!" Madison snaps. "If any of you losers actually *had* boyfriends, you might understand that sometimes us girlfriends have to take a backseat. But then, you wouldn't understand that because YOU are all sad little virgins too busy growing your pubes to realize that boys don't want girls to be hairy. Boys want girls to be smooth-a-licious, like me! Isn't that right, Liam?" She claps the shoulder of the nearest unsuspecting boy, who happens to be the twin brother of Lara Dyson, one of the Normas.

"What?" says Liam, nearly choking on a Dorito.

"Hairy girlfriend or smooth girlfriend?" Madison posits.

Liam's nose turns up at one side. "Smooth, duhhh!"

Lara looks on, proudly, but Madison hasn't finished. "So you wouldn't go after a girl with hairy legs?"

Liam snickers. "As if!" His friends laugh, adding their agreement. Madison's power over boys is clear. When they're not busy drooling over Aliyah and Cole, Liam and his gang are staring openly at Madison's chest.

Suddenly, a voice booms from the loudspeaker, echoing across the cafeteria, the bathrooms, the tennis courts: "For anybody not yet aware, fake mustaches are now banned at St. Joseph's. All pupils wearing them are to remove them immediately. Teaching staff will be enforcing this in ALL lessons."

All over the cafeteria, girls start picking at their 'staches, including the small group behind me.

Madison smacks her lips together. "I think that's game over for the Hairy Muffs' Club. What a shame!" She sidles away, smugness oozing from her pores. "Enjoy your detention, Birtwhistle. . . ."

All words have emptied from my head in the same way that all energy and enthusiasm for life have drained from my body.

Do I have math next? I think I have math. I go to math.

By lunchtime, there isn't a hairy lip to be seen. And I

am back to being solo on my picnic bench, thanks to stupid orchestra.

KAR-LOW CATCH me at the end of the day.

"Sorry to hear about the detention," says Karima, power-walking. I follow, despite the fact the bus zone is in the opposite direction from McGovern's classroom. "Shouldn't you be going there now?"

"Yeah, I'm on my way." I'm clearly not. "Rest of the week too."

"That sucks!" says Lowri.

"Yeah," I snort. "I guess the coup's over."

Karima sighs.

"Did you find Jemima Drake?" Lowri asks.

"No." I frown.

Lowri holds up her phone. "Turns out she's the big sister of someone in brass. Her socials handle is Jemima Marigold."

A girl with an open, heart-shaped face looks back at me, unsmiling but flawless. She has almond eyes framed by two-tone glasses—tortoiseshell and turquoise—and strong, un-plucked eyebrows. Her hair is finger-combed into a blond topknot with dark roots. She looks like a model.

"She's in our year? I've never seen her."

Lowri nods. "She moved here just before break."

"I need to find her and shake her hand."

"Even if she landed you in detention?" asks Lowri.

"Absolutely. Seeing all those girls today was amazing."

"And boys," says Karima. "Rupert too."

My heart skips at the mention of his name. "Really?"

"Yep. Turns out guys also took offense to the trolling. Especially the whole feminazi thing."

The first bus starts its engine and pulls away.

"We have to go!" Karima starts running while Lowri gives me a quick one-armed hug.

"See you tomorrow!"

Jogging backward, Lowri shouts one last thing to me. "Forgot to say: I'm pretty sure I saw Frankie in school today!"

"What?"

"I'll text you!"

I watch, my feet rooted to the sidewalk, as the second bus cruises out of its bay. When Kar-Low's bus drives past, Lowri's thumbs are rapidly tapping away. I've begun trudging back toward the school building when her message comes through.

She had her hood up but I'm pretty sure it was F. She was heading out of the main entrance. About 2 pm. Did you know she was coming in?

No, I did not.

A gray speckled staircase looms before me. I liberate the sigh that's been building all day, then plant my foot on the first step.

THIRTY-FIVE

I AM EIGHT MINUTES LATE TO MY AFTERNOON DATE with Donald, but he doesn't comment. I spend the time doing my history homework while he sits at his desk with a stack of navy exercise books and a scarlet rollerball, barely looking up. There are four other students in the room.

As soon as detention's over, I text Frankie:

Were you in school today?

Yes, she replies later that evening. *I came in for a meeting. Didn't stay long—didn't want to risk seeing anyone. Really sorry.*

WHEN THE final bell rings on Tuesday, I head straight to McGovern's room. Having a designated hour of quiet time to do homework with no distractions is actually pretty useful.

I'm sliding my bamboo pencil box out of my bag when she appears like a mustache-wearing apparition. She is every bit as immaculate in real life as in her profile picture, even with the messy-on-purpose hair. She pulls out the seat next to mine and slides a fake mustache across the table for me.

"Nice to meet you, Evia Birtwhistle. I'm Jemima Drake."

"How did you . . ."

". . . know you were here? Word got around about the weeklong detention. Some of us thought that was totally unfair."

"Some" turns out to be more than a few. One by one, the seats in Mr. McGovern's room are filled as girls—and guys—file in. Rupert raises his hand at me, then silently takes his seat, Cameron following suit. When all the chairs are taken, the supporters start lining the walls, first behind me, then around the classroom. McGovern watches, unblinking.

Finally, when the arrivals cease, Mr. McGovern scurries to the doorway and leans out into the hallway.

"Any more?" he calls, and everyone chuckles. "What's going on?" he asks, stepping back into the room. "You haven't *all* been given detention, have you?"

"No, sir," Jemima replies coolly. "We're here to support Evia." Every head in the room turns to look at me.

My face is suddenly hotter than the inside of a data center. They are all here taking detention with me—*for* me.

"Sir?" asks Jemima. "I know this is detention and everything, but would you mind if I took a quick photo of everyone—you know, for social media?"

Donald exhales slowly. "If you must."

Jemima jogs up to the front before Donald can change his mind, then stands in the doorway and positions herself in a selfie, the rest of us in the background. She leans and stretches but doesn't seem satisfied.

"Sorry, sir—I can't fit everyone in. Would you mind . . ." Jemima hands her phone to Mr. McGovern. I can't believe her audacity! He won't agree to take the shot, will he?!

Mr. McGovern tuts loudly but accepts Jemima's smart-phone. "Quickly," he says, as Jemima squeezes into the front row. He goes to the doorway and shuffles out of it slightly.

"Everyone say Evia!" calls Jemima.

"EVIAAAAAA!" comes the chorus.

My heart bursts. I wish Frankie could see this. As for Donald—what an unexpected legend!

Donald returns the phone to Jemima, shaking his head, then retreats to the safety of his desk. "Now, as we're all going to be here for the next"—he glances at the clock—"fifty minutes, I suggest we *try* to get some work done. Those of you with seats, please take out your homework. Those of you without, follow me next door and we'll find you a desk."

"Here's my number," says Jemima when our hour is up. She slides me a tiny piece of paper, torn from the back of her notebook. "See you tomorrow."

"Seriously?!"

"Yup, we're in this for the long haul."

"Wow . . . thanks!"

"No worries." And she glides off with a gaggle of friends.

Outside the classroom, Rupert is waiting for me.

"Hey," he ventures.

"Hey."

"That was . . . well, something!" he says as we start walking toward the stairs.

"A pretty awesome something! Do you know *why* Jemima's doing it? I mean, I don't even know her!"

Rupert shrugs. "No idea. I just heard about it from someone in music and wanted to support you. Listen, I'm sorry if I came on a bit strong last week."

"You didn't."

"It's just—"

"It's fine, really!"

"I hadn't, well—"

"Really, don't worry about it. I had a good time. I just . . . freaked out a bit when you started talking about a second date and, I don't know, I'm not sure I'm ready for anything, you know, serious. . . ."

He nods. "Understood. Friends?"

I smile harder. "Good friends." I put the emphasis on *good* and hope my face hasn't morphed into a giant grinning emoji.

"I'm happy with that," he says, eyes sparkling. "So, as friends, do you want to maybe hang out this Saturday? Come to mine and watch a movie? Daytime, obviously. Definitely NOT a date."

I try to make my eyes bore through to his brain to see how his cogs are turning. "Saturday's good. But can we meet at mine instead?" I'm not sure how I feel about meeting the rest of the Clifton crew. "How's three p.m.?"

"Perfect." His smile draws dimples in his cheeks. "Oh, by the way, I think I might've seen Frankie in school today. Is she back?"

My mouth falls open a little. "You're the second person to ask me that. Lowri thought she saw her yesterday."

"She was wearing a black hoodie with the hood up, so it was hard to tell. But I'm pretty sure it was her. She was heading toward the tech block."

Then it clicks.

"The Zone," I reply. "I bet she was going to The Zone."

Behind the tech block, on the far parameter of our school, there's a detached building called The Zone. It's for vulnerable students or kids who need extra help with learning, or time with a counselor. Lowri had an appointment there after she came out last year.

"Makes sense," Rupert agrees.

"She mentioned she might have some lessons in isolation."

"But you're not allowed to see her?"

Something tugs so sharply at the back of my heart that it forces me to suck in oxygen. "I guess not."

We come to a standstill, having reached the end of the road from school. This is where our journeys diverge.

"Okay, well. See you tomorrow," says Rupert. "And Saturday."

"Saturday." I return his smile without the dimples.

Then we separate, turning to raise our hands at one another from a distance. The farther I get from him, the harder it is to separate my feelings. Half of me wants to skip home, beaming like a lunatic at the thought of Rupert Clifton IN MY HOUSE. But then I picture Frankie coming into school alone and the beam gets wiped away.

THIRTY-SIX

AS SOON AS I GET HOME FROM TUESDAY'S DETEN-tion, I message Kar-Low about Rupert.

> **Me:** *A non-date sounds OK, doesn't it? He's not going to suddenly pounce on me? ARRRRGGHHH, what if he pounces on me?!*

> **Lowri:** *Evia! Chill!*

> **Me:** *What?! I've never had a boy in my house before! Unless my nerdy older cousin counts.*

> **Lowri:** *It doesn't.*

> **Karima:** *Just act like it's me or Lowri coming over and you'll be fine.*

> **Me:** *Easier said than done.*

Karima: *Well, you've got a few days yet to plan it. Now, tell us about Jemima . . . Who is she and what does she want with the HGC?!*

Me: *You say it like she's a fraudster!*

Karima: *Well, is she?*

Lowri: *I heard she's a wannabe influencer. She's already got, like, 1000 followers!*

Me: *Whoa. Could be useful?*

Karima: *Hmm.*

Me: *What?*

Karima: *I don't know . . . What if she just wants to use us to raise her profile?*

Lowri: *Always the pessimist . . .*

Karima: *Am not!*

Lowri: *Are too!*

Me: *Ladies, ladies . . . Maybe she'll raise OUR profile. It seems like she genuinely believes in our cause. She's a feminist through and through.*

Lowri: *Not to mention that she's hot.*

Karima: 🙄

Lowri: 😏😏😏

Me: *She is, to be fair. Anyone who can get their hair to look that messy yet perfect at the same time is a complete goddess. Oh, by the way, Rupert saw Frankie in school again today.*

Karima: *Whaaaaat?!*

Lowri: *Is she actually going to tell us she's back?!*

Me: *Sounds like she's working in The Zone.*

Lowri: *Ohhhhh.*

Me: *I'm guessing she doesn't want anyone to know.*

Karima: *Not even you?*

Me: *Not even me.*

Seconds later, I receive notification of a tag and follow the link. It's the detention group shot and there I am, in the front row, looking flummoxed. I make a pact with myself to learn the other fifty-nine tagged names. After what they did for me, it's the least I can do.

AS SOON as Wednesday lunchtime comes around, I make a beeline for The Zone and linger outside the entrance. At one point, our school nurse leaves, followed shortly by a kid in a woolly hat—despite it being June. When the nurse is out of view, I do a loop of the building, checking the windows, certain Frankie's in there. But the windows either have frosted glass or the blinds are pulled down. If Frankie's inside, they're doing a good job of keeping her invisible.

I text her: *Frankie, I'm outside the building. If you're in there, please come and talk to me.*

Two minutes later, I hear a strange hissing noise behind me. Frankie's head peeks out through a gap in the heavy doors of the entrance, and she flaps her hand quickly, beckoning.

I grin. "It's so good to see you!"

"Quick!" she pleads, sounding breathless. "I don't want anyone to see me!"

I walk over, puzzled by the urgency. "There's no one else around," I say, gesturing. But Frankie's eyes are wide, and she won't step out of the building.

"Can I come in?" I ask, confused.

But Frankie shakes her head, struggling to keep the heavy door ajar. "I'm not sure you're allowed. I think you need permission."

"What? That's crazy! What if I'm having a breakdown? I might need urgent support for my mental well-being!"

Frankie frowns at me. "That's not funny, you know."

"Sorry, I didn't mean . . . I just want to see you, that's all. A lot's happened."

"Oh yes, your date."

"Not just the date . . . We need to talk."

Suddenly, there's laughing behind me as a cluster of girls appears on the path, followed by another pair and another.

Frankie speaks so fast she makes me nervous. "I can't do this right now, Evia," she says, shaking her head. "I need to go." And she disappears behind the darkened glass.

I stand there feeling numb. Until recently, my best friend had never shut a door in my face.

Now she's done it twice.

JEMIMA'S SUPPORT act appears again at Wednesday's detention and I test myself on their names as they file into the classroom. Five minutes later, Madison Cox appears in the doorway. She stands there, searching the patchwork of heads until she finds mine, then snorts and rolls her eyes before disappearing. That night, she finds the group shot and lamely comments *Weirdos.*

Halfway through Thursday's detention, we have another visitor. Mrs. Chubb surveys the room, arches her eyebrows and shakes her head. Like Madison, she walks away without saying a thing. What can she do? None of us is wearing a mustache during the school day, and everyone else is here of their own volition.

Then on Friday, I turn up to find Donald alone, wearing his own falsie.

"Last day," he says with a conspiratorial wink. "Thought I'd play my part."

"Would you mind?" I ask, holding up my phone to take a picture.

He shrugs. "Why not?"

Wow! I take back what I said about Donald being Chubb's minion.

"I have a teenage niece, Amelia," he explains. "I'd never really thought about the whole body hair thing and, to be honest, it's not something I'm ever likely to talk to her about. I mean, can you imagine your uncle trying to talk to you about female grooming?"

My face fails to repress a hefty wince. My mom's only brother—my Uncle Tristan—lives across the country and we see him about every third Christmas. But even if I *did* actually know him, I can't imagine discussing my maintenance frustrations with him.

"Exactly," Donald goes on. "But it got me thinking about all the pressures there are for teenagers today and how social media makes it so much harder. And I thought, yes! Miss Birtwhistle has a point. While I wholeheartedly agree with Mrs. Chubb that exam season must not be hindered, I do feel that your feminist crusade is an important one. So well done."

The other detainees start arriving and I move toward my usual spot.

A tiny part of me feels like hugging Mr. McGovern, not as his pupil but as his wannabe niece. Because he is right. I do have a point and my feminist crusade is important. Here, surrounded by supporters, I can feel it. My body throbs with it. I should be shouting from the school roof, pinning banners on the building, marching through the corridors. I should be running for school president or some other senior student role. But I can't. Why? Because of exams.

Stupid exams.

Who needs test scores anyway?

THIRTY-SEVEN

ALL WEEK, OUR NUMBER OF FOLLOWERS HAS BEEN growing. Comments on our group detention pic reached six hundred and something.

I want one! they said, about the mustaches.

Go, girls! raved others.

Then BAM.

There it was, staring back at me like an angry hornets' nest, albeit a triangular one.

This hairy enough for you?! read the caption, followed by a load of crying-with-laughter emojis.

Within the hour the post was removed, and I received:

> *Some of your previous posts didn't follow our Community Guidelines. If you post something that goes against our guidelines again, your account may be deleted, including your posts, archive, messages and followers.*

WHAAAAAAAT?!

Ha! I post straightaway. *Whoever thought they'd get us banned, you failed! I'm still here, haters!* followed by the flexing muscle emoji. Someone thought they'd post inappropriate pictures on our account. Someone thought they'd get us taken down. Well, SOMEONE FAILED!!!

Antonia calls me down for tea and I slaughter my cannelloni, devouring it like a feral beast.

Afterward, having barely wiped the tomato sauce from my chin, I call Lowri.

"Did you see it?"

"See what?" she replies.

"The lady garden."

"What?!"

"Someone posted a picture of their, um, bush—online. Under our account."

"Nooo!"

"Yep."

"A pussy pic . . ."

"What?"

"It's called a 'pussy pic,' Evia."

"Ohhh."

"Is it still on there?"

"No, the internet police removed it. Got a warning too. They have a strict policy on nudity, don't they?"

"Jeez. At least it was only a warning, I guess." There's a sliding of wheels along floor tiles, followed by the clunking of computer keys. Top-notch technology is not high on the Edwards' agenda, and even if they were loaded, it still wouldn't be.

"Er, Evia?"

"What?"

"I can't find our account."

"Huh?"

"I can't find it."

"Wait, let me try." I grab my iPad, the browser window taking an age to load. Goddammit, Antonia! I don't want to sound ungrateful, but why do I *always* get lumbered with her ancient hand-me-downs?!

Finally:

ERROR

Your account has been deleted for violating our terms.

My heart launches toward my throat and my ears fill with the *thud, thud, thud* of hot blood. All our followers! All our posts! The words of the message bounce around as I try to reread it.

"But I don't understand! It was there, like, less than a half hour ago! They sent me a warning! It can't just . . . disappear?"

"I think it has."

"But how?"

"I'm guessing another picture got posted. You'd already had a warning; this time was game over."

"Game over . . . ," I echo, remembering the last time I heard those words.

"Did you see who posted the first one?"

"No. Someone who got our log-in details at Young Enterprise Week, I guess. Maybe it wasn't such a good idea sharing them, after all."

"So they must know us. Or at least be at St. Joe's. You don't think it was Frankie, do you?"

"What? No! She wouldn't do that. Hang on, Lowri, I'm just googling. . . . Account deletion, blah blah blah . . ."

Then:

"AHA! We can appeal!"

"Yay!"

"Right, I'd better get to work. Wish me luck."

"Good luck!"

OVERNIGHT THERE is no response to my appeal. I spend Saturday morning primping ahead of Rupert's arrival, and then . . .

Knock, knock, knock.

Cue: me, galloping downstairs, leaping for the door.

Too late.

"Oh, hello! Nice to see you again."

Step away, Mother! I do not need your gigantic nose sniffing around this new, slightly terrifying situation!

Rupert shakes my mom's hand but thankfully does not stoop for a cheek-kiss, or stare in an uninterrupted fashion at her almighty yeti shins like some boys would.

But wait! Why is the smell of cut grass lingering in the air? Afternoon light streams boldly through the still-open front door.

"Hi," comes a confident voice from somewhere behind Rupert. "I'm Cameron."

THIRTY-EIGHT

CAMERON HUGHES STEPS INTO MY HOUSE AND shuts the front door behind her.

"Oh!" says Mom, her eyebrows on the ceiling. "I wasn't expecting . . . Are you the one who . . . ?"

Is in the middle of transitioning? Is Rupert's best friend and might as well be Rupert's conjoined twin? Yes, yes and—regrettably—yes.

"Probably," says Cameron, locking eyes with me. I might be imagining it, but it feels as though she might reveal the top of a revolver beneath her oversized tee at any moment. It's like Cameron's sensed the beginnings of Rupert getting romantically involved with another girl and either she doesn't like it, or she's come to inspect the candidate. My eyes break her gaze.

"Well, congratulations," says Mom. "It's impressive to meet a young person who knows themselves so well."

"Drink, anyone?" I lead the pair speedily toward the kitchen and start opening random cupboard doors, as if exciting new beverages might suddenly present themselves. "We have milk-shake, cranberry juice and more herbal teas than you can find in Whole Foods." I take out the solidified milkshake powder and check for its use-by date.

"We're set." Cameron lifts an unsullied plastic bag onto my kitchen table. She produces a two-liter bottle of Diet Fanta, some toffee popcorn and a four-pack of jelly doughnuts.

My mouth waters and my heart sinks. I hurriedly shut the kitchen door.

"What's wrong?" asks Rupert, clocking my face.

"Take it all out of the packaging—quick, before she sees!" I grab three plates, three glasses and a large bowl from the cupboards. "You'll have to take the trash away with you."

Cameron's mouth twitches. "You're joking?"

"No! My mom's like superintendent of the Plastic Police. I'm amazed you even got that plastic bag past her."

"But it's recycled. . . ."

"I know." My mom has an impressive supply of canvas tote bags under the stairs that she regularly hands out to our guests—sometimes to random members of the public, too. Thank goodness Antonia had the good sense not to follow us into the kitchen. I couldn't bear the lecture in front of Rupert.

Cameron begins to pour out the popcorn into the bowl and place the doughnuts onto plates.

"I hope you don't mind Cam coming," says Rupert, pouring Fanta. "She was at a loose end and, well, as we're all friends here, I thought it'd be okay."

"Of course!" I coax a grin onto my face. "Absolutely. Let's go upstairs, yeah?"

"It's a sunny day," says Rupert. "Maybe we should go outside." But when I glance out the window and see my mom's reusable panty liners waving from the clothesline, I try to block the view with my torso.

"Nah. No Wi-Fi outside," I argue.

They follow me to my room, loaded with the drinks and snacks. Thank goodness I decided against lighting that row of tealights!

Cameron immediately springs onto the middle of my bed while Rupert takes the desk chair. I opt for the end of my bed and reach for the remote.

"How's the campaign going now that detention's over?" asks Rupert while we wait for Netflix to wake up.

"Not great, to be honest. We lost that interview and now our social media's been shut down."

"What?!"

"Someone posted some inappropriate stuff and got us kicked off."

"You're kidding?" says Cameron, mouth full of doughnut. If she gets even one speck of sugar on my duvet, I will push her off the freaking bed. I mean, I eat on there all the time. But other people dropping crumbs near my pillow? Different story.

"No," I reply. "I'm trying to appeal it."

"Jeez."

"Yeah, so between that and The Chubb shutting us down at school, things aren't great. We've got our mission statement and a few ideas, but that's it." I take a swig of Fanta to help wash down the sense of failure.

"I forgot to ask," says Rupert. "Did you manage to find out whether it was Frankie I saw in school the other day?"

I shake my head, swallowing too fast. I think I need lessons on how to drink fluids in the presence of boys. I gulp hard while the bubbles fizz in my nose. "I went to The Zone to see her, but we didn't get to talk for long. She won't even reply to my messages."

"But you are still going to keep going with the club, aren't you?" says Cameron. "You have to!"

"I don't know. Sometimes I wonder if there's any point. I mean, what have we actually achieved?"

"Loads!" Cameron says vehemently. "Every girl who's ever seen one of your pictures, everyone who's posted on the club feed, everyone who's stuck a mustache to their face—you've made them all stop and think."

"She's right," says Rupert. "And not just girls either. You've made guys think too. It's not just girls who have body-hair issues."

"Really?"

"Being a teenage boy isn't a piece of cake either. You've got to have the right amount of chest hair, leg hair, arm hair. Too much and we're Neanderthals; not enough and we're girls. You know what my nickname is, right?"

My mouth twitches up at one side.

"You know how I got it? PE changing rooms. Kenny noticed my, er . . ."

"Happy Trail," Cameron finishes.

Rupert glowers at her.

"What's a . . . ?" I begin.

Cameron points to the zip of her jeans and waggles her finger. "It's that line of hair between your belly button and Bush Country."

"Oh, that! Girls get that too."

"Well, anyway," says Rupert, "I had the faintest one in sixth grade and Kenny nearly yanked my boxers down to show everyone. Then I became Rupert the Bear, and the name stuck."

"And now you have the body of a thirty-year-old man and it suits you even more!" Cameron teases, finishing her doughnut.

Rupert sends her a mock glare, and I'm wondering exactly how much of his body Cameron has seen.

"I keep trying to get him to buy yellow pants," Cameron says to me.

Rupert flashes his middle finger at her while I picture them both in an H&M changing room, wrestling with a pair of mustard chinos.

"What about you?" I ask Cameron, giving Rupert a break. "You must have *all kinds* of body-hair issues. . . ."

"You mean because I'm trans?" she asks bluntly.

"Well, yes."

"Luckily the hormone blockers kicked in before I got too hairy. Also, I wasn't that hairy anyway."

"He really wasn't—" says Rupert, before gasping at his mistake.

Cam's eyes roll. "I'll forgive you—this once. It's not like

Evia doesn't know my backstory. But yes, Evia, I do shave my legs. And probably all the other stuff that you do."

All the other stuff? I think Cameron seriously underestimates my hair-removal routine.

Cameron continues. "I want people to see me as female, so I do everything that society expects a female to do."

"Don't you think that's wrong, though?" I challenge. "Don't you think you should be accepted as female without having to do all of that?"

"I *want* to do it. I want to feel normal."

Normal. My favorite word.

In the next two hours, I learn what the IA+ stand for in LGBTQIA+, as well as garnering a whole host of new words having to do with gender affirmation surgery, which Cam has decided to pursue as soon as she's old enough.

Rupert kicks back and, after leafing through my library book on Hollywood icons, starts playing *FIFA* on his phone. I can only presume that vagina construction is not his preferred topic of conversation.

Meanwhile, Netflix gives up on us and regresses to profile selection, then oblivion.

And so it is that Cameron Hughes—hijacker of nondates—wins me over. She clearly came here to suss me out in an act of protection for her bestie, and for that I cannot blame her. If I were Rupert's BFF, I'd want to protect him too.

On their way downstairs, Cam talks over her shoulder to me. "I did have one idea. For keeping the campaign going."

"Go on. . . ." We hover at the front door.

"You know that giant billboard outside the school gates?

At the moment it's advertising that laser hair removal place in town."

"Yes," I say.

"Hijack it," Cam says simply.

"Hijack it?"

"Hijack the billboard. Graffiti it, add your own slogan, whatever. It's right outside school, so is bound to get everyone's attention. But it's not on school property, so The Chubb can't punish you."

"But it's MASSIVE!"

"Yep!"

"How would we even . . . ?"

"It was just a thought," finishes Cam, reaching for the door.

"No, no!" I reply, wanting to show appreciation. "It's a great idea! It might just take some planning. I was thinking about organizing weekly meetings anyway. It will give us time to plan our next moves. What d'you think? Are you both in?"

"Definitely!" says Cam.

"Sure," says Rupert.

"Great. I'll see if I can plan something for next week. Keep an eye on the HGC group chat."

Just then, Mom bursts from the living room with something in her hand. She extends it in Cameron's direction.

"Noticed your plastic bag earlier," she says. "Take this."

It's a canvas tote.

"Er—thanks," says Cameron, and Rupert shoots me a knowing smile.

After they've left, I follow Mom to the sofa.

"Well, that was my good deed for the day," she says, commending herself for the tote.

"Mmm-hmm," I reply, distracted. Because I already have my phone in my hands and I'm busy texting Jemima Drake. If I'm going to organize a meeting for sixty-plus people and hijack a *mahoosive* billboard, I'm going to need her help.

THIRTY-NINE

ON MONDAY, IT'S POURING, SO MOM OFFERS ME A
ride to school. The journey is delicious: the heater at my feet,
the cozy velour seat, the chipper voice of the local radio pun-
dit. We pass sixth graders with umbrellas and sophomores
with rattail bangs, moms with covered strollers, an old man
with a bedraggled Westie. I am super smug.

There's a roundabout at the end of the road leading to
school, and just off the roundabout is the gigantic billboard
that Cam was talking about. I glare at it through the rain
as we drive past, cogs turning in my head. It's currently displaying an outstretched pair of women's legs—golden and airbrushed to perfection—with the tagline *Get perfectly smooth
skin with laser hair removal.*

Mom follows my gaze. "It's been photoshopped," she re-
marks.

I give a small nod. "I know. I was thinking more about the

wording. Why skin can't be perfect unless it's smooth, as if any other kind of skin is *im*perfect."

Mom smiles in triumph but says nothing. She pulls into the school kiss-and-ride and I lean over for a quick peck. "Thanks, Mom."

She smiles warmly. "Have a great day, love."

"**SOMETHING ABOUT** you is different," I decide, squinting at Karima over lunch. I couldn't put my finger on it in homeroom and still can't now.

"Oh." Karima blushes. "My Aunt Nadia visited over the weekend. You know—the one who works at that Brow Bar in Brooklyn?"

"That's it! Your eyebrows! They look amazing."

"Not just my eyebrows—she basically threaded my entire face. I asked her not to; explained it was sort of against what we're trying to do with the HGC. But there was no stopping her! My mom practically pinned me to the chair."

"Did it hurt?" asks Lowri.

Karima's face withers. "Yeah, it did. And it took AGES! The worst bit was when my mom dug out the baby albums and she and Aunt Nadia sat there pointing and laughing at what a hairy baby I was! I mean, all the babies in our family are born with loads of dark hair, but apparently I was *ridiculously* hairy and my aunt's been dying to get her hands on me ever since."

Lowri sticks out her bottom lip. "Poor Kari."

Suddenly, someone shouts over the ruckus of the cafeteria. "Puss-ay!" calls the voice. "Puss-aaaaay!"

I look at the other two, who've clearly heard it.

"Ignore it," says Karima.

My snack bar turns to concrete in my mouth. I chew on a big lump and swallow hard.

Some boys saunter past, laughing.

"Nice bush, Birtwhistle!" says one boy—Raephe—over his shoulder. He's a friend of King Kenny, although this particular posse is Kenny-less. How many more bush jokes am I going to have to put up with? I try to bury the muff voice under thoughts of Wednesday. Wednesday is going to be our first-ever HGC meeting: a whole room full of allies and not a bush bonehead in earshot.

WEDNESDAY COMES around *slowly*. My phone is basically pinging nonstop in the run-up. About forty people turn up to the HGC meeting, which is pretty impressive, seeing as a lot of them are missing buses and having to find other ways home. Ms. Mazur agreed that we could use her classroom—the original detention overspill zone from last week. She coaches basketball on Wednesdays, so she's not likely to be here.

After about fifteen minutes, Mr. McGovern pokes his head around the door.

"Girls!" he hisses, failing to notice the boys in the room. "If this is going to be a regular thing, I'll need you to exercise more decorum. I have students in detention next door!"

"Sorry, sir," I reply.

"Sorry!" chorus the clubbers, some wearing 'staches, some not.

"We'll keep it down!" I loud-whisper.

Looking skeptical but amused, Donald pulls the door closed.

"We really should keep the noise down," I say, trying not to sound bossy. "We don't want to give Mrs. Chubb a reason to ban us after school too."

Several others concur. I'm standing in front of the smartboard, flanked by Karima and Lowri. Jemima sits directly in front of us, and Rupert and Cameron are in the second row. The walls shout hello at me in several languages, punctuated by brightly colored European flags.

"Right," I begin. "First thing on the agenda is: getting our message straight. Some of you already know that part of my inspiration for starting this club was my best friend, Frankie Smith. Frankie has polycystic ovary syndrome, which means she has more excess hair than most of us. She's out of school at the moment after some girls in our grade shaved her head in a really horrible way."

A few people gasp and whisper to each other, but I'm telling them because I want to set the rumors straight. If we're in this together, they need to know the facts.

"Anyway, Frankie recently pointed out to me that although you have to be brave to fight social expectations—or, in her case, walk around with facial hair—it's really tiring having to do that all the time, not to mention frustrating. Did anyone hear about that plus-sized model recently making a similar point?"

Only a couple of people nod, so I elaborate. "She was angry because people tell her she's brave all the time for posting bikini shots on her Instagram, when they wouldn't say the same thing to a slimmer person. She was just being herself. Well, if we're continuing with this campaign, I want to make sure everyone understands we're doing it because we want to empower girls to own their body hair—to not be ashamed of it. To normalize it. We're not feeling sorry for anyone or telling them what to do. We're simply creating a safe place to be yourself. Does that make sense?"

More nodding, and Karima smiles gently at me. Even though Frankie's not here, I feel a massive rush of relief. I hope she'll see that I'm listening . . . whenever she's ready to talk.

I exhale quickly and roll my shoulders back. "Great. Next up: social media. As you all know, we've lost access to our socials, following some inappropriate posts."

"Boooo!" comes the reprise.

"I know! Well, in case you haven't heard, I tried to appeal the ban. I got a reply on Sunday saying that, after the initial warning, another fifteen so-called pussy-pics were posted under our name."

"Fifteen?" says one incredulous member. "Fifteen people were willing to share pictures of themselves . . . down there?!"

"They could just have been screenshots from porn," says Rupert, immediately blushing. The thought of him watching sex videos makes my stomach churn.

"Can they track who posted them?" asks someone else.

"No," I reply. "The user had our log-in details, so it just looks like one of us did it."

"Probably Madison Cox," scoffs someone.

"Definitely a Norma . . ."

I interrupt their guessing. "Well, it wasn't me, in case any of you heard the rumors. If you hear anyone spreading lies like that, I'd appreciate you setting them straight." The rest of the school even *thinking* I'd post a picture like that . . . Urgh! It makes my whole body shudder. "Anyway, if we can't have an account in our club name, the next best thing we can do is post using our club hashtag. It's not anonymous—you'll have to use your own personal accounts—but if you're feeling strong enough, I think that's our best option at the moment."

Jemima chips in, "Just to be clear, that's #hairygirlsclub, right?"

I nod. "Yep! Use it as much as you can, wherever you can. The internet police can't ban a hashtag!"

Karima looks solemn. "They probably can, if it's inciting violence or mass murder . . ."

I roll my eyes. "They won't ban *our* hashtag."

"Let's get it trending!" adds Lowri, rubbing her hands together.

"Right," I say next, looking at Cam. "One club member had an excellent idea that I think we should definitely pursue, but we're all going to have to work together. Cam—do you want to explain?"

Cameron's cheeks go pink and I instantly feel bad for shining the spotlight on her.

"It's that billboard on the roundabout," Cam says quickly. "I thought we could . . . put it to good use."

I smile. "We *definitely* could. Everyone knows what's on there at the moment, right?"

"Giant legs?" one girl calls out.

"Yes! It's an ad for laser hair removal. And it insinuates that you can't have perfect skin unless it's completely hairless. I suggest that phase two of our Big Plan should be to design our own HGC billboard poster to replace it. But while we all think about what to put up there and how to do it, I'm thinking a phase one might be easier. How about we graffiti what's already there? You know, add some hairs on the legs and change the tagline . . ."

We brainstorm ideas on a giant flip chart courtesy of Karima's dad's shop, and decide on a few tiny amendments:

- **Current tagline:** *Get perfectly smooth skin with laser hair removal.*
- **New tagline:** *Have perfect skin with*out *laser hair removal.*

By tweaking the odd word here and there, we have a whole new message!

"So," I begin tentatively, "I'll need a ladder and a couple of volunteers to help with the, er, adjustments."

Karima immediately makes a face. "My parents would go *ballistic* if they found out I'd done anything like that."

"And mine," says Lowri.

Jemima's hand shoots up. "Mine wouldn't! I mean, I live

243

with my dad, but he won't care. He'd probably pat me on the back!"

Cam tentatively raises her hand. "I'll help," she says. "It was my idea, I guess. . . ."

A girl named Amelie politely speaks up. "One slight problem," she begins. "I think it's illegal for stores to sell spray paint to people under eighteen."

"I'm pretty sure we have spray paint in my garage," Jemima answers. "And if I get caught carrying it, I could say it's for a school project?"

Karima holds up her phone. "I've googled it and graffiti is a criminal offense. You can get an on-the-spot fine—or jail time if it's a lot of damage."

Hmm. Maybe this isn't such a good idea after all. I don't want to be seen to be organizing criminal activity or getting fellow clubbers in trouble with the police!

Jemima detects my reticence and jumps in fast. "It's not a *lot* of damage—it's only a few doodles. We'll just have to do it in the middle of the night and make sure we don't get caught."

"You're clearly not using the spray paint for a school project if it's in the middle of the night," argues Karima.

I hesitate. I'm not sure about this. . . . But then, if you think about it, what's more damaging: a poster telling girls their natural bodies are ugly, or a poster telling girls they are naturally beautiful? Is it really worth breaking the law to get this message out there?

Yes, I decide. It is.

I look at Cam and Jemima. "How's Saturday night for you?"

"I'm not sure I'll be able to get out in the middle of the night," says Cam. "Plus, it'll be dark. How about early Sunday morning instead? Like four a.m.?"

"Works for me," Jemima replies.

"All right," I agree. And before we know it, our first-ever HGC meeting is over and phase one of our Big Plan is agreed!

FORTY

BEFORE HEADING TO BED ON SATURDAY NIGHT, I warn Antonia that I'm going to be up early the next morning.

"I've joined Running Club," I announce. "I'm meeting up with a couple of the other girls for a run in the morning. But they like to get up at the crack of dawn."

"Wow," Mom replies, clearly impressed. "Are you sure you'll be safe?"

"Yep. We're meeting at the end of our road. We'll run the whole route together. I'll take my phone and we'll be totally fine."

Mom's eyebrows flutter. "All right," she says. "I can't believe my teenage daughter will actually be up before me, but if it's in the name of exercise . . ."

~~~

URGH. WHAT was I thinking?! My alarm goes off at 3:50 a.m. (No, you didn't read that incorrectly, my friends, I said THREE-FIFTY IN THE A.M.!)

I feel sick. I have NEVER been up this early before!

I pad down the stairs with shaking legs and a stomach full of butterflies. I can't tell whether I feel nauseous because I'm about to commit a crime, or because my body's in shock at being wrenched from sleep at this totally *unnatural* hour.

With sleep in my eyes and confusion in my brain, I slip on my sneakers, zip up my hoodie then—*click*—close the door as softly as I possibly can behind me.

HOLY BREASTICLES, IT IS COLD!!

Why the hell does it feel like winter?! It is June! Even the air smells cold, hitting my nostrils like a freshly shaken cocktail of pollen and cut grass, all served on ice.

I break into a jog—not to justify the lie I told Mom, but simply to WARM THE HELL UP! My entire body is shaking with a mixture of adrenaline and pure, finger-tingling cold.

At the end of the cul-de-sac, Cam and Jem are waiting for me like a comedy duo, each standing at one end of a long silver ladder. They've carried it all the way from Jemima's garage, along with the creative weaponry currently stashed in Jemima's backpack.

"Morning," I manage, teeth chattering.

"Jeez, Evia! Where's your coat?!" asks Cam.

"I didn't realize it would be this c-c-cold!"

"Wanna go back?"

I shake my head. It's not worth waking Mom and endangering our whole plan for a piece of outerwear. "Let's just go."

I jog along the pavement like a fanatical exerciser out for a run at four a.m., while the other two clatter along behind me with their ladder. The sky is violet-blue with a coral halo. It would be pretty—if it weren't for the fact that the coral halo is broadening every minute, like a ticking time bomb. In an hour's time, it will be completely light and people will start to materialize; not zombies like us, but real, awake human beings who start their Sundays at five a.m.

Finally we reach the roundabout and stand beneath the billboard, looking up.

It is ENORMOUS. More enormous than I had realized. Even with the ladder, we're going to have to do the graffiti at arm's length. The others seem to be thinking the same thing.

"I'm tallest, I'll go up," Jemima decides. "You two hold the ladder."

Cam and I clasp the ladder with numb hands, our ice-cold digits about as much use as frozen fish fingers. Meanwhile, Jemima inches upward, brandishing the can of black spray paint like a pro. She starts on the model's legs, making quick flicks as far as she can reach.

"Wow! This is going better than I expected!" she says.

Cam and I groan. She's jinxed us! As Jemima moves on to the text, we scan the streets nervously. The Jinx-o-meter is about to decide our punishment, for sure. Just as we're starting to relax, a car zooms toward us, flashing its headlights and honking its horn.

Jemima squeaks in alarm and drops the spray can.

Cam looks up.

THWACK!

The spray can smacks her in the face.

"YEEOOOOOOOOW!"

Cam lets go of the ladder to clutch her head. With an almighty wobble, the ladder and Jemima tip toward me.

"HANG ON!" I shriek, pushing back as hard as I can.

Above me, Jemima clings to the ladder like her life depends on it. Which, to be fair, it might. She looks like a frightened koala hugging a eucalyptus tree.

Must.

Save.

Koala!

A burst of determination surges through me and I manage to steady the ladder while behind me, Cam mutters something about brain damage. The boy racer speeds off with a screech of tires, no doubt laughing maniacally from behind his steering wheel.

"Owwww," Cameron groans. "My poor head . . . I think I'm concussed . . ."

"No time for that!" I say. "Pass Jemima the spray can and help me keep this ladder steady."

To my surprise, Cam does exactly as I say. Maybe the clunk really has affected her brain.

"Anyone get that number plate?" I ask.

"Yeah," Jemima says sarcastically between quick squirts of paint. "Because the police are going to be really interested in a complaint about boy racers from three kids vandalizing a billboard."

Fair point.

"What car?" Cam asks. "And where did the elephants go?"

"Right," I say to Jemima. "Let's speed this up. I think we might need to get Cam home to her sickbed."

Moments later, Jemima begins her descent. We stand back to admire her handiwork.

"Perfect," I say, nodding.

Jemima flicks her wrist toward her. "Four-fifteen. Not bad! Right, let's hotfoot it home, ladies!"

Suddenly, I notice the camera on the school gates. CCTV! Why did we not think of that?! I nod in the direction of the camera. "D'you think that's close enough to pick us up?"

The others follow my gaze, Cam squinting.

"Nah," says Jemima. "Come on, let's go!"

And so we turn back, Jemima helping me with the ladder, while Cameron straggles behind with her crimson lump. As we walk, we keep glancing over our shoulders and bursting into fits of giggles. The farther away we get, the more bizarre the billboard looks, the more alien the notion that *we* did it. When one of us stops giggling, another starts, the ladder shaking and rattling in our arms.

Walking into a warm house has never felt so good, (a) because it's warm, (b) because I am relieved at our mission being over, and (c) because it's warm. Did I mention that it's warm? I go back to bed, but not back to sleep. My heart is pumping so hard I may never sleep again.

FORTY-ONE

I SPEND THE REST OF SUNDAY AT HOME, REPLAYING our act of vandalism in my mind. I text Cam to make sure she's okay.

Cam: *Yeah, I'll live.*

Me: *What did you tell your mom?*

Cam: *That I was out early with Running Club and ran into a tree.*

Me: *And she bought it?!*

Cam: *Yep. Perils of running at sunrise, she said.*

Me: *And you've stopped seeing elephants?*

Cam: *I've stopped seeing elephants.*

Phew.

Part of me wants to go back to the scene of our crime to

gauge people's reactions. But another part is scared of getting caught. What if whoever honked that horn knew us? What if they recognized us and called the police?

Late afternoon, the doorbell rings. Eeek! It's going to be the police . . . they've been tipped off and watched the CCTV. They've got us!

I make my way shakily down the stairs, my palm sticking to the banister. A dark-blue shadow looms through the frosted glass.

They might have sniffer dogs!

And guns!

Taking a deep, wobbly breath, I reach for the dead bolt and open the door. There, on the doorstep, are four brightly colored shopping bags, unmanned. Why would the police leave groceries on the doorstep? Are there handcuffs under the hummus? Is the broccoli bugged?

"Can you take those bags in, love?" Mom calls from the street. "I'll bring the rest!"

My heart is just about beating normally when Mom joins me in the kitchen to unpack everything. She has the biggest smirk on her face.

"You'll never guess what's happened," she says, ferrying yogurt to the fridge.

"What?" I ask, rummaging for a banana.

"You know that billboard near your school?"

The color drains from my face.

Mom goes on. "It's been graffitied! Someone's put hairs on the woman's legs! It's brilliant, Evia—you should go see it."

My tongue is itching to take credit but I'm not sure Antonia will be entirely thrilled about her daughter's new venture as a supporting graffiti artist. I take a small bite of banana and try to sound nonchalant, adding a shrug for good measure. "I'll see it tomorrow morning, I guess."

And see it, I do.

The torso-less legs start calling to me the moment I glimpse them on my route to school. *Evia, Evia, Evi-ahhhh! Here we are! Come and admire your handiwork, Evi-ahhhh!* The model's voice is singsongy, her new legs fluttering gleefully as she wiggles her hairy toes in the air.

Rounding the corner onto the school grounds, I keep my eyes on the path ahead. My heart is racing. I still can't believe it was us and we were here, yesterday morning, with a giant ladder from Jemima's garage! What if we get found out? What if Mrs. Chubb makes the connection with the HGC and calls us in?

I had no need to worry.

Monday is awesome!

All day, I am greeted with grins in the hallway, high fives in the dining hall, whoop-whoops in class. Jemima, Cameron and I are like plucky heroes returning from battle—especially Cam with her purple shiner. One girl even offers to buy me a Sprite!

Meanwhile, from their corner of the cafeteria, the Normas watch quietly, Madison's face sizzling like a hot iron. It won't take her long to connect the dots. Why else would the Hairy Girls' Club be buzzing on a Monday morning? Who else could possibly be responsible for the biggest, hairiest legs in town?!

ON TUESDAY, the iron strikes.

"What on earth?" I can see it from down the hallway. One of the lockers—in about the same place as mine—has something on it. Something triangular and black.

"What IS that?" Karima wonders aloud.

We all stand there, peering at the frizzy triangle, trying to decide whether it's real. It's like someone has actually peeled the top layer of skin from their groin, pubes and all, and stuck it slap-bang in the middle of my locker door.

Lowri raises a finger to poke it and I slap it away, harder than I mean to.

"DON'T TOUCH IT!" I squawk.

She prods it anyway.

"It's not real," Lowri declares. "Look . . ." She slowly peels it off of my locker, turning it over for us to see the back. "It's a merkin."

"I thought they belonged in *The Little Mermaid*," says Karima.

"Not a mer-*king* . . . a mer-*kin*. Actresses wear them sometimes. Like, when they're playing a historical role and they don't have enough of a bush."

"Like fake pubes?" I offer.

"Exactly. A pubic toupee."

Karima's mouth shrivels toward her nose, dimpling her chin, while Lowri holds it out for me to touch. I take a closer look. It's scarily realistic—and generous! The "hair" is long and wispy, attached to a meshlike backing.

"How d'you attach it?" I wonder out loud, lifting a corner of the wig to inspect the netting.

"Why? Need a bigger bush?" Lowri asks, grinning.

I summon my best scowl.

"Some kind of glue, I guess . . . Hey! How do you like my new beard?" Lowri holds the merkin against her chin and swings it from side to side.

Karima and I laugh, grimacing.

"Lowri! You don't know where that's been!"

The bell rings.

"What are we gonna *do* with it?" asks Karima.

"Chuck it?"

"No way!" says Lowri, stuffing it into her bag. "We could have a *lot* of fun with this."

But despite Lowri's best efforts to make light of it, I'm being haunted by Madison's face in the cafeteria yesterday. Where would she even get hold of a merkin?! How many people have seen it on my locker? Urgh. Suddenly, I'm back in that hall thinking about growlers and birds' nests. It's like a whole flock of blackbirds is flapping toward my head. I know it's just my imagination, but part of me wants to pull my blazer up over my head and RUN.

ON WEDNESDAY, I am alone when I find a folded scrap of paper in my locker. I unfold it excitedly, in case it's from Rupert. I mean, I know I said I just wanted to be friends, but the thought of another love note from him gets my heart thumping fast.

I read it.

For the first time ever, I'm grateful my locker is next to the girls' bathrooms. I rush in, lock myself in a stall and read it again:

> *There was a young lady named Eva*
> *who ran a hot bath to receive her.*
> *She took off her clothes*
> *from her head to her toes*
> *and a voice at the keyhole yelled, "BEAVER!"*

At first, I give a little snort. Because it *is* funny. But it is also not funny because:

a) someone I don't know slid this into my locker

b) the same someone is imagining me naked, and

c) that someone is *not* Rupert.

"Like it?" calls a voice from above.

My body jumps inside its uniform.

Madison's face peers over the top of the stall. "Kenny found that little gem on the net and sent it straight to me. He's so eager to please! Poor little Ken-Ken . . . Anyway, we tried to make it work with Evia but your name is so goddamn weird that nothing rhymes with it."

She goes on. "I'm guessing you and your hairy chicks had something to do with that billboard out front? You think you're so clever, don't you? Well, you're not. All you've done is made a lot of people laugh—*at* you, not *with* you."

"I don't care," I retort. "As long as I'm making them think."

"Ha! No one wants your hairy freaks' club, Birtwhistle! You're a bunch of weirdos."

"Says the girl with her feet on a toilet seat."

She spits and it lands squarely on my cheek, the glob sliding down before I have a chance to wipe. My eyes fill. Even after wiping, my cheek still feels dirty.

"You get what you deserve, Birtwhistle. Oh, and did you know I caught your freaky friend Frankenstein going into The Zone the other week? She's so sly! And what *has* she done with her hair? She really should get that looked at. . . ." She laughs a sick laugh, then jumps down.

My inner rhino lifts its head and stares out through my eyes. Madison starts pounding her fist on my door so hard that the entire row of stalls rattles. My rhino stands stockstill, then lies down. I guess she doesn't feel like charging today.

"Come on! Come out!"

I hold the lock firmly shut with both hands, my head filling with the things Madison might do.

"You can't hide in there all day."

"Crawl underneath," suggests a voice.

"YOU crawl underneath," replies Madison. "I'm not getting down on that disgusting floor."

"I won't fit," says the other voice. "El? You will."

I picture Ellie's face. Once, in family and consumer sciences, she refused to even put her hands in a mixing bowl.

"Some friends you are," says Madison. "Hey! I've got an idea!" There's silence, then a collective giggle.

"Don't look at me!" says Ellie. "I'm not going anywhere near that thing."

"Fine, I'll do it," says Pixie.

In the gap between our stalls, the base of the sanitary bin disappears, replaced by a shadow. I glance with horror at the bin in my own stall. They wouldn't . . .

Madison chuckles in anticipation. "A special shower to remind our little feminist friend what being a girl is all about."

The top of next door's sanitary bin appears above my stall, like a blue, box-shaped beast. The beast has a big silver mouth, and it's about to spew.

Oh God, oh God!

I push my body against the far side of my stall and lock my arms over my face. Should I crouch? Should I run?

There's a rattling sound, again and again while they wait for the Blue Beast to barf. I keep my head covered, my ears ringing.

"It's not gonna work, Mads," says Pixie. "The little tippy thing blocks it."

"What are you talking about?"

"The slide that sends pads into the bin. When you tip it upside down, it closes."

Madison snorts. "Lucky this is stuck on it, then!"

A long white thing flutters into my stall, then lands, sticky-side-down at my feet. I try not to look at it.

The Blue Beast is restored to its resting place, then there's the rush of water at a sink, followed by the blaring roar of a hand dryer.

"Smell you later, Beaver!" Madison calls before the main door shuts, dimming their laughter.

I wait until after the bell before quietly opening my door. Then I step over the stained pad, silently apologizing to the poor cleaner who has to pick it up.

Gross.

Gross.

Gross.

I wash my hands for a long time.

It's no wonder Frankie was so petrified at The Zone last week. If she clocked Madison stalking her—if they had any kind of run-in at all—she'd be back to square one.

Frankie, I miss you so much right now.

FORTY-TWO

"ARE YOU SURE YOU'RE OKAY TO DO THIS?" ASKS
Lowri on the way to our HGC meeting. Luckily, I had art and
math with her this afternoon and was able to tell her everything.

I nod. "I have to. There's no point going through stuff like
that unless it's for a reason. This club—and Frankie—are my
reasons." I hold my head up and lead Lowri into Ms. Mazur's
classroom before assuming my position at the front.

We start by talking about phase one of the Big Plan, aka
the billboard. There is much excitement among the clubbers,
and congratulations are bandied around.

"I wonder when they'll take it down," says Karima eventually. "I mean, it's pretty embarrassing for the company who
owns that clinic."

"True," I reply. "But when they do, we can come back at
them with phase two! The CCTV didn't seem to pick us up,

so it should be safe. Maybe we could start brainstorming ideas for things we could put up there. Does anyone here have design software?"

A sophomore named Heidi raises her hand. "My mom's a graphic designer. She won't mind me borrowing her computer. Plus, I've got my last final on Friday, so after that, I'm free for, like, the whole summer!"

"Amazing!"

Karima chips in. "My dad can print stuff for us. I think you have to print big signs like that over several sheets, don't you?"

"I don't know, to be honest," I reply. "Would you be able to look into it for us, Karima? Maybe you and Heidi could work together?"

Karima nods. "Sure."

"Shotgun putting it up!" Jemima jumps in. "Sunday morning was so awesome. I got such a rush!"

I spot Cameron rolling her eyes at Rupert.

"We can decide who gets to put it up when it's ready," I say tentatively. "Maybe we should talk about content in the meantime? I thought looking at these might help." I pull out the posters from our Young Enterprise stand and pass them around. "These big razor brands have reigned supreme for over a hundred years, telling us what to do."

"Show them that ad from 2018," Karima loud-whispers to me.

"Oh yeah!" A fresh torrent of rage rushes through me as I remember. "So in 2018, Gillette revealed this new ad campaign featuring people with skin conditions. It was trying to say that all skin was beautiful and we should wear it with pride, et cetera. What it was *in fact* doing was exploiting people with skin conditions to say that no matter what kind of skin you've got, you need to shave it. And get this: it shows a woman (a) shaving her arms, and (b) shaving her abdomen, like it's totally normal. Like everyone should be doing it and if you're not, you should go straight to the bathroom and do it RIGHT NOW! It's like 1915 all over again, but with new parts of your body."

"So that we can make our razors nice and blunt and go out and buy *more* razors to shave even *bigger* expanses of skin!" Karima's eyes have more fire in them than I have ever seen before.

Lowri taps furiously on her phone to find the ad on YouTube, then flips her screen around. "Is this the one?"

"It's the one that begins with the line: *Remember these old Venus ads?*" I say it in a sickly-sweet voice.

Lowri passes her phone around for people to watch while others find the video on their own phones. Shocked gasps and shaking heads move around the room like a rolling wave.

"It's not just Gillette," I continue. "There are loads of these kinds of ads, all aimed at women, all shaming us into action."

"Also," adds Karima, "they photoshop out facial hair, and generally make models appear hairless and flawless and blemish-free."

"Yes!" I agree.

"I have an idea for a powerful image," begins Lowri. "How about we all form a circle with our bare arms, fists together in the center, and then get someone to take a picture from above?"

"A bit like a clock?" asks Karima.

"Yeah, sort of. It would show lots of different skin tones and levels of arm hair, all in a circle, in solidarity. And then we add some kind of slogan about how our bodies are beautiful and how we refuse to shave our arms. What d'you think?"

"Love it," I reply. "Let's try it!"

We gather together and each hold out a fisted arm, spacing ourselves out into a circle. Because there are so many of us, we have to make two separate circles, but each shows an assortment of arms at varying levels of bareness and hairiness. Rupert takes the photos from above, snapping several versions until we're happy with them.

"That would make an awesome poster," I admit.

"I think we should edit out the background," says Heidi. "I can do that. And if Karima can come up with the words . . . ?"

Karima nods fervently.

"Great."

And with that, our second meeting comes to a close.

LATER THAT evening, I get a text.

Rupert: *Great meeting today.*

Me: *It was, wasn't it?!*

Rupert: *You're really good at organizing people.*

Me: *Are you saying I'm bossy?!*

Rupert: *No. It was a compliment.*

Me: *In that case, thanks.*

Rupert: *And maybe a BIT bossy . . .*

Rupert: *You can boss me around any time.*

Maybe I will, Rupert. Maybe I will.

FORTY-THREE

DESPITE A FAB MEETING, THE THOUGHT OF GOING to my locker on Thursday—or anywhere near those bathrooms—paralyzes me. Karima insists on coming with me.

We hear them within about ten steps: Madison and a gaggle of Normas in front of the freshmen lockers, laughing. A nauseating dizziness floods my head as every sinew in my body fights to turn me around. That inner Mom voice bursts into my head. *No, Evia Skye! DO NOT run away from these Nasty Normas! Face them like a fierce, unshakable woman! Come on—step to it!*

My feet move as though they belong to someone else.

"Back for more?!" says Madison, grinning.

The inner Mom roars at her with almighty force.

On first glance, the locker doesn't look too bad. It's been decorated, but not with fake pubes. Tiny jewels adorn the mint-green door: sparkling pink and white sticky-backed sequins arranged in various shapes. No, not shapes, but letters forming three messages:

Kiss me

Enter

Pussy galore

My brain conjures a giant word, bedecked with tinsel and fairy lights: *VAJAZZLE!* Yes thank you, Brain, I had already worked out what those glittery words were—I don't need you to spell it out for me.

Karima folds her arms and glares at Madison, looking unusually assertive.

Madison glares back. "We're just gonna keep doing this until you quit it with your little club. What you did to that billboard was really immature."

"Oh!" My voice appears from nowhere. "Because sticking merkins and vajazzles on a locker door is *really* mature."

Madison merely snorts. "You think girls in this school are going to idolize you with your little freaks club? Girls want someone they can look up to, not someone who gets laughed at. Besides, why would they want *you* when they've got *me*?"

"I don't want to be an idol," I reply.

"And we're not going to quit," says a version of Karima I've never seen before. She turns to me, "Anyway, they'll run out of ideas soon. They're not that creative."

Madison arches an eyebrow. "Wanna bet?"

We stand there, staring at one another. Finally, deciding she's won, Madison leads the Normas away down the hall.

"Don't worry," says Karima, starting to pick at one of the jewels. "They'll come off really easily."

They don't. By the end of lunch hour, the quicks of our nails have been eaten into by dozens—no, hundreds—of tiny vicious gems.

We stand back and admire our handiwork.

"Much better," says Karima, adjusting the last gem on my locker's cute new border.

"Not bad." I nod.

"Best vajazzle recycling I have ever seen."

I gasp because she said *vajazzle*. Karima saying anything even vaguely vagina-related is unheard of.

"How many vajazzles have you actually seen, Karima?!"

"Er, these will be my first."

I take out the books I need and shut my locker.

"Hey, maybe we could start a new business in vajazzle recycling."

Then I smile, my shoulders starting to lower. "Vajazzle Salvage."

"Roll up, roll up! Get your used vajazzle jewels here!"

We're laughing and that sick feeling has gone, but for some reason, we end up walking to the humanities block in silence. I fantasize about bringing a suitcase into school and traveling with my entire locker contents everywhere I go, like a flight attendant.

No, I decide. If I can survive pubic toupees, beaver poetry and inside-your-underpants jewelry, I can survive anything. Besides, like Karima said, what more can Madison possibly throw at me?

IT'S ACTUALLY a massive relief not to have the Normal Normas pursuing us online anymore. I was starting to dread picking up my phone—to the point where a headache would start descending just at the thought of doing it. But now that's gone.

Then, over the weekend, someone starts a new group on my chat app and adds me to it. The group has only three members.

Thought you could hide? says Madison. *Thought we wouldn't find you?*

I don't reply. She'll see I've read the message, though.

We had so much fun decorating your locker the other day. How about we come and redecorate your bedroom next? Or your front door?

Ooh yeah, adds King Kenny. *Good idea, Mads. How about we paint a massive black mustache on her door?!*

My thumbs are beginning to itch, but I say nothing.

Madison: *Come on Evia! We know you can see us!*

Kenny: *Yeah! Come out to play!*

Madison: *I'm not sure she's gonna bite, Ken.*

Kenny: *Oh she will. She won't be able to resist when I own up to the pussy pics.*

He's right.

Me: *What?*

Kenny: *My muffs!*

Me: *It was you???*

Kenny's memoji slow-claps at me while Madison's memoji cries with laughter. I muster the self-control to screenshot our chat as evidence.

Kenny: *Well, it wasn't MY muff. I snuck into your mom's bedroom one night . . .*

My boxing-gloved fist reaches through the phone screen to punch him. Hard. On the nose.

What, no reply Birdy? Madison taunts.

God, I hate you, Madison Cox. I hate that you think you're so clever. I hate how much boys like Kenny worship you and will do anything for you in the hope that they'll get a kiss. Most of all, I hate how you control everyone around you like you're a puppet master—or some kind of god. Well, YOU CAN'T CONTROL ME!!!

I stab Off and slam my phone face down on my duvet. Then I smother it with a pillow and give it a satisfying pummel with my fists. Afterward, I fall back against the cool wall, close my eyes and take long, deep breaths. I force the breath out from my throat like a fire-breathing dragon, just how Mom taught me.

Finally, when I feel ready, I message the others and tell them about Kenny.

FORTY-FOUR

ON MONDAY, I STEP OUTSIDE TO FIND BIRDS CHIRP-
ing and clouds skimming the sky. Somewhere beneath my
phone screen, I'm aware of my feet striking the pavement. I
stare at my last messages to Frankie, the final two unanswered.
Once, we had a chat streak going for 489 days. She's never *not*
replied to me before.

I draft a message asking how she is. Before I get a chance
to send it, some new posters near the school gates catch my
eye. At first, I think they're for an upcoming band face-off.
The upperclassmen hold something called Rock Your Face
Off each term, where they compete to be voted the school's
best band. I pocket my phone and stop to take a closer look.

They're not band posters. They're pictures of me.

Someone has pulled that photo from the website interview,
blown it up and doctored my mustache to make it look like
Hitler's. There's a border made up of red and black swastikas
and, across the top, one word:

FEMINAZI.

I tug the first poster from its tack and reduce it to a lumpy sphere in my fist. Then the second, then the third.

Toward the school parking lot, I notice a design change. From a distance, I can't quite see . . .

Oh my God, oh my God, oh my God!

In case you don't know what Downward Dog is, I'll tell you: it's a yoga pose where your hands and feet are on the ground and your bum is in the air so you're making an upside-down V shape. The graffiti artist has ripped a picture of Mom doing Downward Dog from her yoga website, with her ass facing the camera and, putting it politely, looking absolutely MASSIVE. Then they've scribbled a liberal covering of spikes, not just on her legs, but spiraling from between her butt cheeks.

HAIRY DOG reads the slogan. *HAIRY DOG.*

My ears fill with a loud ringing and the parking lot floods. I try not to blink. I will not cry.

The posters gather in my cold hands, growing into a shaky wad. How many people have seen them? How many have pointed, mocked, laughed? They can't have been up long, or Mrs. Chubb would know about them. I could take them to her, but what would she say? *Well, you can't say I didn't warn you, Evia. Didn't I say that other people might not be as open-minded?*

I break into a half-jog, quickly sketching a map of the school grounds in my head. I won't stop until I've crisscrossed this entire place.

~~~

HALFWAY THROUGH second period, I round a corner too fast and collide with a bulging shoulder bag. It's like bumping into an old friend and simultaneously being put on the stand: Ms. Wallace.

"Evia! You weren't in homeroom. I marked you as absent."

Her voice is gentle. Her eyes are too kind.

The first sob erupts violently, like bagpipes at a memorial.

"What's the matter?" Ms. Wallace ushers me to the nearby Careers Office, where its only occupant—our careers advisor, Mr. Johns—promptly abandons a clunking photocopier.

Ms. Wallace spies a box of tissues on a shelf and passes it to me. Its contents are thin and scratchy.

"Take your time," she says.

I empty my nose into three layers of tissue and still manage to blow a crater in them. Meanwhile, the photocopier sounds like it's murdering a robot.

Eventually, I pull the posters from my bag and silently slide them toward her. I can't even . . .

Ms. Wallace frowns hard. She's been my teacher since middle school. Despite me spurning geography, she probably knows me better than any other teacher in the school.

"You skipped homeroom to pull these down?"

I nod.

"And your first class?"

I nod again, feeling embarrassed.

"Don't worry. I'm taking these to Mrs. Chubb. We need to find whoever's responsible."

"No! Please! I know who put them up. Well, I can guess. . . ."

And anyway, Mrs. Chubb won't want to hear any more about the HGC."

"HGC?"

"Hairy Girls' Club."

"Oh yes. It's not that she won't want to hear about it. She just didn't want finals season being disrupted, that's all. You know how important it is for the school to get good results. But the Nazi comparison is out of line. And this—" She shuffles the sheets to isolate the Hairy Dog poster. She can't even say it.

The lump swells in my throat. More tears follow. I tell her about the trolls, the pussy pic, the locker stuff, the constant laughing and name-calling—everything.

"Oh Evia . . . Have you told your mom?"

"She knows about the trolling."

"But not the rest? Look, let me call your mom and speak to her. Maybe it's best if you go home for the rest of today."

"Please don't tell her about the posters! Or the locker stuff!"

"Don't you think she'd want to know?"

"No! She goes so over the top when it's anything to do with me. Please."

"All right," Ms. Wallace says eventually. "But I'll call to let her know that you're on your way home, at least. You walk to school, don't you?"

I nod.

"All right, then." I can have as long as I need, she says. She will personally scour the rest of the school grounds for posters. She will handle the perpetrator herself.

Halfway home, I get a text.

Karima: *I saw you out of the window during homeroom but you didn't come in. And then you weren't in English either. Is everything OK? x*

Me: *Will explain later. Going home for rest of day. x*

Karima: *Hope you're OK. xxx*

IT TURNS out Mom was in the middle of teaching a class when Ms. Wallace called, so she left a message to say I'd be going home. The first thing I do when I get home is run a bath so hot that the water makes my feet squeal. I ignore them, slide in, then commence my ritual of scooping up bubbles to cover my top half. I am not going to shave anything in the bath today—not in the name of feminism but in the name of Not Caring Anymore.

My phone vibrates against the gray chenille pompoms of the bath mat. I try to ignore it, but end up leaning over to read the name before the home screen turns black.

Frankie.

Frankie!

Relief breaks onto my face. Water sloshes in waves up and down the bath. I reach for a towel and dry my right hand adequately enough to grab my phone.

I've decided I need to move schools. I'll be starting at Mayfield in September: new year, new start. I'm so sorry, Evia. It hasn't been an easy decision so please don't make me feel bad. xxx

My smile dissolves as if it were never there, like footprints in mud, or the warmth of a hand pulled away.

I let the phone fall back onto the bath mat, then take a deep breath and sink down, down, down until my shoulder blades jut against the pit of the bath, the water dissolving my edges. I lie there until I cannot tell what is body and what is water.

FORTY-FIVE

I DON'T WANT TO TELL MOM ABOUT THE POSTERS,
so I have no choice but to go to school on Tuesday. Ms. Wallace looks pleased to see me in homeroom.

"Everything okay?" Karima asks, her dark eyes drilling through my forehead until my skull feels like it will shatter.

"I'm fine," I say quietly.

"Was it the posters?" Lowri's tone is unusually soothing. "We didn't see them, but . . ."

She doesn't need to finish. By lunchtime yesterday, everyone will have been talking about them, regardless of the fact they'd been taken down.

"Ms. W gave us all a lecture," adds Karima. "She wanted to know who'd put them up."

"Three guesses," I mutter, eyebrows raised.

"I'm sure we'll find out soon enough," says Lowri.

And she's right. By the end of the day, we hear that the sequence of events went something like this:

1. Kenny finally asked Madison out.
2. Madison laughed in Kenny's face.
3. Madison got called into The Chubb's office and tried to blame Kenny for the posters.
4. Kenny got called into The Chubb's office and confirmed the posters were Madison's work.

YES! At last, the truth comes out! For once, I feel almost happy about something that's issued from Kenny Fisher's mouth.

IT'S LAST period on Tuesday and one of those rare lessons where we're all together: study skills.

"Anyway," Lowri divulges, "apparently when Madison's boyfriend found out—"

"Ryan," Karima butts in.

"Yes, so when *Ryan* heard that Kenny asked Madison out, he went absolutely nuts! Bottom line is, Kenny snitched on Mad-Mads for the posters and, after that, she confessed. They called her parents in for a massive talk and she's on some kind of final warning or she's out. For good! Can you imagine?!" Lowri's mouth falls open for emphasis.

"That's not all," adds Karima. "Madison's supposed to be writing a formal apology to you and your mom."

My heart drains instantly. What if that letter lands on our doormat and Mom gets to it first? I don't want her finding out about those posters. They were horrible, too horrible.

For the rest of study skills, my head feels like mud, my

brain churning the thoughts over and over until I can't think straight. I keep picturing Madison writing that letter.

And Frankie on her first day at Mayfield, dressed in Mayfield blue.

FOR THE whole of Wednesday, I barely speak.

"Is everything okay?" asks Lowri in art. "You're really quiet."

The kindness in her voice immediately makes me want to cry, but I nod and try to smile. "Do you think people will mind if I skip the HGC meeting later? I'm not really feeling up to it."

"Are you sure? It's only the third one. You could take a backseat and let me and Karima lead, if you want?"

I consider her offer for a moment. "No," I decide. "I just want to go home, if that's okay."

Lowri narrows her eyes at me. "If you're sure . . . We can fill you in later?"

"Thanks," I manage, looking down at my charcoal drawing. I stretch my eyes as wide as they'll go to keep the tears at bay.

FOUR HOURS later, I get a text.

Karima: *How are you feeling, Evs?*

Me: *Alright, I think. How was the meeting?*

Lowri: *Interesting. Jemima's been out at night graffitiing half the town!*

Me: *What?!*

Karima: *She's been sabotaging beauty ads all over town in the name of the HGC!*

Me: *Oh God . . .*

Lowri: *Exactly!*

Karima: *She's actually starting to take over a bit, Evs . . .*

Lowri: *Yeah, we're not sure we trust her. She acts like a dictator. Like today, she was trying to give everyone titles and roles. Without you there, she made herself honorary chairperson. I tried to fight her for it, but she's too good at arguing. Instead, I ended up as vice chair and Karima got social media secretary. I mean . . . THE NERVE!!!*

It's weird, but I don't feel anything about Jemima. It's like I don't have the headspace to think about anything except my mom and Frankie. Every time I try to concentrate on something else, Frankie pops into my head in that ultramarine school blazer. She waves at me in a detached, empty sort of way, then turns and walks away.

FORTY-SIX

TUESDAY IS MOM'S BIRTHDAY. AFTER UNWRAPPING
her chocolates and scented candle, and praising me for using
paper tape, she looks at me straight.

"Is everything okay, hon? You've been so quiet lately."

I smile and nod. "I'm fine, Mom." Part of me wants to tell
her about Frankie, but I feel like I've been burdening Mom so
much lately, and I don't want to spoil her birthday.

"Really? Because if it's those trolls again . . ."

"It's not. I'm fine, honestly." I plant a kiss on her cheek.
"Happy birthday, Mom."

She lets me go off to school, no further questions.

BY THE time Wednesday comes around, all I want to do is
skip the HGC meeting again. But missing two in a row would
not look good for me. Plus, Kar-Low have an after-school
music rehearsal to practice for the summer concert, so if the

three of us were absent, it's a surefire bet who would run the show.

THERE ARE only eleven of us at the meeting. "Probably because you weren't here last week," Jemima points out helpfully. "And now Karina and Lowri aren't here."

"Kari-*ma*."

Kar-Low were right: Jemima can be pretty irritating at times. Now I'm back, I'm allowed to resume as chairperson (yes, thank you, Jemima, so magnanimous of you seeing as I SET UP THE CLUB IN THE FIRST PLACE), but because Kar-Low aren't here, she immediately usurps Lowri's role as vice. Plus, she tries to talk over me—a lot—and she comes up with pretty cray-cray plans, too. Despite having defaced ads all over town, she keeps asking for more and more things to graffiti, like some kind of feminist Banksy. I swear she actually *wants* to get caught.

"What exactly have you been doing to these ads, Jemima?" I challenge.

Jemima looks taken aback. "Just replicating what we did to the one outside school. You know, adding spots and bits of facial hair here and there to make the models look . . . less perfect."

"We need to be careful," I comment. "We don't want people to think we're being unkind. Our message isn't supposed to be that the models look *bad* with body hair, just more natural. I think you need to add some words too."

"Like what?" asks Jemima.

"There's this cool skincare brand," says a small eighth grade girl named Bea. "They use models with actual body hair rather than using smooth, pre-waxed ones like you see in most ads. I can't remember their hashtag, but it's something about championing body hair. Maybe you could direct people toward that?"

"Okay, cool."

"Or," I add, "maybe just some messages about body positivity. Body hair is only one issue when it comes to the beauty industry and fighting the patriarchy. There are loads of other points we could make about how we're all expected to look a certain way—"

"—and spend loads of money in the process," finishes Rupert.

"Exactly!" I assert.

Bea looks eager to speak again. "Maybe we shouldn't be using so much spray paint, either, Jemima. It's really hard to clean off."

Jemima glares at Bea, but Bea isn't perturbed. "My little brother has these special crayons for drawing on glass and plastic. They're completely washable so they don't cause any long-term damage. And if the billboards are inside bus stops and stuff, the crayon won't get washed off when it rains."

"Perfect," I say, smiling. I like this Bea girl. "Now, with Karima and Heidi both absent, I'm afraid we can't recap on progress for the Big Plan today. So how about we come up with ideas for other things we can do as a club instead?"

Those ideas turn out to be:

- Targeting razor and beauty brands on their own
  social media feeds

- Reproducing prints of the original hair-removal ads, adding our own slogans then displaying them wherever we can get away with it
- Making posters with messages about female body hair and body positivity and putting them up around town
- Continuing to use #hairygirlsclub wherever possible.

After the meeting, Rupert escorts me out like my own personal bodyguard. "Jemima likes the sound of her own voice, doesn't she?" he says.

I turn to check Jemima is out of earshot. "That's not all. Last night I was browsing her recent posts and saw that she's now trying to take credit for the entire campaign, like it was her idea in the first place. She's posting pictures from our meetings and creating graphics of our slogans like they're her own words."

"No way!"

For some reason, I find myself staring at the hollow of Rupert's neck, where the skin is smooth and white.

I swallow. "Where's Cam today?"

"She's doing something with the Lambda Alliance. Want me to walk you home?"

I find myself shrugging. "Okay." Even though I know it's in the completely wrong direction for him.

Suddenly, I feel something warm DOWN BELOW. What the hell?

Oh no!

My period!!

With all the drama lately, I'd totally forgotten about it and it's late! OH GOD! What if it starts running down my leg? What if the lateness makes it a MEGA PERIOD and it starts pouring out of me like an angry red river?! I feel sick.

"Uhh, can I take a rain check on that walk?"

"What?" Rupert looks worried. "Are you okay? You've gone really pale. . . ."

"I'm fine. I, er, just need to visit the, um, ladies room."

"Oh. Right. Do you want me to wait?"

NOOOOOO!!!

"No, it's fine. I might be a while."

Great. Now he thinks I'm about to puke or do the world's longest poo. Either way, not a winner!

"Okay," he says. "If you're sure. See you tomorrow, then?"

"Yep!" I walk backward, reaching out my arm for the bathroom door. Why is it so very far away? Realizing it is in fact half a hallway away, I turn and start jogging.

"Bye!" I shout into the air.

"Bye," comes his confused reply.

FORTY-SEVEN

ON SATURDAY MORNING, I'M ENJOYING A LOVELY leisurely shower when I hear the front door bang. We have this timer in the shower to help us save water (for the planet as well as the water bill, Mom argues), but with Mom out at yoga, I didn't use it. I hurriedly turn off the water and grab my towel.

"You're home early!" I shout through the open bathroom door.

"You're up late!" Mom calls back.

I dry off, get dressed and head down, gently squeezing at my curls with a microfiber towel. Mom's blocking the foot of the staircase, reading something. The mail must've been delivered while I was upstairs.

"Don't you usually go for brunch after your Saturday class?" I ask, two steps above her.

"Café's closed for a refurb," Mom replies, still staring straight ahead. The sheet in her hand is lilac, with a matching envelope by her side. "What posters is she talking about, Evia?" she asks, turning to look up at me.

Oh crap.

My face drops into my chest and my heart flops down to somewhere near my knees.

When did *that* arrive? I've been watching the mail slot for days! Madison must've literally dropped it through the door while I was showering. I take the envelope and check the front. *Mrs. and Miss Birtwhistle* read the neat, looping black letters. Great, I can't even accuse Mom of reading my mail! She pats the carpet next to her and shuffles toward the wall so we can sit side by side.

"Mrs. Birtwhistle, indeed." Antonia scowls. "Who *is* this Madison girl and what is she talking about?"

"I didn't want to . . ."

"Tell me?" Antonia raises her eyebrows at me.

"Can I read it?"

Mom hands me the lilac paper with its crisply folded lines.

Dear Evia and Mrs. Birtwhistle,

This is a formal apology for any hurt caused by my posters. They were insensitive and I shouldn't have made them.

To be honest, Evia, I never expected your club to take off. You guys were doing something so weird, and everyone thought you were so cool. I didn't get it. But even if I don't like it, I think I'm beginning to understand now why you're doing it.

Anyway, I know writing this was part of my punishment, but I really am sorry. My posters got too personal.

I hope you'll both accept my apology.

Yours sincerely,
Madison E. Cox

PS: Sorry about the locker stuff too. Ken and I are a bad influence on each other and sometimes we get a bit carried away.

Wow. She actually sounds genuine and not at all like the Madison Cox from the bathroom. Could it be that she puts it all on—a show for the Normas? Who's the real Madison? The one at the lockers or the one who wrote this letter?

"So?" Mom prompts. "Are you going to show me these posters or not?"

"I—I don't have them," I say quietly.

"Oh-kay," she says slowly. "But why were they insensitive?"

Something tightens in my throat, making it hard to swallow.

"They were pictures of you, Mom, and—and—" I can't look at her. She puts her arm around me and squeezes. The throat tightness explodes in a loud sob and once I start, I can't stop.

"It's okay! Evia! Whatever they were, it's okay!"

"But they were awful, Mom! Really awful. They drew hair . . ."

"It's all right. You don't have to tell me if you don't want to. I just wish you hadn't carried the burden of this on your own. Did this *Madison* girl get found out? At school? Was she punished?"

I nod. "Writing this letter was part of her punishment. I didn't want you to see it. . . ."

Antonia cocks her head at me and laughs. "You don't need to protect me, you big oaf! I'm a grown-up. I can deal with this sort of thing. What I can't deal with is my baby girl hiding stuff from me and suffering on her own!"

Suddenly, my phone pings in my pocket. There's message after message on the group chat.

We're back online!

Check the socials!

Nice one, Evia!

What? I haven't done anything! I tap on my app and wait. There it is! Our whole account—undeleted and wholly present. But *why* is it back? It makes no sense.

There's no sign of the incriminating images. Everything is exactly as it was before. So weird. Then I spot a new picture, added only today. It's the lower half of a girl's face. She's wearing a tiny, white-jeweled nose stud and a mustache. Not a fake mustache, but a real one, thin and dark. The hair isn't just on her upper lip, but along her jawline and around her chin: unapologetic centimeter-long stubble. The other thing she's wearing is a black bobbed wig.

The one I bought from the costume shop.

"Wait," says Mom, peering over my shoulder. "Is that . . ."

"Frankie?" I say, grinning. "Yes, I think it might be."

FORTY-EIGHT

RIGHT ON CUE, A MESSAGE POPS UP FROM FRANKIE:
Dear Mia & Maya, My best friend and I haven't talked much lately and I feel really bad about it. How do I tell her I'm sorry? xxx
It takes me about five seconds to tap out a reply:
Dear Mia & Maya, I've been really stupid too and have missed my BFF like crazy. Do you think she'll have me back? xxx
Yes! Frankie replies instantly.

Me: *Was it you who got our SM accounts reopened?*

Frankie: *Yes. I wrote to them and explained what the HGC was all about. I sent them some pictures of myself . . . Then I posted that photo. Hope you don't mind?*

Me: *Don't mind?! It's amazing! Thank you soooo much.*

Frankie: *They made me agree to change the log-in and password to avoid more troll pics. Can you re-add me to the group chat so I can send it around?*

Me: *Of course! THANK YOU!!*

Frankie: *Do you want to come over? It'd be so good to see you . . .*

ANTONIA INSISTS on driving me there.

"I know you haven't seen Frankie for a while," she says on the way over. "I really hope you two can patch things up."

Something pulls inside my chest. "I hope so too."

There's a pause.

"Evia, I've been thinking . . ."

I watch her while she stares straight ahead.

"About what you said about your father, not knowing where he is, whether he's dead or alive . . ."

"Mom, that was ages ago!"

"I know, but it's been playing on my mind. It's just . . . I . . . If you wanted to start looking for him, you can, you know. I'd help you." Her gaze flicks from the windshield to me, and back again.

I freeze, staring straight ahead. So *this* is why she offered to drive. Thank goodness we're in the car, so we don't have to look at one another.

"What are you thinking?" she asks, after a while.

"I don't know," I manage. "I . . . I hadn't really thought about it. Not seriously. I'm not sure how I feel. . . ."

She smiles gently. "That's fine, love. I'm just saying—if you want to, think about it. If you don't want to, that's fine too. Whatever you decide, though, I want you to know that you are enough for me. The two of us are enough."

Her words flow into me like warm milk soaking into a cookie. I let them lie there a bit longer, feeling like an oozy puddle of chocolate chips.

Before I know it, we're outside Frankie's. Mom pulls on the hand brake.

I unclip my seat belt and reach over for a car hug. "I think we're enough too," I whisper to her shoulder. "Love you, Mom."

It's only when I pull away and notice her full-to-the-brim eyes that I realize I haven't said that for a while. "I love you too, Evia," she says, her chin dimpling with a smile.

I blow air out through pursed lips and try to gather my chocolate chips. Then I put one hand on the door handle, feeling like I'm about to climb out of one emotional roller coaster and get straight onto another.

"Thanks for the ride, Mom."

"No worries, sweetie. Let me know if you want picking up."

And suddenly, I'm walking up the Smiths' path and taking deep breaths, willing those chocolate chips to solidify— fast. The combination of my little chat with Mom and the anticipation of seeing Frankie is making my heart wallop hard against my chest.

I don't even have to knock and Frankie's there at the door. She looks so different, my lungs sort of judder. Her hair is closely cropped now, all over her head, she's wearing thick eyeliner and she's got the beginnings of a dark beard.

Stepping into Frankie's house is like re-entering my second home. It smells of the Smiths' laundry detergent and lunchtime toast. We go up to her room and it's still the same even though, somehow, everything has changed. I smile at the faces on her wall like they're old friends: Ziggy Stardust, Maximo Park, My Chemical Romance.

"Suits you," I say, nodding to Frankie's face.

She strokes the beard a few times. "It's a hell of a lot easier than shaving every day."

"When did you stop?"

"Soon after I gave up school."

"What happened? You stopped coming to The Zone."

"I know, I'm sorry. The day before we spoke, Madison saw me going in there. She followed me . . . started thumping on the window. It was really freaking me out. I think I had a panic attack. After that, my anxiety got really bad, I couldn't sleep. . . . Ruth's been coming here ever since."

"Ruth?"

"My therapist."

"Oh." A small pang of jealousy pinches my heart at the thought of Frankie confiding in someone I've never met. "How's it going?"

"It's amazing, Evs! I feel so much more positive about everything. She's only coming once a week now."

"Have you been out?"

"Out of the house? Not since I started growing this." Frankie taps her chin. "I'm not sure I can. I just wanted to sort of . . . see what it looked like. And give my skin a break."

I waggle my toes in her direction. "I know it's not much, but . . ."

Frankie squints at them. "Oh yeah, Evs. *Really* hairy!"

"They look hairy to me."

She rolls her eyes but smiles. It's ridiculously good to see her. Suddenly, I can't stop talking. Everything pours out of me: the posters, the lockers, Rupert and Cam, Madison and Kar-Low, Jemima—

"Evia! Hi!" Louise leans around the door, bringing two lemonades. She comes in and hugs me. She calls Dom up, too. Followed by Jake, who instantly turns me into a giant lobster. We haven't locked eyes since the bowling alley. He winks at me on his way out. "Catch ya later, Evvy-Wevvy," he says, smiling.

My lobster face goes redder.

"What was that about?" Frankie asks once they've left.

"No idea," I lie. "New nickname, I guess." Then, quickly changing the subject, "How do they feel about the . . . ?" I spiral my chin with my forefinger.

"The beard? It's okay—you can say it! Jake's totally fine. Dad wants me to be happy. Mom's . . . not sure. She doesn't want me to get hurt again. AND she wants me to get married and give her grandchildren one day, not that she's said that, of course."

"You CAN get married and have children one day!"

"Yeah, but my chances are slimmer with this on my face."

"Not true. You just need to find the right person."

"Hmm . . . I'm not sure I want kids anyway. I want a career first."

"Cheers to that!"

We clink lemonade glasses.

294

"I'm glad your family doesn't hate me," I say, after a bit. "Because of the campaign, I mean."

"Not at all," Frankie replies. "When I showed them some of the trolling and how you were basically taking the flak for me with the HGC, they were all really impressed."

"So they're on board with the club?"

"Yep."

"What about you?"

"Oh, I'm on board. Totally. Sorry about what happened with Lucy. . . ."

"It's okay."

She pulls her phone out, taps it a few times, then hands it to me. "I got this the day before. It's part of the reason I canceled."

I stare at it.

It's a screenshot from a video, showing a close-up of Frankie's head with Madison's hand poised over it with the clippers.

Hey Frankenstein, says the message. *Remember this?! I've still got the original . . . Quit your BFF's club or I'll post the entire video to my feed where it'll stay FOR GOOD.*

I recoil, my jaw clenching. "Why didn't you tell me?" I ask, handing her phone back.

Frankie leans back and massages her neck with both hands, then sighs. "I didn't even show Mom. She would've marched straight into school. I just wanted it all to stop."

"You should've told me, though. I would've understood."

She shrugs. "It doesn't mean anything anymore. Things can only get better, right?"

I nod. "Does that mean you're coming back to school?"

She doesn't answer. Instead, she squeezes her mouth into a thin-lipped frown.

"Pleeeease . . ."

This time, she shakes her head. "I've been talking to Ruth about it and I'm not sure I can. I can't risk another panic attack. At least at Mayfield there's no Madison. I get a fresh start."

"Sophomore year isn't exactly an ideal time to move schools."

"Yeah, well. Life isn't ideal sometimes."

FORTY-NINE

ON WEDNESDAY MORNING, FRANKIE ASKS TO JOIN that day's HGC meeting over speakerphone. But in homeroom, Kar-Low are looking more than a bit sheepish.

"We're really sorry, Evs," says Karima, "but we can't make it . . . again."

"Yeah," adds Lowri. "The concert's next week and Mr. Harkness is putting pressure on us to attend all the rehearsals—you know, set a good example to the younger kids."

"It's not just orchestra, it's wind band and jazz band too."

"Jeez!" I reply. "How many different types of band are there?!"

"He said that if we want to take AP Music—"

"Which we do—"

"—we can't miss any rehearsals from now on."

"Ouch," I say. "What about the billboard, though? We haven't carried out phase two."

"I'm so sorry," Karima says heavily. "Heidi finished designing it ages ago, but my dad's been really stressed about work—the shop's not making enough money–and I've been putting off asking for his help to print it. I'll do it this weekend."

"Are you sure? I don't want to give him more work."

"He hasn't got *enough* work; that's the problem."

"Oh."

"It's okay, honest. With all these meetings I'm missing, it's the least I can do. I'd better not help put it up, though. I'd be in deep trouble if we got caught."

"Don't worry," I say. "I'm sure Jemima will offer."

Lowri raises her eyebrows. "Good luck keeping *her* under control."

"Thanks," I say, sighing. "I'll need it."

"HOW ABOUT a flash mob?!" shrieks Jemima, jumping in the moment we start discussing new campaign ideas. "In the mall! In the summer!" She looks like she might explode.

I nod a couple of times. "Could work."

"I'll get my dance group to choreograph something!"

Of course she has a dance group. She'll be showcasing us on a major talent show next.

"Maybe we should do some fundraising," says Frankie over speakerphone. "You know, so we can do bigger and better stuff. Buy some ad space in the local newspaper. Make ourselves look more official?"

"Great idea!" I reply, wishing Frankie could be here in person. "Following up from last week, has anyone had a chance to make any posters yet?"

A girl named Paige raises her hand. "I put some up in town over the weekend. I meant to share the pictures but I forgot." She pulls out her phone and starts scrolling through. "They said things like: *Men have body hair. So do women.* And *Shaving should be a choice, not an expectation.* And *Be Proud of Your Body.*"

"Brilliant!"

"Aliyah Dobson saw me putting one of them up. . . ."

"No way!"

"I honestly expected her to pull it down."

"She didn't?"

Paige shakes her head. "Turns out she was just waiting for someone—that Cole guy? He works in that big sports store on weekends."

"That's good. Aliyah's more interested in him than Madison and the Normas at the moment."

"An old lady stopped me, though," Paige goes on. "She said what we're doing might be something called fly-posting. Even though we're not trying to sell anything, if we don't have permission to put the posters up, we could get in trouble. We might have to stick to using bulletin boards."

Suddenly, the door bursts open and an eighth grader rushes in. I'm ninety percent sure her name is Sally.

"AMAZING news!" Ninety Percent Sally gushes, dropping her bag to the floor and whipping her phone from her pocket. "Guess who I spotted over the weekend going into the Laser Hair Removal Clinic?"

She holds up her screen for me to see. It's taken from across the street, but it's definitely . . .

"Madison Cox?!"

"Yep! Anyway, I went up for a closer look and read the plaque by the door. The clinic is owned by doctors Andrew Cox and Anne-Marie Cox! Madison's parents!" Ninety Percent Sally is basically squealing by this point.

"Wow," I reply, my face going cold. "That billboard poster was for her parents' clinic. We destroyed it. No wonder she hates us."

Ninety Percent Sally shrugs, shuffling her bottom onto the front-row table. "Oh yeah, I guess. But that's not the best part!"

"What d'you mean?"

"Well, at first we thought maybe Madison was just visiting her parents at work. But me and my friend were intrigued to see what the clinic was like inside, so we followed her in."

"You what?"

"We followed her from a safe distance. We went in and spoke to the receptionist, asked for a consultation—you know, doing some research for the HGC—and she told us to sit in the waiting area. It was very swanky. AND GUESS WHAT." She scrolls through her camera roll, then holds her phone up again. "There were pictures on the wall, before and after shots. The head shots only showed the lower part of the girl's face, but look. . . ."

I peer at the images on the screen. It definitely *looks* like Madison.

"AND the photos weren't just of Madison's legs, but her arms and her stomach too. . . ."

"They could be photoshopped," Jemima points out. "Someone might've airbrushed them to look like that."

"Yeah, but . . ." I'm a bit thrown, contemplating what this might mean about our nemesis. "Did Madison see you?!"

"No. But we saw her. She disappeared into one of the treatment rooms—for two hours!"

"You waited for TWO HOURS?!"

"Not in the clinic itself, no. After about thirty minutes we got bored and took some pamphlets. Then we went and sat in a café across the road and waited. Madison emerged two hours later."

Jemima's face lights up like a wily-eyed pumpkin. "You know what that means, people?"

"Je-mi-ma . . . ," I say slowly, as a warning.

"It means the leader of the opposition is a TOTAL AND UTTER LIAR!"

The response is deafening. Meanwhile, my mind flicks back to the PE changing room and Madison claiming she was naturally smooth, as if she was born that way, when in actual fact she was once as hairy as me.

"Everyone! Hey! PEOPLE, SHHH!" I clap my hands once, like a starting pistol. "I know this is pretty exciting, but we don't want McGovern on our backs."

"*Pretty* exciting?" replies Jemima. "This is HUGE! We could take down the Normal Normas, like, right now!"

That lilac envelope flutters into my mind's eye. "I don't know . . ."

"Evia! Are you serious?!" Jemima is loving this a bit too

much. "Have you forgotten about those posters and what she did to Frankie? We HAVE to share this!"

I stare at my phone, where Frankie lies silent, listening.

No, I haven't forgotten about the posters, or being trapped in a toilet stall, or the time Madison asked me to stroke her arms. *Some of us don't have to worry about hair removal,* she had said, when really, underneath it all, Madison had the same issues as the rest of us. Maybe she's under pressure from her boyfriend or parents. Maybe having a hairy daughter isn't good for business when you're a dermatologist specializing in hair removal.

"I think sharing it would be wrong."

"You're joking? After everything . . ."

"The Hairy Girls' Club isn't about shaming people. We set up this club to make people feel better about themselves, not worse."

A few people murmur in agreement.

"Frankie? What d'you think?"

"I agree," she says over speakerphone. "There's enough hatred in the world already."

"She's right," adds Rupert. "No one deserves to be outed like that, not even Madison Cox. This just shows she's got insecurities like the rest of us."

Jemima returns to her chair and slumps into it. "Well, it was a good bit of detective work, Sal."

One Hundred Percent Sally smiles wanly.

"Yes," I bolster. "Really good. But I think we need everyone in this room to promise they won't breathe a word of this to anyone."

"Not even other HGC members?" says Jemima.

Hmm . . . I *would* quite like the chance to regale Kar-Low with this little tale. "Okay. We can tell other HGC members. But it can't go any further. Agreed?"

Jemima sighs heavily. "A-greed," she chants in a low voice.

"Good. Now, what's next?"

FIFTY

"TALK TO YOU LATER," I SAY TO FRANKIE AT THE END of the meeting. I hang up and find Rupert milling around outside the classroom.

"Want to try walking me home again?" I ask. "Maybe we'll make it out of the school building this time."

He grins at me. "We can try."

We're out of the school gates before I even notice.

"You did the right thing," he says. "About Madison. I mean, part of me wants to get that picture and send it around the whole school."

"Me too."

"But she must be pretty messed up. I mean, she's leading a group called the Normal Normas, but she's having to work pretty hard to be 'normal.'" He makes air quotes with his fingers.

"Exactly. She's doing what she thinks society wants her to

do. I mean, assuming Sally is right, who wants to get laser hair treatment on their whole body at fifteen?"

"I would, to be honest!"

"Ha! But you're a guy—you can be hairy and get away with it!"

Rupert's face turns all serious. "Yeah, I'm all right at the moment. But if I'm like this at fifteen, imagine what I'm gonna be like at twenty. Or thirty."

Don't worry, Rupert, I'm imagining. . . .

The smell of sunbaked wood chip hits me as we near my old playground. It's full of tag and scabbed knees.

"I like that I can talk to you about this stuff," Rupert says suddenly. "I've never really talked to a girl like this before."

"Not even your sister?"

"She doesn't count!"

"Cam?"

"I guess. But I see her as more of a sister too."

My chest floods with a mixture of relief and excitement. "I like talking to you too." I smile at him, heart throbbing.

We pass the bus stop with the ad for "perfect" nude foundation and admire Jemima's handiwork. She's doodled a couple of zits on the model's face and added a new tagline: *Nobody's perfect.*

Suddenly we're at my street and my house has leaped across the cul-de-sac to land in front of us, like something out of *The Wizard of Oz.*

"Well, we're here, so . . ."

Why can't I stop looking at him? My Dorothy shoes are stuck in the pavement. I can't move a muscle.

"Oh. Oh yeah. There's your house."

I manage to pull my feet from the pavement and take a small step toward him. "Yes, my house."

He moves toward me so that our toes are nearly touching. "Can I . . . ?" he asks.

I answer by standing on tiptoes and pressing my lips really, really softly against his. He kisses me back, putting one hand on the small of my back. But it's kind of awkward because I'm carrying my giant art folder and all I can think is I AM HAVING MY FIRST KISS RUPERT CLIFTON IS KISS- ING ME AND I REALLY WANT TO PUT THIS THING DOWN AND OH GOD WHERE CAN I PUT IT I REALLY DON'T WANT HIM TO STOP!

And then we do stop and I hope we've just paused because I still haven't put my wretched art folder down and—oh. We've definitely stopped.

He smiles.

THAT was totally awesome. I think I might actually be bouncing on the balls of my feet, i.e., not playing it cool in the slightest.

"See you tomorrow," Rupert says—coolly.

"Definitely," I reply, uncoolly.

"Bye, then, Evia Birtwhistle."

"Goodbye, Rupert Clifton!"

As he moves away, a small figure on the pavement oppo- site comes into focus. She's wearing a blue gingham dress and has clearly been watching us. As soon as Rupert is gone, Lola whizzes over on her scooter.

"Can you teach me how to do that?" she asks.

"Do what?"

"Kiss. How d'you do it?"

I smile and shrug like the answer is obvious. "When the time comes, you'll know."

"Oh good," she says. "I'm planning to kiss my boyfriend soon."

I roll my eyes and start heading for my front door. "All right, Lola. Good luck."

"His name is Harvey!" she calls after me.

FIFTY-ONE

A WEEK (AND A WHOLE LOAD OF KISSING!) LATER, IT is our penultimate day of freshman year AND our final meeting of the semester. The room is packed.

"Nice to have you back," I say to my wingmates, who performed their hearts out at the summer concert.

"Nice to *be* back," says Lowri, grinning.

"So," says Karima, "what's on the agenda?"

TURNS OUT, the agenda is:

- Talking about the total cliché that was Sports Day and how the Normal Normas managed to make their PE skirts shorter than ever
- Deliberating over the next total cliché that was Enrichment Day and how totally unfair it is that only sixty pupils from the whole school get to go to

Hersheypark, which is basically the only thing that ABSOLUTELY EVERYONE wants to do

- Chatting about campaign plans for the summer, like doing our flash mob in the mall, coming up with fundraising strategies, and getting everyone we know to post using our hashtag.

And there's another thing to talk about too, because on the way into school on Monday—Enrichment Day—there was a surprise waiting for me at the end of the road. As an apology for missing meetings and not knowing what was going on with my mom, Kar-Low organized a whole team to put up our new billboard poster!

Karima's dad printed it off and Heidi, Cam and a few others (without Jemima, interestingly) volunteered to put it up—early on Sunday morning, like before. I nearly cried when I saw it: a whole, wonderful circle of arms, outstretched with fists and emblazoned with a tagline saying *We love who we are.* Simple and perfect. Plus, Madison's parents' spray-painted poster had been stripped down and the billboard was bare, which meant we weren't technically graffitiing anything this time. Hopefully no one will prosecute us for borrowing a bit of advertising space.

"Where's Jemima?" I ask, suddenly noticing her absence. People turn to one another, looking blank.

Lowri shrugs. "She's gone a bit quiet on the group chat too."

"Maybe she's annoyed about not helping with phase two of the billboard," I suggest.

"It's not like we didn't ask her," replies Karima. "But she never replied."

"Weird."

"Oh well," says Lowri, rummaging around in her bag. Eventually her hand strikes whatever it is she's looking for and she wiggles her eyebrows mischievously. "For our last meeting of the year," she says, "I thought we could have some fun with this. . . ."

The merkin!

We pass it around, taking turns posing with it, sharing pictures on social media and cracking up with laughter. It gives me an idea.

"Hey! Everyone!" I holler, trying to shush them all. "You know how the Normal Normas always use filters on their photos?"

"Yes," groans Karima. "ALWAYS."

"Well, maybe we should have some fun with them too. I know filters can be bad because they exaggerate . . ."

"And lie," adds Karima.

"And make us feel like crap about ourselves," says Lowri.

"Yes," I continue. "Well, that's because celebrities and influencers post filtered pictures of themselves all the time. So when *real* people with the slightest imperfections see those filtered photos, they hate themselves. They're suddenly too spotty or not tan enough and voilà! Before you know it, every time you look at yourself, the real version of yourself is never enough."

Silence.

"Anyway, maybe it's time we had some fun with filters too, but in a different way."

So we do. We use any digital hair-related accessories we can find and post pictures using our club hashtag, adorning our faces with neat mustaches, bushy eyebrows and lengthy sideburns. We draw in nasal hair, create monobrows and beards. *It's just hair!* we write. *What's the big deal?*

Then I read Karima's caption from over her shoulder and my mouth drops open.

"Love is in the hair? LOVE IS IN THE HAIR?! Karima Bakshi, where was that little gem when we were brainstorming in my bedroom?!"

Kari shrugs at her own poetic genius. "It just came to me."

I am still contemplating Karima's brilliant wordsmithery when Ms. Mazur dashes into the classroom in her jazzy sportswear. She has a quick rummage in her desk, pulls something from a drawer, then looks at Lowri, bemused, before zipping off again.

Lowri is sitting there, arms folded, with the merkin flopped over the crown of her head like a black, wiry toupee.

I have never loved my friends more.

FIFTY-TWO

ON THE LAST AFTERNOON OF SCHOOL, I'M NEVER sure how they manage to get everyone into one room, but somehow they do. The remaining upperclassmen are assigned the tiered seating at the back; the rest of us relegated to—yep, you guessed it—the floor. With the seniors already gone, we occupy the space at the back of the hall where they used to sit. It feels alien. We get a flash forward—a glimpse of how it feels to see school through their eyes.

We're sitting there, waiting for The Chubb to appear, when tiny pinging noises start echoing around the hall. Hands reach for blazer pockets, mine included.

It's AirDrop, asking me to accept two pictures from Jemima Drake. Everywhere around me, people are elbowing one another and laughing. I open the images.

The first one is of Madison, walking into her parents' clinic, and the second is of Madison's before and after shots— the ones Sally showed us. Jemima has edited the first picture to add the word *Smooth-a-licious!* in bold luminous pink across it.

Karima leans over to peer down at my phone. "Oh no . . ."

Lowri turns her screen toward me, to confirm we're looking at the same thing.

I puff out my cheeks.

A few rows behind us, Jemima and Aliyah give one another high fives, as if they're best buddies. So *that's* why Jemima went all quiet!

Madison springs up from the floor, brushes a yellow curtain of hair over her face, and bolts toward the exit, tripping on her way. Everyone's laughing; nobody stops her.

"Looks like the Normal Normas are no more," says Lowri, chuckling.

"Looks like Madison and Ryan are no more, too," adds Karima, signaling toward the upperclassmen, where Ryan Avery looks like he wants a trapdoor to open up beneath him.

Part of me—the part that knows Madison hurt Frankie—feels satisfied and avenged. But another part is thinking about how I'd feel if my own parents encouraged me to doctor my entire body at fifteen years old—or made me think I wasn't good enough any other way.

I jump up and head for Jemima's row, Kar-Low following in my wake. By now, a lot of people are watching us. Jemima looks up, making her eyes wide in mock-innocence.

"That was out of line, Jemima," I say, trying not to spit while I talk. "We agreed that sharing those photos was *not* consistent with our ethos."

Jemima scoffs at me. "Oh, come on. She totally deserved it!"

"It was cruel, Jemima. Really cruel. Leaking those pictures to make fun of Madison's hairiness is exactly the opposite of what we've been trying to achieve all this time."

"Exactly," echoes Lowri. "We've been saying that body hair is normal and natural. *Not* something to make fun of."

"Not to mention point seven on our mission statement," adds Karima the lawyer. She glares at Jemima. "Don't you remember?"

"Erm, let me see," Jemima muses, finger to chin. "No."

I help Karima out. "Always be kind, no matter what."

"NO MATTER WHAT," repeats Lowri.

Jemima rolls her eyes and I look at her in disgust. "I'm sorry, Jemima, we can't have members who don't respect the basic rules of the club. You're out."

Jemima shrugs. "Your loss. You're the one who needs *me*, Evia. I have followers, you know."

Aliyah suddenly pipes up from her side. "Yeah, that's right. And she's gonna get even more followers when she takes up the modeling gig my mom got her!"

Jemima smiles sweetly at Aliyah, then turns back to me and wiggles her eyebrows. Suddenly, their friendship makes more sense.

"Let me get this straight," I posit to Aliyah. "You introduced Jemima to that sportswear company and she got work out of it?"

"Yeah," says Aliyah. "And she's gonna be great at it!"

Lowri guffaws nearby.

"You don't see how she's using you?" I point out. "Just like

Madison used you to set up the Normas, then stole back her throne as soon as she came back to school?"

Aliyah starts to look uncomfortable.

"Speaking of Madison," adds Lowri, "wasn't she meant to be your *friend*?"

Aliyah growls an actual growl. "Queen Cox had it coming. She was the one who let my skin get burned from that leg cream, then paraded my pictures around school for a laugh. Madison Cox is *not* my friend."

"SAINT JOSEPH'S!" bellows a voice all of a sudden. Mrs. Chubb has mounted the stage and is gripping the lectern. "I don't know what all this HOO-HA is, and on the last day of the school year, quite frankly, I'm not sure I *want* to know. But will you all take your seats and put your phones away THIS INSTANT!"

Watched by what feels like the whole school, Kar-Low and I return to our places with distinctly red hues to our cheeks. Even Lowri the unblushable goes pink. I glance back at Aliyah with her arms folded, and Jemima, smiling smugly.

"I can't believe Jemima," I whisper to Karima. "If being an influencer is more important than being a good person, she seriously needs to rethink her life."

"QUIET!!!" booms The Chubb.

Slowly, the murmuring dims and devices are pocketed.

"Thank you! Right . . ."

The big Last Day Assembly begins with the usual stuff: looking back on key events; saying goodbye to a retiring teacher; recognizing big achievements; dishing out awards.

Then comes the award for the year's most successful Young Enterprise team.

"This award," says Mrs. Chubb, "goes to the enterprise with the most original idea and the team who showed the most initiative. Its leader is creative, driven and ambitious, with a real flair for looking after the customer experience."

- Creative? Check.
- Driven? Check.
- Ambitious? Check.
- Customer experience? Er—

"And the winner is . . . Bartholomew Hedges!"

Bart struts up to the front to accept his lame certificate (not that I'm bitter). Oh, and an Amazon gift card (not bitter at all).

He's just finishing his acceptance speech when the doors at the back of the hall swing open so hard that they bang against the bricks.

FIFTY-THREE

FOR A MOMENT, I THINK IT'S GOING TO BE MADISON, coming back for revenge. But it's not. Frankie makes the long walk through the hall toward the stage. She's wearing her usual jeggings and black T-shirt with her favorite lightning-strike Converse. As she passes, I notice a new piercing in her nose. Her cropped head is uncovered and her face is unshaven and I'm petrified for her. I want to run up and throw my arms out to stop her.

My BFF climbs the steps onto the stage and strides toward the lectern, where The Chubb steps aside. Frankie straightens the bendy microphones, their squeals ripping into the sea of whispers.

"Oh my God!" people are hissing. "It's THAT GIRL! She's got A BEARD!"

What are you doing, Frankie?! I feel like a tall glass of Worry Juice, about to spill over. But towering over the lectern and standing next to stumpy old Chubb, Frankie suddenly looks really tall. She appears confident and empowered and, for the first time in a long time, comfortable in her own skin. My Worry Juice goes down a bit, as if someone's had a good slurp.

"Some of you might not know who I am, so I'll introduce myself," my BFF begins. "I'm Frankie Smith and I'm a freshman. A couple of months ago, some girls came to my house and shaved some of my hair off. Quite a lot, actually. I guess they wanted me to be embarrassed by my own reflection."

Some kids at the front giggle nervously.

"It's okay," says Frankie. "Laugh if you want. I know it's not *normal* for a teenage girl to have a beard. The only reason I have one is because I've got something called polycystic ovary syndrome. It's actually really common—about one in ten women have it. I just have it worse than most."

I beam at her, willing the pride to shine out of me like a beacon. I can't believe it's her: MY Frankie. I'm not sure how, but it's like she's been given a blast of super-strengthening radiation. If she wanted to, I bet she could pick up that lectern and swing it around her head like some kind of incredible hulk.

"Anyway, since then, my best friend has been doing something pretty awesome. In case you don't know who I'm talking about, here she is. . . ."

Holy Roly Poly!

My face has appeared, as wide as a bus, on the back wall of the stage. It's a photo from my fifteenth birthday. I'm rosy and grinning, with two thumbs up and crossed eyes.

People laugh.

"Her name is Evia Birtwhistle and she is my hero." Frankie picks me out in the abundance of faces, and waves. I flash the palm of my right hand to her. What feels like the entire lower school turns to stare. The boys directly in front—Raephe and a boy called Jack—turn to give me a double thumbs-up with mocking, closed-mouthed grins.

Frankie continues. If there's a script, it's in her head. "I admit, I wasn't sure about the Hairy Girls' Club at first. But then, when I understood how much it might help other girls like me and even girls with just the tiniest bit of body hair, I realized how important it was. No one is out there telling us it's okay, that it's normal and everyone has it. All we get is celebrities on social media showing us how perfect they are, using about a billion filters and making us feel horrible." She stops and takes a deep breath. "Anyway. Some of us want to say thank you to Evia on behalf of all the hairy girls out there. Actually, no: ALL the girls out there, period."

Frankie's eyes flit to Mrs. Chubb. "I'd like to play a song now, if that's okay?"

The Chubb nods and goes to her seat off stage. Frankie raises her hand to her forehead and peers beneath it in a "Land ahoy!" kind of way.

Except it's not land she's looking for, but Lowri—at the back of the hall, holding up her phone and recording.

Karima walks onto the stage from somewhere in the wings, leading a load of people who I think constitute the school choir. Mr. Harkness stares at them with knitted eyebrows.

Then the music starts. Part of me hopes Frankie is about

to sing, like she used to do in our performances to her family. But instead she steps to the side of the lectern, to the middle of the stage.

Keala Settle's voice enters the hall. It's Frankie's favorite song: the one from *The Greatest Showman.*

Somebody in the hall groans loudly, but Frankie is a statue, head bowed, letting the words wash over her. The choir is silent, reflective.

Keala sings about scars and shame. About loving those scars. Finding a place.

One of the choir members passes Frankie a large piece of white cardboard. She raises her gaze to look out at us, then turns it around.

I can grow a beard says the placard, in large black letters.

So what? says her face.

From the back of the hall, a lone male voice whoops loudly and I spot Jake, on his feet, hands clapping above his head. His exams are over so he must've come in especially for this—for his little sister. My heart flutters for a second. Then I remember Rupert and it flutters again. Aww, I am so conflicted!

While Keala sings, Karima steps forward and reveals her own board: *Girls have body hair too.*

Rupert goes next: *Hairy and proud.* I want to run over and hug him!

Then Cam: *I'm not scared.*

Suddenly, the whole choir joins in, stampeding into the air. "Oh-oh-oh," they chant. "Oh-oh-oh." The volume is

INSANE. It's like someone's blown icy air on my neck and arms. The whole hall vibrates with the noise of them.

Members of the HGC pop up all over the choir, holding up placards as they sing.

I don't notice Ms. Wallace until she's halfway up the steps. She goes to stand next to Frankie and holds up her own piece of card, announcing—to the whole school—that she shaves her toes.

"Whoop, whoop!" I shout, cupping my mouth with my hands.

Next is Mrs. Hubbard—the soft-spoken science teacher who donated the ancient wax bomb. Her sign reads: *I pluck my chin.*

I'm aware of people beginning to clap, slowly at first, then faster, hungrier. I join in, heart hammering.

Ms. Mazur joins the stage next, followed by a social studies teacher, Mrs. Fletcher. *I used to bleach my face* confesses Ms. Mazur. *I trim my nasal hair* says Mrs. Fletcher.

Cheers pop up all over the hall. The snickers fade. My eyes keep returning to Frankie. I am so happy I could cry!

Mr. Jessop—the retiring woodshop teacher—is the first man to join the line of teachers. He flips his sign. *I trim my ear hair* his statement reads, and the hall erupts. I didn't even know ears could grow hair!

Mr. Wall is next. *I love my monobrow* he declares, followed by a PE teacher, Mr. Kitchen. *I wax my pecs* he announces, and everyone dissolves again, some laughing, some cheering.

Finally, Mr. McGovern takes to the stage. The Chubb's

face is a picture! Her eyes wide with alarm, she moves toward the edge of her seat.

I have a hairy back says his sign. But no one jeers. No one makes ape noises. People are cheering him on!

Then I notice Frankie beckoning to me. Lowri pulls me out of my row, one hand still on her phone, and leads me onto the stage until the choir is pulsating in my ears. Heidi hands me a sign. I look down at it and smile before spinning it around.

We are glorious!

Half the school is on their feet, clapping; some of them singing along. Lining the walls, some of the teachers are off their chairs, doing cheesy above-the-head clapping. Other teachers remain firmly glued to their seats, probably wondering how all this might affect the dynamic in the staff room and whether they will ever be able to look their colleagues in the eye again.

The song fades to Frankie and me hugging and laughing—laughing so much I feel sick!

"You're amazing!" I tell her over and over again.

The rhythmic clapping dissolves into applause.

Mrs. Chubb shuffles toward the lectern and grasps it with both hands, waiting for the din to fade.

"Well," she says finally. "That was quite . . . something. Thank you, Frankie, for a point well made. Does this mean you'll be returning to school next year?"

Frankie nods cheerfully and relief ripples through me. She'd already hinted to me that she was thinking about it, but seeing her confirm it to our principal makes it real.

"And thank you, choir," adds Mrs. Chubb, without turning to face them. "That was very . . . rousing." She pauses uncomfortably. "I must admit I was not at all sure about Miss Birtwhistle's campaign when she first explained it to me. But, well, I think we women—and everyone, for that matter—have all been too busy for too long performing our beauty rituals in secret because we have been made to feel ashamed. Well, no more! So far as I can tell, feeling ashamed about yourself only breeds more and more self-loathing. And I for one would like a little less self-loathing in society!"

Everyone bursts into a fresh round of applause while Mrs. Chubb smiles, close-lipped. Most people can only see her controlled smile. But from where I'm standing, I can see her eyes, and they're as glossy as an ice rink in the sun.

"Well," she says, signaling an end to the clapping. "Nothing else remains to be said, so I hope you all have a productive, restful summer, and come back raring to go in September! Thank you, everyone."

The unthanked teachers file off the stage, followed by a gabbling choir.

The hall doors open and upperclassmen start to file out. Frankie, Kar-Low and I hang back and wait for the hall to empty. Teachers pass us, smiling, while HGC members wave triumphantly and give thumbs-up. Ex-Normas refuse to meet our gaze, while Rupert—lovely Rupert—mouths "See you later" in my direction, over the sea of heads.

Finally, the hall is deserted, and we're left standing like a four-piece band after our own concert.

"Wow," I say, still buzzing. "That was awesome."

"It was super awesome!" says Lowri. "And I got it all on here." She taps her phone. "So we can go home and watch it all over again!"

"Can we?!" asks Kari, with a tiny squeal.

I look at Frankie. "Why didn't you *tell* me you were planning . . . THAT?!"

Frankie lifts one shoulder, coolly. "I knew you'd freak out."

I feign offense.

"You totally would have," adds Lowri.

"I totally would have," I agree.

"Nice surprise though?" Frankie asks.

I grin at her. Then I take her hand and give it a squeeze. Frankie takes Lowri's hand, then Lowri takes Karima's. And we stride out of there together—through the double doors and out into a summer that may or may not feature hairy legs. And I realize that whatever happens next with this club, in this school, in this life, I am ready. Because I am strong.

WE ARE STRONG.

ACKNOWLEDGMENTS

I've already thanked my parents for the hairy genes, but in all seriousness, without those genes, I couldn't have put myself in Evia's head to write this story. Being at the hairier end of the spectrum is rarely fun, but it did inspire me to want to help all the teenage girls out there who think they're the hairiest thing on the planet (like I did!) or, quite frankly, anyone who is working out their feelings about their natural body.

Secondly, I'd like to thank the bullies on the bus in 1996 who unwittingly inspired me to write this. That mortifying episode where they pointed and laughed at my unshaven legs for what felt like an eternity ended up securing me a literary agent and a book deal. So ha!

Thirdly, to my lovely sister-in-law, Alice—thank you for lending me your mustache! For several years, Alice wore a fake mustache to raise money for Movember in memory of her dad, Rick Dorrington. Yes, she got stared at on the tube; yes, it must've hurt like hell every time she peeled off the falsie; but

Alice soon became a proud MoSista who raised thousands in the name of prostate cancer awareness. When I told her about my idea for this book, she was immediately on board. Alice, you are one strong, courageous, clever lady, and I am proud to call you my sister-in-law.

Lastly, I want to acknowledge my husband, who has put up with a lot of talk about female body hair over the past few years and supports me regardless! That support may be entirely fueled by a misconceived notion that all authors get Netflix deals (he's holding out for a cameo), but I acknowledge him nonetheless. Thank you, Doug!

Now, down to the nitty-gritty . . .

The idea for this book surfaced during a writing workshop run by the Golden Egg Academy in 2019. So, a big shout-out to children's publishing guru Imogen Cooper for setting up the academy, running that workshop, and triggering my epiphany!

Next, to Abigail Kohlhoff, my Golden Egg editor, for helping me shape those first drafts of the story and highlighting early sensitivity issues. Thank you, Abi.

My Golden Egg mentor gets the next mention: Kathy Webb, editor extraordinaire! Thank you, Kathy, for all your help and advice through various edits, and for your unswerving passion for Evia's story. Your wisdom and support undoubtedly helped me to secure an agent, which leads me to . . .

RACHEL HAMILTON! Being a published author, successful copy editor, and creative writing lecturer wasn't enough for Rachel, who decided to try her hand at literary agenting. And thank goodness she did! An abundance of gratitude goes to her—and to the rest of the team at the Ben Illis Agency—for showing such enthusiasm for my novel from the start, and for persevering with its submission at a time when, post-pandemic, the publishing world was eerily quiet.

And finally to Alison Romig, who read my manuscript and offered it a home at Penguin Random House. Without Ali, this story would still be languishing somewhere in the deep, dark brains of my laptop! Thank you, Ali, for seeing the story's potential, for reining in my (sometimes inappropriate) humor, and for making the strengths of the story really shine. I will be forever grateful for your invaluable input and for that all-important offer of publication. A huge thank-you to the rest of the Delacorte team, too, for coming up with such a catchy title and a stupendous cover design. I'm not sure I will ever meet you, given the size of the pond between us, but I send my hearty thanks across that pond and hope they reach you undiminished.

Finally finally, thanks to you, the reader. I'm not sure anyone ever reads the acknowledgments, but if you have, you must've really liked the book! And that makes me very happy indeed.

ABOUT THE AUTHOR

GEMMA CARY grew up in Somerset, England, and earned her degree in English at the University of Exeter. She worked as an editor in children's publishing for many years before realizing that, rather than editing other people's words, she'd prefer to write them herself. Her debut, *Love Is in the Hair,* is the result.

@gemmacary